# I Was
# Dora
# Suarez

# THE FACTORY SERIES
## by Derek Raymond

# I Was Dora Suarez

The tragedy with help is that
it never arrives.

## Derek Raymond

AVAILABLE
PRESS

BALLANTINE BOOKS • NEW YORK

An Available Press Book
Published by Ballantine Books

Library of Congress Catalog Card Number: 90-93024

ISBN: 0-345-36852-5

Cover design by Don Munson
Cover illustration by Larry Schwinger
Manufactured in the United States of America
First Edition: October 1990
10  9  8  7  6  5  4  3  2  1

# FOR

Gisèle, Chopin, Claude and
Marie-Pierre Franqueville:

•   •   •

*I could never have got through this
without the four of you.*

# I Was Dora Suarez

# 1

Interrupted by her because she had come to see what was happening next door while he was still finishing up with the girl, the killer came up to the old woman without a word, got hold of her as if she were a load of last week's rubbish and hurled her through the front of her grandfather clock, which stood just inside the door of the flat, using strength that even he didn't know he had. He saw that that had worked OK: she died as she hit it. After the splintering crash that her body made breaking the clock—the shocking, sudden damage, the liquid slap of her head hitting the inside of the clock case—she sighed once, death's sister to a sob; and the sound, as she died with her head hidden inside the clock, outranked every other sound in the place.

However, the killer heard nothing. He stood, unaware, for a good minute; absorbed, absent and distorted with ecstasy and by the excitement of the two murders that he had just committed. He had a long, blank time to make up for; months, pitiless chains of days and nights of hideous, iron struggle, of ruthless training and punishment; there had been nights when he had moaned and screamed out of his broken window into the night of College Hill, wondering if he ever would get into action again, his hands jammed round the black frames.

As for his second victim this evening, Betty Carstairs was eighty-six, and that was how she died that night. She had never truly asked herself if the long and arduous history of her life had been worthwhile, or whether indeed it had had any meaning at all; but she had at least supposed that she owned some right to her own body, to give or withhold it while it was still worth looking at, and to continue to live on in it even after it was not. She had endured two wars, accepting in both the losses of people close to her that wars entail; she had been less afraid of the bombing than of considering why it was that so many of those who made up her personal world should perish in an apparently random way, and why it was that she should have expected patience from herself, and found it, each time her husband, long dead now, had invaded her physically—for she was Scottish, and had never been an awakened person: all she had ever really enjoyed doing was walking. And then, lately, when she had fallen seriously ill with her heart and knew that she was spent, she marvelled and wondered, when she was not in pain, why she need feel so afraid and alone.

Well, now she had been killed in her own clock, so that was that, and that was the squalid and miserable end of Betty Carstairs. She was to pass later, after the autopsy, through the diesel flames of a London cemetery in a recuperable coffin, a graven angel passing through a moment of fire, at a price arranged on the cheap by her great-nephew Valerian who knew a few people, and who, having been through the flat with a mate of his directly we had finished, took such pickings from it as he could down to Chelsea in two of her suitcases and got pissed on the proceeds.

Now there was one of your promising lads who thought he knew everything, except that much later I indirectly got him nicked by readjusting his head for the hat on another case which was looking for someone to wear it; it carried two years in the shade. I didn't appreciate Valerian somehow; I'm fucked if I know why.

• • •

Anyway, that was the end of Betty in our world.

When he came to himself again, the killer looked at the clock vaguely; it meant nothing to him. He was breathing hard, straining, fit and ready for more, and it was disappointing, it disquieted him, that there was just silence in the place now. He stroked the back of his hand across his lips; they parted stickily, with a crust of effort and desire on them. His lips gaped open with pleasure, only he didn't know that.

The face of the grandfather clock showed a view of the Thames with Windsor Castle behind it in the distance; the river was as it had been in 1810. It was a cottage clock. It had never been valuable; now it was a wreck. Whatever it had stood for, whatever the skill that had gone into making the clock, the Roman figures on the white enamel dial, its river scene: all that was gone now. Without its dusty glass, which the killer had smashed, each detail of a little rowing-boat, painted on a separate strip of copper and then geared to the second-hand pinion with which it agreed, now stood out quite new and fresh. The three hands of the clock, hours, minutes and seconds, the tiny boat and the two people in it had been built to indicate time's passage as it was experienced in that era—in a slow, invariable way. But that, too, was over now—the needle broken off its spindle, the thin steel snapped off its bearing.

Yet time, which had always stepped in a rigidly constructed and formal manner round its face, though arrested now, had in one sense not really changed; for the painted rowing-boat, the kind that on the Thames they used to call a perfect, was still there, resting far out on the tidal river. This swaying toy ferried a miniature couple from a vanished age, a boy and a girl, across the top of the clock face; each leaned eternally gazing at the other with a bare arm lying across an oar. Lovers, they looked into each other's eyes with an adoration which a hundred and eighty

years could not efface even though the flaking faces were no longer clear—either because the little brush had not entirely captured
them, or because it was sunset, or else because the scale was too
small—anyway, you could only in part make out the lovers' features. But still the motionless blades lay dipped in the white-lead,
scrolled waves, the boat lying across the crawling drift of the
river—and if the clock could have been set going again, the boat
with its dreaming cargo would have gone back to dipping and
ticking with the clock as it always had done, rocking and nursing
them each time the pendulum swung. Only of course that was
impossible forever now; for so great had been the killer's strength
that Betty Carstairs's head had smashed through the clock door,
smashing it in two, and there was no revoking that.

Then, after what seemed like a long pause, the strike weight
suddenly slipped and fell on Betty Carstairs's face. In response to
the new change of balance, the whole clock frame strained gravely
outwards, and its pointed hood slid very slowly off its runners
and crashed onto her legs, so that when this new sound was over,
there she had been turned on one side forever, buried in wood
and glass. There was plenty of mess around, too. There were the
shards of her chamber pot, for instance, that she had been carrying to the bathroom when she heard the noise in the other
room and looked in, that he had kicked out of her hand the
second he killed her. There was also the smell. He held his nose;
for if there was one thing the killer detested, it was the smell of
anybody's piss but his own.

There was her blood, too. Everything that he had done re-
solved itself into abominable little details: for instance, in her
ultimate spasm, she had half spat her top denture out through
her lips, which lent her the smile of a lunatic criticising bad the-
atre.

Now the killer cupped his hands round his mouth; it was cold
in the flat, and he blew hard on his fingers. He half noticed his
lips, for which he had a passion, in a gilt mirror, and was full

pleased to see that they were as thick and red as ever, ready to draw any woman. Only his hands dissatisfied him; for in spite of his gloves, which he peeled off for a moment, the palms were marked from the drainpipe he had scaled; they were dry and rust-coloured, and that was a detail that clashed. He quickly put the gloves back on: 'It's bloody freezing in here!' he shrieked. 'There's sod-all heating on in this bleeding barracks, fuck this for a lark.' He pointed a long, loose finger upwards and shook it at the place as though it had threatened to fight back—but already the second's pleasure he had had of 'handling' the interfering old git was over: so she was weighed off wasn't she, and who gave a fucking green banana? The mistake the little beldame had made was to stick her stupid face round the sitting-room door to see what the noise was about while he was finishing the girl up; he wouldn't even have known she existed otherwise. But she had seen too much. It was logic. He couldn't afford to let Granny live, and anyway he hated being interrupted when he was intent on a piece of work, so it added up to the old cow had to go.

'It's time you were off yourself,' he said out loud. His voice bounced back at him like a scream off the wall.

Still, talk of screaming, the girl had started by half screaming her fucking head off, silly little tart—but then she always had been one to kick the milk over, no matter what, he remembered—and good riddance to her. But, underneath, what he was really trying to ask himself was whether he could get through his present situation; he knew he had to launder it somehow now so that he could get out clean. But although he knew what 'get out' was, he didn't know what 'clean' meant, so that he had some kind of a problem for a minute. He had no conception whatever of the term 'guilt.' He just obeyed his power, the impulses. He didn't know how to frame these impulses in language at all but just automatically marched when the impulses said to do it, and it was this improbability that turned him into a wild card hidden in the social pack that of course made him so vastly dangerous.

He turned soundlessly on ultrathin soles; he had put on a thin pair of brand-new racing pumps for the job. Thinking of women in any way at all transferred him immediately to a vital, if ill-defined level in himself and filled him with the instant desire to punish himself by wanking. He stroked enquiringly at his cock, which still hurt after the last time; but recently, while he had been in training, he had been damaging it more subtly, because he didn't want this cheeky (because apparently independent of him) and self-important other little self of his to clack on him now; rather, he was going to murder it slowly, and the way he was now appearing (but only, like an interrogating copper, *appearing*) to give it a bit of margin meant that the suspect would soon have plenty of mileage in it again and then it would have to go on trying to give an account of itself as it had always had to. He touched it, found it was bleeding and abandoned it temporarily, putting it back into his sports trousers. Then he walked back into the room where the girl's body was.

He leaned against the doorjamb of this room, his black hair making an intense splash against the dead yellow wall. From there he surveyed his principal work, taking no more than a quick look in the mirror to admire his sated eyes, which, he had to admit to himself—though he went through the solemn, absurd ritual of asking himself if it were true—looked pretty terrific. He never realised the truth about his eyes because he was accustomed to believing that their dominating gaze was unique; objectively, though, they were not in the least as he conceived them. Far from it. Far from being attractive, as he was convinced they were, they struck others as eyes that had perished violently centuries ago, and there was also some form of lacquer over them that lent them the expressionless look that you see in the eyes of the dead.

He whispered, looking down at what he had done: 'I could have been a lot neater than that, matey—really a lot neater.'

There was no one there to answer him, of course, and yet again there was no question but that he was dead right.

Mind, the place had looked bad enough anyway already, even before he had erupted into it. The high, icy old room he stood in had already been reduced by neglect and the losing struggles of its occupants to the point where it was now just a decayed, filthy relic of mouldering plaster, the wallpaper sliding towards the floor in the damp—in fact it was so wet in there that the killer's breath emerged as fog and hung motionless in the jaundiced air until in the end it rolled slowly away from him towards the wall like bad jokes emerging out of the mouth of a cartoon character. Two grubby beds with plates and the remains of food on them stood eighteen inches apart, each under an Indian counterpane worked in red tapestry and adorned with small glass discs sewn in, and it was in the gap between these beds, on a square of greasy carpet, that he had felled Suarez. She lay with the left side of her head half split off, and her left breast, severed from the rib cage, had slithered out of the front of her low-cut dress and lay not far from her, partly in her blood, partly inside its bra.

'Yeah, well now, that *was* a real carve-up wasn't it?' the killer screamed. 'A right royal fucking shambles! You could have done better than that, my friend—an unbelievably whole lot better, couldn't you, you fucking amateur?'

Yes, well he could have, only he had totally done his pieces when she put a hand out to reason with him. She started to say 'I love you anyway,' but the mere mention of that word, compared to his intentions, sickened him, so that he had impatiently cut into the arm extended to him at its shoulder with the cutting edge of his axe; at times he still listened with the keen pleasure of a music lover to the clean steel grinding through wet red bone. But where he had gone wrong was that the wound made her hoot and howl, of course, and so made it that much more difficult for him to get her into the position where he wanted her for his main stroke—and besides it made blood too soon just when, like any lover, he wanted to take his time and move slowly towards his climax. But, on the other hand, who the fuck needed to listen to anything she had to say when all he wanted from her was relief for his raving passion, to get the clean scent of her blood in his nose, to get his face, his mouth, his cock down into her?

And so, overexcited by her terror and her pitiful efforts to avoid him, he had let the short, serviceable fireman's axe he had turn in his hand, which was sweating because of his fury and excitement, so giving the girl that fraction of time to pivot as the blade came for her—and even then when, having missed his trick, he appeared to quieten down, half smiling and saying to her (in some imitation of a Midlands accent, remembering a former occasion in Nottingham where that had worked really well): 'Let's be calm, let's calm down now, shall us?' trying to soothe her as a groom does when he approaches a nervous young mare to gentle her, humming absently and pleasantly, she still wouldn't accept the axe when he showed it to her again, ritually presenting it to that white neck of hers—so that in the death he had to come for her pretty well any old how in one of those great curving rushes of his. Silly little bat, she kept trying to get away from him long after there was nowhere for her to go, telling him over and over that she had made her peace with the world, which infuriated him in a delicious way—and yet all he achieved by the panic he had caused in her was make her trip over one of the trailing sheets between the two beds, which created a prize cock-up, because all she did then was fall with a thud on the floor and a bit later, even when she did finally manage to get up again, she had by then got her stupid little head in totally the wrong position for him, so that instead of his being able to take her head clean off, bag up and leave, he somehow got in a fluster. And now look at the fucking place, a shambles, shit order! It wasn't a question of the blood everywhere or the smell of her entrails in the frozen room that upset him so much as the mess he had made of her. She was sad to look down at, like a fuck that hadn't come off; the assorted bits of her lying all over the toffee shop left him with an emptiness, they left him wanting to take the whole scene back and play it again.

He'd be punishing himself for this, of course—still, in the meantime, *whew!*

He got jerked off over her all right in the end, though, just the same, even though he nearly bit his bottom lip off doing it. The pain he was in down there, the state it was all in, didn't make it easy; however, he had been pretty sure he would manage to come for her all right, make her in the end all right, the minute he slammed the door behind him at College Hill, hoisted his bag onto his shoulder and started slamming his feet passionately down to South Circular Road. Yes, of course coming had been painful for him, but just look down now and see what had happened! It had been bloody hard work and he had had to bend double over her, racing away at the meat, but when the sweet relief did come, you could see where he had literally sprayed all over her: sweet Christ, what power he still had!

And then what about that bit after his first go at her when his axe had simply smacked into her right arm just like that, like almost casual—and she had burst out crying and bleeding, holding back from him like a little bride while she clung to her bright wound that had already aroused and excited him like a pig—and then they had then both danced swiftly around almost like lovers, backwards and forwards, barging into the furniture and things. He felt quite simply exalted, so that he just could not help himself getting down to her on the floor again and licking her blood again just once more, peering into her wounds, which he opened gently with his fingers, to see where his semen had gone, and how he and she mixed, murmuring love words to her because she was still alive. Then, when he had finally had enough, he pulled her up to him with her bleeding face to his and told her, 'I'm ready now, Dora, this is it, love,' and he cut her straight across the throat with the wrong, blunt edge of the axe as she held on to her bad arm like a bad swimmer hanging on to the lip of the pool and he gazed at the stains of his sperm on the skirt of her new dress as he did it to her. Then, after she had died, he had an idle go at decapitating her, but because she could no longer react, the game bored him straightaway. Presently, though, there arrived his detached interest: didn't these people make an extraordinary noise when you did it to them just? Jesus, yes, that was yet another snap for the old souvenirs—he had really conquered tonight! It was more like a gargling squawk they made than a scream really; and then there was like a short noise like a kind of gasp they made as the throat parted in smiling, pouring lips. The noise was like when his dad used to do it to a chicken, only a great deal louder.

Now he felt like inching back in a ratlike posture, bold but careful, to the spot by the window where he had left his shoulder bag and listened, but there wasn't a sound to be heard in the flats as he got a rag out of the old Adidas carryall and began to wipe his axe, taking care not to cut himself—Christ, it was sharp! As for the silence in the flats, that didn't surprise him at all, for they stood in a prime residential area where the big property combines had forgotten very few places indeed and catered for the old and rich, who didn't care what rent and rates they paid as long as, in return, they didn't have to be pestered over the unemployed, ethnic minorities, handicapped people or anything else even re- motely disturbing. It was, as a matter of fact, because the tenants in Empire Gate didn't want to know about anything unpleasant at all that the killer had been enabled to behave more or less as if he were at home. *The Times*, like Axel's servants, did the ten- ants' living for them, and the slavish need to sell newspapers that lay behind their intellectual and other pretensions meant that all the really dirty washing could be kicked downstairs to some base court or other where all that nasty kind of thing belonged. For Empire Gate was a street filled with doddling old millionaires whose wallets fitted their porticos and facades, and the whole district, therefore, shut down early at night with not a taxi to be had except for sweet pickups from the Japanese and Arab hotels where the man on the door copped for his drops. The flat where the killer was now, leased for ninety-nine years by Betty and Billy Carstairs when they married in the risky days of 1940 (and sensible folk such as occupied the street now were nowhere to be found at the time because they were afraid of taking a German bomb and so had 'regretfully left for Canada' as the formula went then until the poor stupid bastards that had stayed on got the lights working again). Betty Carstairs's was the only flat in the block, therefore, which, because of her lease, the developers had been obliged to leave out; then, too, it was also sandwiched between the embassies of two mad countries whose revolutions came and went in the evening papers—but who cared anyway? There was the good old British police, wasn't there? And look at what that cost!

Meantime the killer stood icily, his presence, luckily for the tenants' sleep—besieged as it was by dreams of wigs, sledgehammers, blackmailing ex–daughters-in-law etc.—unsuspected. He felt replete, thanks to his activities, a hungry man with a full belly at last amongst this load of selfish old people in the evening of their days who had never done anything in life except invest their money and keep their heads down. He knew what sort of people they were because he had been keeping an eye on them from the abandoned basement garden for several weeks and could well imagine the scream that was going to go up when this lot was discovered. And there was no doubt it would be soon—for the weather was rainy and fairly warm, and the neglected dead made their decay known just as definitely in Kensington as they did in College Hill.

The killer knew he ought to be leaving himself now, only he couldn't bring himself to do it straightaway; for how could he bear to turn his back on a feast of new blood like this one as perfunctorily as if he were simply refusing a beer? To him, the scene, the collops of her flesh, her blood everywhere, encompassed all the elements of a marriage. It had just been celebrated. He, the groom, had just ritually drunk her blood, trodden in it and masturbated into pieces of her warm flesh, thus finally owning her; and no, there was no question of his leaving his bride just like that—it would have amounted to an insult! And then, what was more, the shotgun-marriage element of the ceremony appealed to him as a bandit as running water does to a man dying of thirst—running things fine, after all, formed a deep part of his thrill at being active again after being months in limbo at College Hill, suspended like a bat in its sleep, clutched upside down to a beam in winter. Looking around the flat, at the blood, at the two women's bodies, yes, he felt like a married man, the head of a family who had rightly been provided for by his womenfolk, had eaten and drunk his fill, had been truly and richly served, and was now enjoying his afters while awaiting coffee. Now what he really hankered after was a cream chocolate. Like other multiple killers he fluently transposed the negative language of death into an appetite for food. The evening was very nearly a masterpiece, so that at last he really felt like the sturdy, exhausted young lover that he had to believe he was, climbing softly out of bed while girlie sleeps to raid the fridge. He never for an instant believed that he would be caught, and would have been as contemptuous of any lecture or punishment for his evening's work as any man would be if he were threatened with imprisonment for having a fuck.

There were glaring differences, of course.

Everything would have been all right (in fact lovely, he said to himself) if only it hadn't been for his balls-up with the girl. Naturally, it wasn't the girl herself he was bothered about (she belonged to him), but something more abstruse. Somehow the evening had gone wrong. It was not a hundred percent to his satisfaction, and in his opinion it was all the girl's fault: it came down to her stupid obstinacy, her trying to stop him doing what he had to do to her. For the killer was really like the worst kind of soldier that every army dreads but has never been able to avoid; he receives orders from somewhere above, no matter where, that literally have to be executed. He has no capacity whatever for analysis (he believed that in killing the girl these were his desires that he was obeying, since he was that true ace of folly, the murdering fool). However, he had brains of a kind. He had to have, because of course he was a one-man army. He was the planner at GHQ—but he was also the man in the trench with the bomb and the rifle. The killer was really, in his head, like a clerk gone mad with a weapon that by some appalling freak he knows how to use. Using it made him feel useful, it kind of helped him get his solitary little rocks off, so that he could return to his frigid home at the death of the day rubbing his hands, having coldly and logically obeyed the plan received from, er, somewhere, rubbing his hands and smiling at his wife with a warmth, derived from the superb order reigning in his files, which is absurd only to others. The needs of the other mean nothing to people like that. The one thing that matters to people like that is that the plan presented from above, no matter what it says, must be obeyed to the letter at no matter what cost; it is the only orgasm such a person will ever know. For any authoritative plan assures the existence of those who have none, which is why many make love and war; in the meantime it also, if you do what you're told in it, produces a cheque at the end of the month. Killer or clerk—but then after all, if you're born dead, nobody costs anything anyway. These wretched people (clerks, killers, anyway absent people) would be laughable if it weren't for the immense damage they do; and of course it is because we do laugh at them, switch them off the telly whenever they appear, and so on, that they do the damage because of that self-despair which they can never afford to acknowledge.

Now the killer found that he was at an interior point in himself, looking down at the blood-puddled floor, at the girl's body, where his self-image (of which he was immensely proud) bothered him vaguely; he felt that something inside him was hammering to get his attention from the wrong side of his steel door—some entity that was starving, excluded and ignored. It was himself, of course, though he had no means of realising that. He had always had very serious problems with himself indeed on practically every level and always would have, because he possessed no equipment whatever by means of which he could identify any problem. Problems manifested themselves with him, as they do with the residents in a lunatic asylum, as no problem, which is why they are in the asylum. The problem is themselves, and it is too great for them to solve—that lust, that vague unidentifiable sadness, the sudden lost feeling or the savage desire to kill or pick someone else's nose, shit in a crowded train. Well, if you have no idea what a problem is, it is extremely unlikely that you will ever be able to solve it. In this case, the killer presented the classic bore's syndrome: that of literally clinging to existence through having no memory of it—in other words, by having an exact memory of the present and none whatever of the past. This provided him—but only him—with an illusion of living: everyone who detected that it in fact was nothing but an illusion had to go, and that was when the sports bag was unzipped. The only way he managed to fill this gap and exist at all was by his exact memory in the present, and none whatever of the past, which provided him with the illusion of living while he absently suffered and caused pain. By definition, however, there was no possibility whatever of his changing, let alone improving his position in any direction—for how can anyone ever hope to be freed from a situation that he doesn't understand?

Bores and killers are much the same; dullness and despair explains most murders. Killers kill because they spew out far too much energy on being polite in a way that normal people never do. Most killers are of bourgeois origin or, worse still, have been forced in a working-class atmosphere to making a copy of it. I have never met one single stimulating killer in all my time with

A14; and if you've never met one there, then I very much doubt if you will meet one anywhere.

With this killer, there were very, very serious sexual problems of whose origins he had no idea, of course, since he was unable to analyse them. One form his trouble took (if it had just stopped there!) was the absolute, though unconscious hatred he bore towards the one part of himself over which, even though it was attached to him, he had no control: his prick. He had started to punish it on that account while he was still very young—ever since the first time, in fact, that it was challenged by a woman to do its stuff and failed. It let him down like a flat tyre the first time he ever tried it out when he was fifteen, at that first dread moment in a young man's life when, thanks to its steadfast and utter refusal to come up, part of his body proved him not to be the superior being that the rest of him thought he was. Quite the contrary: this shrunken yet vital little portion of him lolled feebly, as it had done ever since, with a negative yet controlling insolence, given the situation, against his thigh like an old pisspot leaning on a bar, more or less winking at him as it were in a sly manner, daring him to do something about it. In the end he had given it such a stout slap that he screamed with his self-inflicted pain and the girl fled before the negative glory of his impotence, so that the first penal blood he ever shed was his own. The being that he had already thought he possessed very sensibly rushed out of the room and away from that cheap Caledonian Road hotel.

He made an error and wept with the next girl, having waited, psychically asleep, for nearly a year after that. May was on the fat side and wore glasses that steamed up—she was known as Preshy to her very few friends, Fleshy to her numerous enemies, since she was a known grass and had already taken one heavy beating for playing out of her league. Her new error was to take this sport on because no one else would despite his good looks, and besides she was getting a bit desperate for a fuck. These looks of his, though, she gradually noticed, soon kind of vanished under inspection and she also found herself having to deal with other problems such as his spontaneous outbursts of maniacal fury; they were of an order she had never come across before. Her own problem was the twin one of both being sly so as to encourage trouble and then lying back to try and enjoy it; she was too stupid ever to realise that he was silent and well behaved in the boozers they went to only because he was trying to understand what natural behaviour meant through watching the people around him with exactly the same purpose and intensity as a bad actor, in an effort to make a copy of what he could never become.

Anyway, the first time they did both find themselves flat on a hotel bed at the end of an evening of half bitters, she expertly unsnapped her bra and black dotted clingers and knickers and kicked her flat heels into a corner. They started to cuddle, half-clothed; but the preliminaries seemed to her to last for an awfully long time, which depressed her. She was still sorry for him, but physically his efforts made her start to go off him; she thought, This is getting to look like the makings of a disaster area here if blokey doesn't perform soon and he's so sort of boring—only, being stupid, she was innocent and had no idea of what she was literally playing with, no idea how urgent it was with him that he should conquer her. Hers was a very dangerous ignorance indeed—indeed it was mortal, for when he broke out weeping to her after hours in the dark, complaining of not being able to make himself work in spite of hours of sweating effort, she committed a truly majestic error; she flung herself off the mattress and gave him the raspberry because she was exhausted, dissatisfied and fed up with struggling under him.

It was the last thing she ever did. As with all his past and future women—he was never sure right up to the end whether it was eleven or twelve—May died; and she died because what she had asked of him was not the extraordinary, but the impossible—a good, square, old-fashioned fuck. She had no idea at all what she was dealing with; it was as if you had asked a schoolteacher to defuse a rotting but live bomb. Indifferently, the killer still remembered her at times, sniffed the knickers he had worn on that occasion, which he kept at College Hill with his souvenirs, then shook his head and smiled at the idea as though she were just part of a story he had read in a book or seen on television, saying to himself, Just look at that now, will you? She must have been like that little mystery in that serial on Channel 4 that he watched silently in the pub, where the feller cut just a shade too deep, so that she bled too fast and was gone too quick. That was the trouble with nearly all of them, they were hardly any of them up to it, except just one or two little toughies in some kind of training who put up something like a battle; the rest of them just sliced up like wet fish, gave off that gargle of theirs and died before you were anywhere near your own climax, might you be so lucky, mazel tov.

So that's how it was. He took no more precautions than the normal not to be caught, any more than a girl does going on and off the pill. He performed whenever he knew he had to perform, which was when he was unable to control himself, and then read about it next day in the press, casually, even with the attitude of a serious citizen, since, because he was now asleep again, there was no way, no way at all, that this creature folk were describing as a monster could possibly be him. Also, the reporting was really lousy, and the police work made you wonder how the fuzz ever nailed anyone for anything the stupid way they set about it.

And that was why he had never had his collar felt. As far as he was concerned the culprit was someone totally and absolutely unknown to him despite the shocking litter of relics, the smell, a head from time to time that stood around on an old plate for a while till the pong really got too fierce and it had to be junked. There were even moments, when he read about the exploits of this person in the press, when he muttered to himself, You bet, this bastard's got to be caught, he's a fucking animal. True, he had fleeting feelings that whoever had gutted this poor little bat

here on page one was some other geezer that he might know just
vaguely; he wasn't sure, but didn't he go out with a very nice-
looking dark feller that he met in the boozer from time to time
and then they both went out on a dragging spree? He would have
to have a word with this feller about it next time they met,
whatever his name was, he probably had lots. Still, give the mate
a bit of margin—after all, just like himself, he was only going for
a stroll, ripping off a bit of bird, it was the kind of thing the
whole world did the whole bleeding time, why be choked if a bit
of vinegar gets upset?

All right, laddie had let his passions stray just a little bit too
far; still he was certainly pretty terrific as an operator.

'Your funny little thing really is tiny, isn't it?' May said to him,
looking at it with interest the first and last night in her life she
saw him naked. She bent down, doubled up in her fat clumsiness
and tried to give it a kiss. He shrank away from her with the
whiplash speed of a viper and she said: 'It's all right, don't get
your knickers in a knot, I was only just looking at it, love, it
looks sort of bruised or something, doesn't it hurt?' She added: 'I
thought you would be huge, like Daddy's, the way you came on
in the pub.' She was a working-class good-works vicar's daughter,
only oversexed. 'I've seen all kinds, but yours is just sort of nothing, isn't it,' she said, 'all sort of black and hurt looking, does it
work? I can hardly even find it, see, I'm looking for it.'

She intended these remarks kindly—affectionately, as if he could
ever have understood what that word meant. These words—her
last—were only casually thrown off, like many a death warrant,
and like every other death warrant, they worked. He remembered
how the bulb her side of the bed at the cheap hotel—twenty-eight
quid for two, cash, no questions—was too bright; also, with
detached affection, the way the back of her head had looked as
her nose dived suddenly into the Schweppes ashtray on the night
table as he cut her and she died. At the same time he dealt with

that thick red crease across her stomach where her panties went which had always made him feel so ill; he also seriously re-arranged the broadening line through the back parting of her hair which meant that May would have gone bald if she had lived long enough, which she really had no valid reason for doing. Even so, like a faded photograph of someone's family that he had half known, the memory of her made him feel nostalgic from time to time—it was a shame, who on earth would have bothered to kill her, she must have been just a pickup in a pub. Well, anyway, she should have been glad to be spared all future indignity—only why should it be he who, as he thought of her, remembered wiping his knife off, putting it back in the black sports bag and leaving by a rusty fire escape?

Still, what could it matter? All these things were just some of those things, images from some second-rate film dug up from somewhere years ago that left you frankly cold—no starring roles.

Well, now the killer felt impelled to leave—not on safety grounds, but because he wanted to preserve the precious afterglow of his rich dinner and take its savoury memory back out into the cold with him—and yet that was the very minute when his vast ban-quet suddenly turned sour in him. It was just as he made up his mind to go that the great rich meal he had indulged in, its pon-derous, heavy, bloody sauces, suddenly rose and boiled in his gut, bringing his stomach heaving up into his mouth. He managed to get to the jacks and spew up most of what he had just supped on and then, when he got back, he found that there was nothing left to gloat over but the revolting litter of an abandoned feast; all at once it was clearing-up time. The scent of the girl's blood had lost its bouquet, its spicy, fresh fragrance, and all of her which, through fullness, he had not been able to enjoy of her lay congealing on the floor, her blood now smelling sharp and acid, like stale wine. Her sprawling limbs admitted only one image. They were what they could only be—joints of chilling, upset meat—and her bloodstained grin, the fixed, yet slack absence of her dark eyes were the worst of all sentences, the one that condemned a killer by looking past him. Yes, something had gone wrong this time. Now the place chilled him; it had acquired an intensity of its own. Since he was in no way equipped to face the appalling result of his butchery, raging, he blamed the room. While he was out of it, being sick, it must have found a subtle opportunity to plot against him, and that was why now the motionless air in there, the feeble electric light, had become thickened, slyly menacing him. That was also why the various smells in there, recalling cold food, gas and green peas all together, the sweetish stench of the old woman's underwear, combined to bring the frightful scenario back into his throat again so that he instantly found more vomit on his tongue. He glanced into the mirror at which he had so lately smiled in triumph. He shouted: 'I look pretty good!' and flexed his muscles, but any third person would have registered nothing more there but a bent and hollow shadow, a seamed, yellow face and eyes that would have made even a trained nurse turn away in horror.

It was true he felt frustrated and cheated. All he had wanted to do was what he always did when he could—take the girl's head off in one, bag it up and get straight back with it to College Hill. There he would have put it on the floor on a dinner plate facing him, just as he had done with the others, so that she could watch him while he punished himself. He would have kept her there as he went into training for as long as possible, but it was always the same in the end, of course—sooner or later it all started to go bad until in the end the lot had to be smashed up and junked, leaving an absence; it was like being thieved of an ornament, a memory, until there was a next time.

Because there was no question of taking this head back—look at it! It was like the day Father papered the parlour—what a fuck-up!

Suddenly he began to hear noises outside; someone was knock-

ing on the front door. He didn't care; there was something else
he had on his mind anyway which would soon make him feel
better. Still, he rapidly picked up his old sports bag, slung its
handles round his neck, raised the bottom sash of the kitchen
window and dropped out onto the drainpipe that he had come
up by. He was already a quarter of the way down when he paused
to listen to a timid rapping on the front door of the flat and an
elderly female voice saying: 'Betty? Mrs Carstairs? *Mrs Carstairs!*
Betty! Dora! Are you all right? Can you answer me, please?
Please!'

The killer smiled as he shinned on down the wall, his mutilated
cock, roughly bandaged to halt the bleeding, forced to grate
against the iron pipe; he whimpered at the pain, already planning
out the ruthless exercises to come.

(We immediately discovered that the old lady who had tapped
at the Carstairs door was an elderly neighbour, a Mrs Drewe and
that, as turned out to be invariably the case with her, she had
nothing useful to tell: 'Like Cupid, I'm very shy and rather blind,
you know,' she explained to me, 'though of course, like any mod-
ern woman I may look very *mondaine*.' I had a feeling she wasn't
entirely sure what that word meant, so I settled my face into a
keen look and hoped she might say something interesting if I
gazed at her long enough. She didn't, though. She set her cracked,
red old lips in a considered manner and said: 'I just fire my little
arrows, Sergeant, never truly knowing where they might land—
but I must bare my soul to the police and admit that in my time
I have had several exciting little adventures. Now when I was in
Buenos Aires in 1953 . . .'

However, as she finally admitted, she had never really had a
single useful thing to say since she had left Tunbridge Wells in
1938 except common gossip, which was why her husband had
dumped her in a Shepherds Market bar one pink-champagney
night in 1949. She added that she was frightfully rich but very
lonely, and that although she had rather lost the habit for young

men like me, we might perhaps just steal upstairs to her flat and have a very small gin and It, one each, no more.

But I was several light-years away from her and I cut her short, assuring her that if she had been three minutes earlier at the door of the Carstairs flat instead of three later, the killer would have opened it to her, in which case she would be dead; it was her instinctive sense of mistiming that had undoubtedly saved her life.

I also told her while I was at it that she had no chance of achieving her one ambition, which was quite obviously to live to be two hundred years old, unless she cured herself of her terrible habit of listening at people's doors and peeping through keyholes, since there were people like me paid to do silly things like that anyway.

The only tangible result that that rather strict little lecture had was to make her ring in to the Factory and complain about my manners, which got a dusty answer from the desk sergeant; he copped a deaf one to her just as he did the day he got a voluble tourist in a lightweight two-piece and wig in front of him who spent a whole hour patiently explaining in Swedish that his brown poodle, which answered to the name Hooki, had last been seen straining its greens against a pillar of Albert Bridge.)

Meantime the killer, in his exalted state of excitement, gave off a dreadful smelly fart as he reached the bottom of the drainpipe, which, the traces of it bright yellow in colour, were afterwards found by us in a pair of his old underpants at College Hill, together with other stains. He crossed the little wreck of garden, littered with empty cement bags and other rubbish less easy to name and found a slice of shadow beyond the reach of the street-lights; there he pulled his sports sack away from around his neck and adjusted his lower clothing, which had taken a good beating, together with what was inside it, during his descent.

What had happened above him was already becoming blurred in his mind. Like any man who has enjoyed a great many women in his time, he had trouble counting all his conquests and seldom tried. He stripped his soaking red gloves off and shoved them into the sports bag last, telling himself to get real racing ones next time with a proper grip; then, having stepped back, he took a run at the low wall between himself and the street and neatly vaulted it.

The street was empty except for the fog that swept slowly round the lights; the pillars were surrounded by rubbish sacks that lay slumped against them, waiting for the garbage truck like old men who had been shot. The killer thrust his bloodstained gloves deep through a rent that gaped in one of the sacks, then crossed the street to a pink Fiat Uno that was parked there.

Although he had only nicked it three days before in Kennington he dropped into it as easily as if he had had it for years, giving the starter an easy time with plenty of choke, because the battery was on the weak side.

The killer drove away looking really excited now because he was by no means exhausted. He was in real training, so it was therefore going to be one of those rich nights that collide with major dying. What he was doing now was motoring over pretty fast to Felix Roatta's palatial house on Clapham Common North Side, as he had some business outstanding there. When he arrived, one in the morning was well gone. There was some fog, and it was thickening. He stopped the Fiat in Marjorie Grove, taking a place at the parked-up kerb by bumping two cars about, then walked back to Roatta's place in his little racing pumps with his usual quick, jerking steps. He met no one. He sprinted up the steps two at a time to the smartly varnished real oak door and rang the buzzer at the base of the answerphone. After the killer had repeated the code twice, Roatta's voice growled into the tin speaker: 'Who is it?'

'It could be Tinkabel,' the killer said, 'so don't fuck me about.'

'You know what time it is?'

. 'I didn't know money cared,' the killer said.

Roatta evidently agreed, because the lock on the heavy door clicked open and the killer went in. His body was glad of the sudden warmth of the pretentious hall, his thinly-soled feet in their sporting pumps grateful for the sumptuous carpet. Roatta said from the head of the stairs: 'Come on up,' but he needn't have bothered to say that at all because the killer was already there. He went up close to Roatta, who sniffed at him.

Roatta said: 'You smell funny.'

The killer said: 'I am funny.'

'In here,' Roatta said, indicating his massive drawing room. A Conservative on his local council, a leading citizen, he feared and detested his visitor, only they had shared interests, so that Roatta had to put up with him whether he liked it or not. Roatta didn't like it. He was too soft now to like anything much except his comfort. The shared interests consisted of a West End club called the Parallel Club which had been doing very very well, but was now suddenly glowing red hot because of some stupid fucking newspaper story, so that even the law, though it had been extremely well seen to, was getting anxious. Roatta wanted to get out of the business cash in hand while it was going, and he believed that because of certain things the visitor had done there, of which he had photographic proof, he had got him into a jam, so he wanted a lot of money for the matter to be like settled. Roatta was a man who wanted a lot of money anyway, but sometimes you can't know what it's wrong to want till it's too late, can you?

'First time I've dropped by here,' the killer said, 'and a nice place it is, too, if you can stay alive in it.'

He reached down between his legs. A little blood was leaking through his crotch; he wiped it away with his forefinger.

Roatta was mesmerised; stupidly, he gazed at the blood spot.

'Now you shouldn't be so indecent,' the killer said softly. 'You shouldn't go showing your eyes around where they don't belong.'

He took a drop more blood away from the place with his finger; only this time he held it under his nose and sniffed it. Then he looked at Roatta again—not at his outside, but at his inside. It was a look that moved on through Roatta and far away. Roatta waved at the big liquor cabinet across the room and said: 'A drink?'

The killer said: 'No.'

'Well, sit down then and feel at ease,' Roatta said; secretly, though, he dreaded for his cushions because at heart he was rather an effeminate person.

'No,' said the killer. He just stood there in front of Roatta, much too close. He stood utterly still, appearing not even to breathe, and saying nothing for such a long time that in the end Roatta, getting nervous, had to bridge the gap.

'All right, then,' Roatta said, 'have you got it?'

'Got what?' the killer said.

'My money,' Roatta said. 'My reddies. Have you got them ready?'

It was the bad joke of the century, but Roatta laughed at it as if he were sitting well back to enjoy—which was a lucky thing for the joke, because it was obvious no one else in the room was going to laugh at it.

'Yes, OK,' said the killer, 'here it is.'

He produced a big 9mm Quickhammer automatic with the tired ease of a conjuror showing off to a few girls and shlacked one into the chamber. He told Roatta: 'Now I want you nice and still while all this is going on, Felix, because you're going to make a terrible lot of mess.'

Roatta immediately screamed: 'Wait! Wait!' but his eyes were brighter than he was, and knew better. They had stopped moving before he did, because they could see there was nothing more profitable for them to look at, so instead they turned into a pair of dark, oily stones fixed on the last thing they would ever see— eternity in the barrel of a pistol. His ears were also straining with the intensity of a concert pianist for the first minute action inside the weapon as the killer's finger tightened, because they knew that was the last sound they would ever hear. So in his last seconds of life, each of them arranged for him by his senses, Roatta sat waiting for the gun to explode with the rapt attention of an opera goer during a performance by his favourite star, leaning further and further forward in his chair until his existence was filed by, narrowed down to, and finally became the gun.

At the same time great changes took place in him. As age goes in the world Roatta was fifty; but as he detected the first, barely perceptible sound in the gun's mechanism he was suddenly a hundred and fifty, then a thousand and fifty, and then two hundred thousand and fifty until, when the killer fired, Roatta's face was bright yellow and he was a million years old, his face hardened in iron concentration before the bullet even struck.

The ammunition was old, like the gun, and the bullet for Roatta had a cross cut in its soft tip. The gun was silenced, but it was a big gun all the same, so that even though it only made a discreet noise like *fup!* when everything happened, a sound between a sneeze and a fart, the effect that the gun had on Roatta was much, much more precise and spectacular than either.

A dizzy series of happenings occurred. The upper part of Roatta's head entirely disappeared; it vanished in a red screen of exploding blood and bone, and when that cleared away, there was nothing left of his head at all except his lower jaw, from which a sly tongue with things running off it dropped sloppily over his chin like a grass trying to sell a phone number. Roatta now resembled some mad orchid—its perimeter decorated with gold fillings in the front but just National Health amalgam in the molars, which didn't cost much and didn't show—or else you could compare him to a wobbling great egg cup if you liked, the red bowl of his throat a squalid crown for the rest of him, which still leaned attentively forward in its real leather armchair. At the same time as his brains were beginning to run down his tasteful walls and slide across the glazing of his well-chosen pictures, a block of hard matter that had been in what was his nose while he had one whirred flatly through the air and went *whack!* onto an occasional table like the hand of one of those very determined women that want an immediate divorce—except that the hand was bright green. Meanwhile, other splinters of Roatta's head, bone, a lot of liquid matter, marrow, stuff that a team of twenty top surgeons would have a hard time putting a name to, rang, splashed, slid and pattered round the room; they rained onto the vulgar, expensive furniture, into the cushions that Roatta had been so worried about, onto the carpet, where they presented as showers of crimson sick—Christ, the bits rained down just about everywhere.

But the killer laughed, because he found it totally hilarious the way the sitting body still had its once white trousers carefully pulled up to preserve the sharp crease. It wasn't the kind of laughter any normal person would want to hear. While it lasted, the expression on the killer's face never varied, and it was a face where laughter didn't frankly work.

If Roatta's death proved anything one didn't know already, which was unlikely, it reminded the investigating officer of the unwisdom of pushing business interests too hard with a multiple killer—in other words, since Roatta was strictly bent, of trying to put the arm on one. A man who is already dead kills freely, and the proof of this adage was all over Roatta's sitting room.

The killer stopped laughing as suddenly as he had begun. He wiped the Quickhammer free of splashes of Roatta with cotton waste, ejected the empty shell and dropped it into his black sports sack next to the axe. Then he took a plastic bag out of it which held a change of clothes; he put these on in Roatta's bathroom. Finally, when he had packed everything up, he walked straight down and out of the house, closed the door, ripped off his gloves, put on another pair and went back to where he had left the car. He abandoned this a mile from College Hill and jogged back the rest of the way, holding himself between the legs with one hand

and his bag with the other, meeting no one in the deep fog. When he got back to College Hill, he tore up the back wall of the burnt-out factory he squatted in by the fire escape and slipped through the glassless window. He wasn't even out of breath. He went straight to his corner where his jute sack lay, stripped to his knickers and lay down on the cement, using his sports sack as a pillow. There was no light or water in the place but that didn't matter, he wasn't civilised. He very seldom needed water, and what he loathed above all was light. Where he could fold into himself and stay suspended like a bat during such little ease as he knew was in the dark, and there was plenty of that here. Only a far-off streetlight diffused some orange glow through the fog a hundred yards away where Lovelock Road joined College Hill, and the set of traffic lights there snapped regularly on and off. Yes, the squat would do till the council meddlers came round for a shufty, but that wouldn't be tomorrow; it would do him for a time. He no longer consciously remembered the two women as he prepared to sleep; even the image of Roatta's head, not an hour old, was getting blurred. Training would begin when it got light at seven; punishment tomorrow evening.

He closed his eyes.

He dreamed he was by the sea; there was no sky. The colour of the sea was brown, and as well as the waves rolling in frowning lines towards the beach, brains tumbled about in the slow breakers, seamed with red threads. The dream did not disturb him, but he woke on his damp and freezing floor because the punishment he had inflicted on himself going down the drainpipe at Empire Gate had made the shreds of his penis bleed again, and he had awoken because he was in pain.

As soon as he was half-awake he slipped his knickers off. Holding them close to his face, he handled them loosely for a moment with an absent expression, then suddenly buried his nose in them, his dark eyes huge, his face monstrous with the wisdom of evil. As well as the blood and the seepage from last night's ejaculation he had shit himself lavishly in his sleep, a sloppy, yellow liquid. Having spent a while burying his face in them, he folded the knickers up and put them carefully to one side on top of a stack of others. He would never wash them; he would never wear them again. Every secretion that had occurred in his underclothes before, during, or sometimes just after a moment of action was a souvenir to be preciously kept and safeguarded. He wasn't a clean person in any sense of the word; he was absolutely connected to his bodily smells as though they alone proved to him, for want of other evidence, that he existed. From these excreta he would from time to time select an example years after it was dry, consulting it, scenting its associations, and then turn generally back through the pile slowly, nostalgically, as a man turns back through time—stroking, sniffing at the fetid little crusts much as any of us might look wistfully at the flowers that he pressed between the leaves of a book when we were a child. Finally he laid the knickers away and jerked his way to the window. There he shook his tangled face and said, half aloud:

'There really are times when I frankly don't know how I keep a firm grasp on my reason.'

His lips, grey and sharp, were bent sharply downwards in the shape of a sickle. His eyes compelled the other because they bore the stare of someone entirely lost on the earth, and he was the most hideous thing that you prayed you might never see.

# 2

I was down at Brighton for the day. The front enclosed the sea, which wasn't a bad idea; the only thing wrong was the town behind it, which I thought was a pity. I thought it would have been pleasant to have had just Sussex countryside, narrow lanes leading to a village or two, but there was no more hope of that. I stood some distance from the sea at the top of the stony beach. It wasn't that I minded getting wet, since it was raining anyway. The sea grumbled greenly around inside the old harbour walls and the breakwaters, under the pier. It looked as fed up as I was, so that in the end I decided that the best cure would be to go and massacre a beer in a pub I had spotted not far off actually open for trade called the Fishing Smack, as our seafaring big London brewers call practically any pub within the smell of seaweed if the opposition hasn't already got away with the title for one of theirs. I noticed there was a door at the side as I entered; what was left of the word GENTS on the heavy-glazed pane was well scarred, someone must have cracked a bottle against it, or more likely a head.

There were few folk in there just yet since it was early, so I ordered a pint of the Kronenbourg and went over to the window with it to sit at the end of the long bar and watch the sea again in its troubled equinox movement. The rain was coming down really hard now, I saw, without the red-coated young barman polishing his pint pots about half a mile away having to remind me of it, so I watched the sea practising really, like a county-class cricketer who doesn't have to try very hard for the match but with a batting problem at the nets, slogging plastic bottles from the cap of one glutinous wave to the next. I drank some of my beer and watched three local men of a certain age wearing macs, sou'westers and gumboots, walk slowly down the steep slope of pebbles to examine the same scene. I watched it with them from the bar and then farther out, beyond them, southwards until the water stopped being shore green and turned a freezing far-out Channel blue, rolling backwards with the outgoing tide until I supposed it must get to France or anything else solid enough to stop it.

I didn't especially know why I was down there; it was a Sunday, and I had merely woken up that morning, immediately got up and dressed as though I were still in a hurry to get round to A14, only to remember as I always did, once I was well awake, that I was beached. But today, on an impulse to get away from Acacia Circus, I had just got the Ford off the weeds that were gnawing its tyres away by the kerb and come down to Brighton because it was near. It was something to do—something that helped me forget, at least for an afternoon, that I was permanently prevented from doing my proper work. I had one key phrase against being bitter about this. I thought always, and was thinking now as I drank my beer: 'Well anyway, if Frank Ballard, brave man, better mate than him I never had, and he paralysed from the waist down for life by a gunshot wound, if he can take it and not go mad, then I can bloody take it.' Finishing my beer, I thought: 'After all, what's the alternative?' I was both a human being and a disciplined police officer, and so because I had combined what I saw as justice with my duty, I had struck a fellow officer, been judged by the police and fired. It was to do with a case called the Mardy affair. After I had repeatedly warned him not to give in to an excess of zeal and to keep completely out of my way, for his own sake and notably for the accused's own, and he still interfered because he had been promoted inspector and didn't like the way I invariably handled my work on my own, I hit him and broke his jaw, and so I was brought before a police disciplinary board, was heard by three senior officers from the north country where nobody knew me, was found against and fired—that's getting on for a year back now.

But if it were all to do over again, I would do it all over again; I know my hands are clean.

I felt like going outside for a minute, so walked down to the bottom of Palmyra Square, where long ago I had been sent down to see into the deaths of a young couple who had lived in the top flat at number eight. There had been no point in my going, really, because they were both dead, and there was nothing I could find out or add to what the Brighton police already knew, that they had been credit-card ripping and it was catching up with them— had caught up. They had a great lunch at Wheelers, where they had invited people over to their table for brandies, after which they walked hand in hand down the pebble beach where I had just been standing and then on out to sea. The sea did for them what they had asked it to do and then afterwards brought them back to the beach in its own time, wet as fish and green with weed, their faces greyish white and their arms still half trailing round each other, and I don't know why, but when I saw them like that in Brighton morgue, I was convulsed with what I felt in myself to be a rightful fury.

I looked out to sea again. It was the end of February, the twenty-sixth, and all at once the short afternoon had had enough; it scattered its way off towards the night chased by short, dirty clouds. I remember I got home to my wife Edie in the end at about two in the morning and she said: 'You look dreadful, what was it?'

'A double suicide at Brighton, boy and girl. Banks, credit cards. They asked the Factory to send someone down.'

'Why get in a state?' said Edie. 'It happens all the time, you've only to open a paper.'

'I know it does,' I said, 'and I always want to know why.'

'Well, that's what they pay you for, to find out, if you call that pay, what you draw.'

'That's what I've just been doing,' I said, 'and it isn't that, it's a question of two deaths down to a square of fucking plastic.'

'The public has to be protected,' she said.

I said: 'They were the public, you stupid woman.'

'They tried to get their hands into the till and it didn't work,' said Edie severely. That was always one of the troubles with my wife Edie. For her and for her father the low-grade police was beneath her socially; she wasn't the daughter of a big wheel in the fruiterer's trade for nothing, apples by the ton up from Kent. 'Scratch my back for me, will you?' I remember she said then. 'I've got an itch between my shoulder blades where I can't reach it.'

We went to bed and I said: 'I've seen them.'

'Seen what? Look, just settle, will you? Why won't you settle?'

'Seen their bodies,' I said.

'So?'

'The sea had turned them surprisingly fucking little,' I said.

'Oh?' she said. She added: 'I do wish you wouldn't swear.'

'You just can't help it in my job, Edie. Don't you see, the words sometimes take the place of tears.'

'I wish you'd just go to sleep,' she said, 'it's nearly four.'

'I can't, Edie,' I said. 'Oh, why can't you just be a wife to me for once, just hold me quietly for a while and don't say anything more just now.'

But she said: 'I think you really ought to know it, and Dad agrees with me, you're a dreadful load on me at times—all this perturbed thinking of yours and you nothing but a detective sergeant who'll never go up in rank because you insist it isn't rank that matters.' She sat bolt upright in the bed, pointed to her stomach and screamed: 'Well, all right, then, if that's the way you want it, look at the load I'm carrying thanks to you, Mr Police Officer with the Lofty Ideas—I think you're altogether too sensitive for the police sometimes, I really do, and now there's the child due in May with all the expenses it'll bring, and a fat lot you care! She's due on the twentieth, the doc says, and I tell you I am near the point when I don't want to know!'

But presently she lay down again and her voice faded; I was glad of that. That night I realised that I had married Edie for her fatal, extraordinary body, not her opinions. I understood that no body could ever be enough if it held opinions in dead opposition to my own. I already knew that I wanted the coming child, who was, for nine short years, to be my daughter Dahlia, far more than Edie did; I loved Dahlia even before she was born, which may have been why Edie always hated her, who knows, and my love for the child meant that I would always find a means of tolerating Edie on account of Dahlia; I would find some means of growing deaf. All I had wanted that night was to hold Edie against me in my vulnerable hour after that day in Brighton. It was her primitive security that I needed; just a fraction of what Edie's body was giving to the child she bore. That was all I needed to recover and so, through being reassured, feel enabled to get into perspective that greenish couple still in their trailing decomposed embrace, their swollen, expressionless faces nibbled by fish— what I needed from Edie then was her kisses, her comfort, just for a few minutes, and so prove to me that love can banish the frozen, lazy rottenness of eyes that have been eight days underwater.

We all have our weak moments.

·  ·  ·

When I got in to Acacia Circus, the phone was ringing. I got my
key into the lock quickly, but by the time I got the door open
the bell had stopped. But I had a feeling it would soon start again;
I just had a feeling when I heard it ring, that's all. It wasn't just
intuition either. One, people hardly ever ring me, and two, on
my way home I had stopped off at the Princess of Wales over in
Battersea for a Kronenbourg; and it happened that three men
came in, one of them with a Sunday-edition copy of the *Recorder*,
which he put on the bar beside him open at an inside page. The
headline read: REVOLTING DOUBLE MURDER—AXEMAN STRIKES. I
said to the man whose paper it was: 'Do you think I could just
have a look at that?'

'Feel free.'

I flattened the page out on the bar and leaned over it.

Mrs Betty Carstairs, 86, of 19, Empire Gate, South Kensington, and a woman of about 30 whose identity the police
have yet to establish, were both found murdered in appalling
circumstances late last night by a neighbour in the Victorian
building, Mrs Philippa Drewe. There is no doubt that the
killer entered the flat through the rear sitting room window,
and left the same way. The flat is on the ground floor, but it
is some distance from the back of the block to the ground,
and Poland Street police are satisfied that the killer made
use of the drainpipe which descends to the waste patch of
garden twenty-five feet below. Mrs Carstairs died through
being hurled into her hall clock; her friend or lodger was
literally hacked to pieces with the killer's axe. Chief Inspector Charles Bowman of the Serious Crimes squad, who is in
charge of the enquiry at present, told us in his usual ener-
getic way: 'You can hardly expect me to make any com-
ment on this disgusting business yet, as I have only just
arrived, and may well hand over this matter to colleagues,
because I am on the missing Yugoslav princess affair over in
Walthamstow.'

It was only a few lines of newsprint but a strange feeling came over me when I read them; I quickly finished up my beer and left.

As I drove back to Acacia Circus I thought of the nights, far back, when I had made love to Edie. She told me once, just before she did what she did to Dahlia, I mean killing her, that out of all the times we had made love, there were only three when she had ever felt anywhere near me; the other times she told me she was completely absent. Somewhere inside me I knew it myself; there were nights when my hands knew, even while they were caressing her body, that she was immersed solely in thoughts of hatred and new curtains. Because of her mental trouble which, until it was too late, I never would admit that she had, she was never sincere with me about anything, but responded to any approach I made to her with a perfunctory sweetness, which in the end I found I couldn't swallow, no matter how hard I tried on account of my unending physical desire for her; until, towards the end, even such grim coquetry, which was all that madness had left her where others were concerned, could only begin after an evening of rum and cokes at the Maid's Head. Or else she might just as easily start screaming if I so much as touched her, with the child sleeping next door.

I found that these days, so many years ago now—eight—since Dahlia's death and Edie's admission to Banstead, I now only thought of Edie when I felt that something abominable was about to happen—something capital and irrevocable in my life; and now tonight, for the first time since I had been discharged from the police, as I drove, Edie, in my mind, was treading heavily towards me yet again in her unrippable dress, drivelling her disjointed evil. Since she was a murderess, Edie, who had impregnated me so deeply with herself that I shall remember her forever with no hope either of peace from her or replacement for her, made me understand murderers better than I ever otherwise could have: their lapses, the vile din of their fugues, the whole negative concerto of insecurity expressed in absent violence, their desires expressed in ways that were thought to have died; but evil never dies. In the old days, as I reached my climax with her, Edie moaned, shouted or screamed as if in delight; but I subsequently understood that she had never understood what that word meant. I was always too hard at work, also emotionally involved with her, ever to consider her objectively, but what I slowly understood was that she was patiently trying out a range of approaches to me, all copied; and that from her point of view I was a piece of flat cardboard cut out roughly as a man. Like all murderers she knew that she must not make too many obvious mistakes, so she worked intelligently and patiently, suppressing her real drives for as long as it took her to formulate those copies of love which would blind and subordinate me to her. She held the ace of hearts after all, my passion for her, and so became my master in the end, the way she played me, knowing that her hatred must never show on those nights, rationed, when she realised that I had to have her if she were to pass, unobserved, as normal; so that when I came to her, her long hair was always arrayed on the pillow and she would immediately surround me with her thick white arms, spreading her apparently hot, solid thighs and stomach, which were in complete contrast to the thin lecturing lips and spurious eyes that she has when I go to see her at Banstead now, and muttering her love for me.

Love which, even with the plunging sensation of my heart and mind, I could never accept was false, because I did not want to live without her body, as I should have had to if I had judged her by her mind.

Now, having passed through what I was hard taught, I have for a long time made use of it in my work to judge and place the actions and motives of others and see how the catcher, to be a true arrow against assassins, must at some time in his own life have personally had to do with one.

I got a can of beer out of the fridge, stripped it open and sat down at the kitchen table with its chrome legs and bitter blue Formica surface. I took a swallow of the beer, trying to conceive what it meant to be murdered. I tried to imagine Carstairs's and

Suarez's terror at the killer's sudden irruption into the flat on Saturday night—until in the end, for an instant, I became Suarez physically as the killer came for her, and felt as paralysed as she did as the axe bit into her arm at the swinging finish of its parabola.

The phone rang again. I picked it up and said: 'Yes.'

The Voice said, as if I had never been away: 'There you are. You're back on the police.'

'A14?'

'Yes.'

I said: 'It isn't to do with the axe murder of those two women over in Kensington at all, Carstairs and Suarez, is it?'

The Voice said: 'It is. What have you heard about it?'

I said: 'I read about it in the paper tonight coming back from Brighton.' I added: 'I'm a private citizen; I don't have to be dead easy about going back to Poland Street just like that.'

'Yes, you do,' said the Voice, 'so get round here now.'

'It's not on,' I said. 'There's the Fox matter, the disciplinary board, all the breakage you get when you try and string me round with a load of cunts.'

'It's all arranged,' the Voice said. 'The Fox affair is forgotten because I'm shorthanded.'

'You make me feel really wanted,' I said.

'Nobody particularly wants you,' the Voice said. 'I need you; there's a difference. So get over to the Factory, get your arse in gear. By the way, there's a mate of yours, Sergeant Stevenson over on A14, who's dealing with another death over at Clapham that happened within hardly an hour of Carstairs/Suarez and he wants to talk to you. You come in now, ask for my deputy, Detective Chief Superintendent Jollo, sign some paper which'll give you a warrant card, then get onto Chief Inspector Bowman, Serious Crimes, he was first on the scene; he'll take you over to Kensington. Also see Stevenson as soon as you can. Now come on, move—I've no one obstinate enough but you to put on this, so hurry—I'm having my wig twisted over this one from upstairs.'

'Why's that?' I said.

'You put your questions to the dead,' the Voice said. 'No point your putting them to me.'

It rang off.

I got to Poland Street and found Bowman. He wore a brand-new black leather jacket which made me understand what sixty-year-old hippies were going to end up looking like, and his face was sort of a funny colour.

'What's the matter with you,' I said, 'have you got flu or something?'

'Don't start,' he said, 'now just don't, Sergeant, that's all, and let's get going, the car's waiting.'

I felt sorry for him, and the trouble between us always was that it showed.

Even though Empire Gate was a mile long, running south at right angles to the Thames with Kensington Palace and the Soviet embassy behind it, it was easy enough to pick out the stucco porch we wanted because there was a uniformed officer standing under the portico at the foot of the steps going up to the block. It was eleven on Sunday morning when we arrived, and the February sun, the colour of a fake guinea, shone down palely on the quiet, dirty pavement, on the big Mercedes of third secretaries parked in front of dubious embassies. Bowman said to the copper on the door with his usual charm: 'Bowman, Serious Crimes, open up, son.' He added, pointing to me: 'And tell your folk that this officer is taking over the case so that they'll know, all right?'

'All right,' said the officer, looking at me, 'I make him.' He led us indoors and along a worn carpet that ran along the ground floor to a dark door under the staircase.

'Everybody been and gone?' I said to Bowman, meaning the technical people.

'Yes,' said the uniformed man. He got the flat key out of his pocket and handed it to me.

Bowman said to him: 'Now go back to the door and stay there till you're told to do something different.'

The officer answered: 'I've had an offer of good work in this big bakery over at Camden Town.'

Bowman said: 'Take it then, sonny. You're dead right, why stand out here in the cold freezing your bollocks off?'

When he had gone, Bowman said to me: 'Are you going in first?'

'You're the major general,' I said, 'the way you just came on.'

'Yes, only it's my second time in here,' said Bowman. He swallowed.

I said: 'It's that bad, is it?'

He said: 'Yes.'

'All right,' I said, 'then stay out in the hallway with the uniformed baker there.'

Bowman said: 'No, but I'd appreciate it if you went in first.'

I had never seen Bowman like this before; but anyway I took the Banham key I had been given, set it in the lock, opened the door and went in. The first thing I took in were the lower limbs of Betty Carstairs because there they were directly under my feet, lying outside the bent clock which sprawled against the filthy wall inside the front door like a drunk that had been beaten up. The top of the clock had collapsed on her head and chest and one of its lead weights, pieces of a chamber pot, wood, glass and blood lay spread round her; I noticed fleetingly that the dial of the clock bore some kind of miniature boating scene with Windsor Castle in the background.

I took in the shambles of the dark, cramped Victorian hall next. There was a pervading smell of urine everywhere. A pointed old woollen hat lay under a table where the phone stood with its

cable ripped out. There was blood on the hat; it must have fallen
off Carstairs's head when she hit the clock. Immediately beyond
her body a narrow corridor wandered at an angle to a kitchen
door kept open by a rug swollen with damp—all this back part
of the flat, the hall and the kitchen, was bitterly cold.

I went into the kitchen; it was still lit by one feeble dirty bulb
high up in the ceiling. It was a tall room, but it was crammed
with rubbish that reached right up to the remains of its moulded
plaster cornice. Trunks, old TV sets dating back to the days when
God was still yelling for his bottle, supported stacks of battered
suitcases and boxes overflowing with the kind of junk you tried
to avoid at the Harrow Road end of Portobello Road; heaps of
cracked dishes rose unsteadily from hard armchairs upholstered
in British Rail. The floor was littered with rusting fish forks in
mock-ivory handles, lengths of material, a pile of men's homburg
hats going back to the thirties, serge skirts, rayon stockings, pink
underwear which was making a comeback after seventy years—
all this was bursting out of suitcases with broken latches marked
*P&O—Not Wanted on Voyage* or out-of-council rubbish sacks, so
that the only free space was an enclave under a window blinded
by dark red paper. The sweet, rotten odour that infested this place
came from a trailing, unmade bed with two mattresses supported
by books; I uncovered the bed and found the mattresses to be
soaked with urine and encrusted with human dirt.

At right angles to the bed stood an old General Electric fridge
with its motor humming ceaselessly; it would go on humming
until it fused because the case of the fridge had long ago rusted
out. Opposite the fridge stood a greasy old New World cooker
in speckled grey enamel stamped *Mark I Series 1940*, its oven
jammed with enormous dishes such as large families used fifty,
sixty years ago. A dented aluminium kettle stood on one jet of
the cooker next to a slab of bacon that had been forgotten about
and rotted, and there was a gas leak somewhere, probably from
the fifty-year-old heater that fed the hot-water tap to the sink.

Directly I felt able, I turned back to the hall and knelt down beside Betty Carstairs. I absorbed every detail of her position, judged the force with which she had been thrown into the clock and took note of every inch of her clothing. What I observed first was a short, naked expanse of withered thigh, the skin and bone showing between a half-length lisle stocking; then a thick old tweed skirt up round her waist—only now, whatever she might once have held precious in herself was as meaningless as a dead soldier after a battle; whatever she might once have believed herself to be was exploded by the violence that had been done to her.

There was a crumpled piece of writing paper lying near the body and I picked it up, straightened it out. I could see at once that the handwriting was not Mrs Carstairs's, but a young woman's. There was just one line on it: 'Now I need a long rest.'

I got my flashlight out because the flat was so dark and examined next, as I had to, the angle of Mrs Carstairs's head to her shoulders and then, having gently felt her neck, confirmed that it was broken. I turned her face just a little in doing so and her denture, that had been forced halfway out of her mouth, slipped back to its normal place as though in gratitude, and the old lips, though fixed, appeared to me to smile. Otherwise her face had been obliterated by terror and disfiguration—wiped out and replaced by the sly look that the dead assume after just a few hours.

I said to Bowman behind me: 'Have they timed this yet?'

'They say Saturday between eleven at night soonest, one o'clock Sunday morning latest, but of course we haven't had the results of the autopsy yet.'

I said: 'I want that soonest.'

He said: 'You know what they're like down there, you'll have to push them.'

I said: 'I'll push them, if they need pushing.'

Bowman said: 'You're going to have to polish your buttons over this one, there's a right flap on upstairs over it.'

'It's the press that bothers them up there,' I said, 'not the bodies.' I added: 'And as for my buttons, I'll polish them to where they're likely to blind someone.'

'You'd better come and look next door now,' he said.

I stroked Betty Carstairs's half-open right hand and said: 'Yes, all right, let's go into the other room now and see the girl.'

He said: 'Wait, let's take our time.'

'What difference will that make?' I said.

Time? How long had my encounter with the dead woman taken? What had it done to me? How long had it really taken me to lean over Betty where she lay in the clock and stroke her smashed face and hand and then pick the splinters off her concave chest?

'Let's go in,' said Bowman, but he was very white, and I stopped him by putting my hand gently on his shoulder and the gesture felt strange, made towards someone I normally so intensely disliked.

'No,' I said, 'stay where you are.'

There was no putting the moment off, so I walked forward into the dark yellow room where the girl lay. As I pushed the door slowly wider open I saw a few fingers of blood that lay drying on the mat. In the dark February light they looked black, as did the red smears on the scaling yellow edge of the door and the jamb, and I was so chilled by what I saw that I found myself behaving like someone in a bad dream, so that I felt I glided, propelled rather than walking normally, over to where the girl lay between the two beds. The smell of her entrails was already very noticeable, but after a time I bent and touched the pool of blood nearest her. It was already cold, with scabs forming on it due to the low winter temperature; underneath it was sticky, oily. The blood lay on the uncarpeted parts of the floor, soaking into the planks; it lay in blots on the bedding, on the furniture, shattered by poverty, on the walls, with thicker lumps and gobs stuck to surfaces here and there; as I pursued my examination I discovered that the murderer had licked and eaten small pieces of her; he had also ejaculated against the top of her right thigh. Something over by the boarded-up fireplace attracted my attention, and I walked over to find a small curl of blackish shit lying there.

Bowman came over and we stood looking down at the hard little turd.

Bowman said: 'Why do so many of them feel they have to do that?'

'It's egoism and overexcitement,' I said. 'It's part of a very complicated way of getting your rocks off—it's also like someone illiterate signing some document with an $X$.'

He stirred the stool with the tip of his Regent Street boot. 'What chance do you think you've got, catching him?'

I said: 'I'll get him.'

'We think so, too,' said Bowman, 'but don't think we're going to do you any out-of-the-way favours.'

'I'll find my own way of getting any help I need,' I said, 'and as for favours, you may find that by putting me on this you won't have done yourself any.' I added: 'Just fuck off now, Charlie, will you? I want to be on my own.'

'Watch your tone, Sergeant.'

I said: 'It's my case. Go outside. I want to be alone with her.'

When he had gone, I got down on my knees beside Dora's body and at once felt close to her, but also separated from her by a distance that I had no means to describe. She was very slender, and wore the bloody remains of a new dress. It was pink and white, with dark flowers on it; its skirt just covered her knees. At first, as I looked at her legs lying folded under her, it seemed to me that her body from her thighs down to her feet was swollen, too heavy in relation to the rest of her—that her dark head, slight shoulders were too elegant for them—but then I realised that that was how, propped up against the bed, she had drained—the law of gravity had filled her like that with her blood, like a sausage with meat, and that was how death had left her.

It was a long time before I could make myself look closely into her ruined face with the terrible hacks, gashes, bruising and broken bone on its bad side. I wouldn't do it until I was alone, and yet to be alone with her was really worse to begin with, because I was afraid that I might get so far out of touch by looking at her that I might never get back; I was as frightened to look at her as I would be to drown.

And yet I found, far from being afraid when I did look into her face, that I was in tears. The good side of it, except for one smear of blood down her cheek, was intact. The axe had struck her across, and then down the face, the bad side. Her eyes were not damaged; they were black, ironic and three-quarters open—blind almonds turned in towards a corner of the high ceiling with the sly pointlessness of the dead.

Presently I got out my flashlight and shone it over her, because the place where she had collapsed and died between the beds was so dark, and the old white light-shade overhead, thick with dust, was wrongly placed to shed enough light on her. In the glare of the torchlight her indifferent eyes glittered coldly past me. On these eyes, the dust of our great capital was already beginning to settle. She was still a very beautiful girl for a few more hours yet as long as you looked at the untouched part of her, for she was only newly dead. Only her brow, drawn in the stiff frown of terror, spoiled her expression, and her lips were unnatural; they were slightly but slackly parted to show her teeth, as though she were finally bored with some argument. Death had already been at work drawing shades across her cheeks up to the widow's peak of her black hair; but the saddest thing to me, because it was totally incongruous, was the outflung gesture of her unhurt arm, which seemed to be waving to everyone in the world, telling them not to be afraid but follow her—and it was only when I touched her back and felt the arch of her spine impossibly bent against the side of the bed that I saw how, in her last abominable agony, the poor darling had wanted to try and stand up again, to escape death for just one second more so that she could explain everything that she was so suddenly having to leave.

A short way from her, three feet from the beds, stood a low table which had not been overturned in the struggle; on it lay a magazine open at a travel agent's advertisement offering cut-price charter flights to Hawaii. I felt it was the last dream of escape that Dora had had before she died, and as I read it I felt her whole presence, a vast sorrow, concentrated on the double-page spread. In the bright photograph palm trees arched outwards, their fronds racing seaward in the wind, reaching for the brilliant waves; just under the trees, a young couple stood staring out across miles of empty beach at the Pacific, which receded so far that it finally vanished into the coupon that you had to send off now to qualify for the reduction that was valid till the first of July only.

It was then, and only then, that I understood what it really meant, the feeling of people's rightful fury and despair, and it came together with my desire to bend over Suarez and whisper, 'It's all right, darling, don't worry, everything'll be all right, I'm here now, it'll be all right now'—and the feeling was so strong in me that I knelt and kissed her short black hair which still smelled of the apple-scented shampoo she had washed it with just last night; only now the hair was rank, matted with blood, stiff and cold.

I went out to the squad car parked across the street and said to the driver: 'Get through on the radio and tell them they can come for the bodies now.'

Bowman was bent over double in the back of the car. 'What's the matter with you?' I said.

'Ulcer playing up.'

I said: 'While the ambulance is on its way I'm just going back in to look through their things.'

'That's all been done,' Bowman said.

'A14?'

'Of course not. No, the real mob. Serious Crimes.'

'That's not good enough,' I said.

'You cheeky bastard,' said Bowman. 'What do you mean, not good enough?'

I said: 'I'll do it my own way, Charlie. You needn't wait—I don't want to keep you from your Yugoslav princess.'

'It was a mistake getting you back, after all,' Bowman said. He clutched his stomach and grinned with pain.

'You ought to see a doctor about that,' I said. I added: 'It wasn't a mistake—I want whoever killed Carstairs and Suarez badly. I solve my cases, but I do it a lot faster when there aren't a lot of unnecessary people about. If you don't believe me, ask Inspector Fox.'

Bowman left in a fury, slamming the car door which he had opened to spit out of. He was always the same, a glutton for other people's punishment—only it never worked with me and he knew it, not that that stopped him, his obsessions being a good deal stronger than he was.

I phoned Stevenson at the Factory. I liked Stevenson. He had come over to A14 from Camberwell not long before I was fired, and we got on straightaway. He was a pale, blond man in his thirties who looked as if he were hard into sport—he wasn't, though. What he was hard into was nailing a free pint, psychopath or villain—he was also, like me, into cutting grasses' price to the bone, which may have been his Scottish blood coming out. He gave the cigarette firm that churned out Westminster filters no peace by smoking practically their whole production through each revolution of the sun. Whether night or day, he blew this vile smoke into the faces of people who had tripped up in the wire somewhere; he blew it at them over at the Factory in Room 202, and was generally noted at all levels as an intelligent, nonviolent man, and yet best not fucked about. In fact, Stevenson was a man rather like me, which meant we could have a word without having to get the dictionary out.

'Well,' he said, 'how's the morale? You on Empire Gate?'

'Yes, that's why I rang you,' I said. 'The Voice said to. And is that right you're into the Roatta death over at Clapham?'

He said: 'Dead on.'

'How was it?'

'Depends if you like the living room done out in grey and red—I saw in the *Recorder* it's up-and-coming fashionable, the new macabre style. But what interests me is the short space of time it took between your job and mine.'

'It would have to have been really brutal for it to be the same feller,' I said.

'Don't trouble your soul over that,' Stevenson said, 'it is.'

'Well,' I said, 'I reckon Empire Gate to Clapham Common North Side to be not even two miles' worth, and don't villains love wheels? Yes, it could sound cosy, who knows? The time it takes for a few sets of lights to change, crossing the bridge at one in the morning. Roatta, how was he done, you say? Nasty? I've not read it.'

'Top of his head blown off,' Stevenson said, 'just the bottom jaw left, the rest of it part of the wallpaper, no extra price. Done with a Quickhammer, nine-millimetre, bullet was a dumdum, if you call that nasty.'

'Well, I don't call it polite,' I said.

'These maniacs just cannot seem to learn manners,' Stevenson said.

'On the other hand I can't say my heart's bleeding over the fact Roatta's gone,' I said. 'We all know about Felix, on the local council, virgil, father and friend to all, also high up the ladder in West End clubs and prostitution, only try and nail him. Still, the killer's the wet twat to get into, so yes, let's have a chat about it like straightaway, because if our luck was running for once, it could turn out to be the same individual, you never know— anyway we've got to start somewhere.'

'Who was this Suarez girl of yours anyway?' Stevenson said. 'Anything known?'

'That's the problem,' I said. 'I'm having her checked north, south, east and west, but as far as I can tell so far, she was clean for us, not a day's form.'

'That blows our theory to bits, then,' said Stevenson, 'because if she had anything even remotely to do with Roatta, she can't have been clean, therefore we're looking for two killers, not one, and that's a pity.'

'Don't be too sure,' I said. 'I went through Empire Gate really close-coupled and found a notebook she'd written which I'm working through, only I haven't had time to finish it yet—but Suarez wasn't clean. She doesn't come out sunny-side through her own writings, anyway not to me.' I added: 'There's something weird in this from my end altogether. These two women were axed to death, but I don't swallow at all, after reading her note-book, that it was just the casual nut, the passing axeman who loves to drop in. I think Suarez was a whore. I think she was in love with someone on a one-way basis. What I know by reading her was that she had had enough. What I saw in the flat with Bowman was that she was dressed to kill or die. Her notebook never gives dates, just days of the week, but I feel pretty sure that the Saturday where she writes that she's going to top herself was the same night she was done. She was also, going by the notebook, physically a very sick girl, and the whole thing stinks to me.'

'It would help us if it stank of Roatta as well,' Stevenson said.

'Well, Carstairs/Suarez does have that kind of stench,' I said, 'if we can just find something like a link.' I added: 'Well, I'll be round as soon as the traffic permits, I'm starting now,' I said. 'Do you know where they've put me?'

'You're back in 205.'

'Bet my plastic tulips have gone.'

'Yes, some cunt left the window open and a vulture did a hot cross out of the zoo, flew over and shat on them, so some pure little WPC held them at arm's length and took them down to the garbage.'

'Oh well, they were getting faded looking anyway,' I said. 'Too bad—I'll buy some more with my first pay cheque if I ever live to draw the fucking thing. By the way, you seen Charlie Bowman around the buildings anywhere?'

'Well, fancy that now,' Stevenson said, 'hold on, here he comes bowling in right now asking for you, and judging by the look on his face, which is all red and funny looking, you'd better do the same. I'll wait for you.'

'I'm on my way,' I said.

'Well, it's good you're back,' said Stevenson, 'it means there'll be a few brains around the place for once.'

'Some people won't be happy about that,' I said.

'Fuck them.'

On my own at last, thank God, I went back into the flat and walked round its half darkness very quietly. The folk from the lab had left everything as they had found it. The back window, by which everyone was agreed the killer had entered and left, still stood half-open, the dust on the base of the frame still smeared by his hastily departing glove.

I walked round and round the flat; I was beyond the two corpses now because I was already with them.

I knew what it meant when Serious Crimes said they had been through a place. They were thorough, all right; the trouble always was, though, that they were thorough but not absolute; that was because they often didn't take enough time to think out what they were looking for. Thus, they would ignore what I would seize on, thinking it unimportant; conversely, they would preciously gather up in their special bags items that turned out to be of no interest at all.

What I wanted from Betty and Dora immediately was traces they had left—writing, letters, a scrawled note, even—anything that spoke of them.

Locking myself into it against all interruption, I began existing in that golgotha. I searched among the boxes, trunks and suitcases. There were over a hundred of them in the kitchen alone. But except for a few of her clothes at the end of her bed and a bra and slip hung out to dry in the bathroom on a line, there seemed to be nothing of Dora's.

What was it Wilfred Owen had written on the Sambre front in 1917?

> Oh what made fatuous sunbeams toil
> To break earth's sleep at all?

It struck me that rooms like these, situations like these, were the front line of the eighties—but this flat seemed to me to be worse than what I usually got, because the very people that the dead armies had fought to protect had been murdered in their turn, and this time there had been no one to protect them.

Such light as there was in the flat faded as I searched it and waited for the ambulance to come until I had to turn the lights on; the afternoon assumed a short, steep winter slant, dulling the high windows a grimy yellow and blackening the plane trees outside, while in the basement flat someone played the same Chopin prelude over and over and over.

I had the most marvellous dream the night before I went down to Brighton; in it I met the sweetest woman I am sure I have ever seen. I was lying in bed in a strange room in a hot, foreign country; but the southern light was dimmed, altered by half-closed shutters, and the high room was cool. I was just wakening in the dream with a feeling of regret at some absence, but tenderly and without sadness, when suddenly she came in and knelt beside me on the bed.

It was most certainly a very old-fashioned room I was in, I should say at least a hundred years old, with a green iron bed standing on a six-sided, tile-patterned floor, terra-cotta, perhaps; I seemed to be in some foreign country hotel. She wasn't beautiful or even all that young; she was well dressed and thickset. She smiled at me, reaching out to stroke my face, and said: 'I have no name.' But I had only to look at her when she appeared in the dream to think, 'Ah, good, you're finally here—now there's two of us, together we can get something done at last'; and thinking this in the dream had a deeply pacifying effect on me. The single swift movement with which she gave herself to me in her day-clothes gave me no time to think, and I couldn't be expected to know the whole of what she conveyed in the space of the dream; but there was nothing hurried in the first close look of our faces. I really just remember my astonishment at the slenderness of her hands, at the intense bronze shade of her face, and at her hair, which was short, knotted quickly and practically at the back of her head. Also her hair was scented in a way I couldn't recapture afterwards; she was the face of a goddess on a thousand-year-old coin that has never been touched, found, damaged or exchanged. Smiling into my eyes, she pulled the skirt of her street suit swiftly up over her hips and we met immediately in my arms. We had no time for anything more, but I managed to say: 'You are the most heavenly woman I have ever met,' and she said: 'I know, and you have been looking for me for a long time, and so I have come because you believed and knew I would come'—and so we made love and I woke in a state of great peace, knowing that somehow I was sure to be all right.

Later in the dream I sat in a white restaurant, the brilliant sunlight that struck through the glass roof dulled by dark shades. I was sitting alone at a table when she came in with her many children and sat down at another large table at the far end, carrying herself with that same superb assurance. I was perfectly happy, though, to sit on at my own table, smiling at her—indeed, I had never felt so happy. The minute she saw that I had noticed her she put her chair at the table in a position so as to face me squarely; and when she was sitting there, pointed straight opposite me, she suddenly opened her thighs wide so that I could see her sex, and then her innumerable children, excited and pleased, crowded round me, jostling each other, and she said with her shining eyes in mine, saying it with her eyes since we were too far off to speak: 'There! Does that please you now?' I didn't know—I only knew that mercy, love and justice were the same.

• • •

Before he left Bowman had said: 'Is there a chance the killer could have been a woman?'

'Christ no,' I said, 'even Squeaky Fuentes never killed like that. You remember her, and she was as nutty as a shopping bag full of monkeys on heat.'

'All right,' said Bowman, 'it was just a theory I was spinning off at random.'

'Well, luckily it missed me,' I said.

He saved a cartridge on that one and said: 'Anything else I can help you with?'

'Probably,' I said, 'only not with your thinking, more the practical side.'

'I'll give you some of that in the mush on my night off,' he squawked.

'Why don't you just go on losing money at snooker with Alfie Verlander,' I said. 'That way you'll only fibrillate, and avoid the major stroke.'

That was when he slammed the rear door of the squad car on my nose and left for the Factory in a smelly roar of exhaust.

I thought how extraordinary it was the number of people that didn't like the truth and went back into the flat. My wife Edie had said to me one night: 'You'd be amazed the number of people who don't like you,' and I remember I answered: 'No, I wouldn't, but I find that the people who don't like me don't like themselves, that's all.'

'You don't expect to get on in the police with that attitude, do you?' she said.

'No,' I said. 'That's not what the police is for, and I do wish you'd stop worrying about my career.'

'We need the money,' she said flatly, turned over with a loud thump and slept.

I had come out of the flat for a moment's air and to think; now I turned to go back in again, moving round a team of builders on the damp pavement who had just finished loading a skep with rubbish, seen it off the truck, and were now going down to the Queen Anne round the mews at the back of the block for a few pints of Swan, and why not? In their bright yellow helmets with the Wimpy slogan on them, joking away together, stacking their gear for the night, slapping and punching each other, they made me feel better just to be around them for a second or two like that. They were all young men and, I imagined, must be just like I was at their age—either married, going steady or anyhow hoping to get their end away after next Saturday's match; they made me feel less lonely as I came back to you, Dora.

For I kissed your hair and I can't understand why, but I am bound to you.

Dora, I don't know how far into the dark I shall have to go to find you, but try to help me reach you, help me to find you, don't just slip away. Try your hardest to help me.

I'm not afraid of your killer, Dora. Listen to me, I'll try to explain this through the words of another man—one of my best friends, a police officer called Frank Ballard who was shot in the back down Fulham Palace Road opposite the Golden Bowl by a little cunt with a sawn-off twelve-bore who was ripping off a take-away, which has left my mate Frank paralysed from the waist down for life. Well, Frank has organised his new life as a cripple wonderfully, and I wish you could have met him because he would have done you good. He knows how to explain difficult things; I respect Frank and I like him and always ask him for advice when I'm in a jam; we were on A14 together and worked on some tricky things. Well, just after he was shot and he was in the Charing Cross hospital with flowers and books round him which we brought in, I saw him alone one afternoon and he said: 'It seems to me that the worst of a serious police enquiry—by which I mean enquiry into a murder—is that too often the investigating officer, and he can be the best you like, can't stop unconsciously thinking about how he is getting on with his enquiry in relation to his superiors—he will always tend to commit the error of thinking of himself. The result of this is that it blinds the officer to the dead person, and since he is generally unaware that he is committing it, it is a very hard fault for that officer to correct. Yet he must most certainly do so; for if he did not, he would be deprived of his objective sense of justice, and so would not be a proper person to be an investigating police officer. He could not be because, if the dead do not count sufficiently with the officer, then how would that officer weigh at a bar, supposing that the dead were to be sitting there? Supposing that they could still form an opinion in our world where they, too, used to live, the dead would want to know: *Where was this officer's true interest?*

Do you know, Dora, Frank smiled then and said, 'Excuse me for running on like this. . . .'

But I never forgot what he said because it was what I have always believed myself, and Frank knew it.

I knew I would find Dora's things in the end if I looked long enough, and I did, in the fortieth box I opened in the kitchen. There were just a few papers in it—her National Health Insurance card and an old black-and-white photograph, with its corners bent, of her dancing with a man in a club somewhere with his back to the camera, a dark-haired man, and an exercise book. I opened the book; it was about three-quarters filled with her handwriting. I wanted to read it immediately, having looked through everything else in the flat and found nothing else significant of hers. For I one was certain of one thing—that Dora was the key to both the deaths, not Betty Carstairs.

# 3

When I got into Poland Street and said who I was, the sergeant on the main desk looked up sharply and said: 'You're to go straight up to the fourth floor.'

The fourth floor was where the Voice lived. I thought that for the first time in my life I might meet it, but I was right out of luck there. I took the lift up to Room 471, and there the Voice's deputy, Chief Detective Superintendent James Jollo was waiting for me.

I said: 'Well, here I am.'

He said: 'Yes. And it's usual to address me in a proper way, Sergeant.'

'You'll soon stop bothering about all that once you get to know me better,' I said. 'Is the commander away?'

'What do you care?' Jollo said. 'He don't move in your shitty little world.'

'I know,' I said, 'that's the trouble with him—not knowing what's going on gets him just like you, all kind of confused, and that's when he sends for people like me and not you. Silly, isn't it?'

'I didn't send for you to have an argument,' Jollo said.

'Good,' I said, 'let's not have one, then. Let's get on to the Carstairs/Suarez murders.'

'You've been, have you?'

'Yes, I have,' I said, spreading them out. 'Look, I've got their blood on my hands.'

'You really are a horrible man,' said Jollo. 'You don't give an amber light—I find you're everything Chief Inspector Bowman says you are.'

'That comes from the dead I mix with, Jollo,' I said, 'so why don't you try it yourself one day instead of dressing up as a detective chief superintendent and licking arseholes and stamps?'

'Don't you ever talk to me like that,' he said, 'and your first warning's your last, cuntie.'

'Well, that's how I talk to most people,' I said, 'so don't bother warning me, it's breath wasted.'

'How do you get away with it?' Jollo said. 'What's the great secret?'

'The secret's simple,' I said. 'The secret is that I don't fucking care.'

He started to open his mouth but I said, 'Don't open that, Jollo—you used to be a good detective before you bottled out. Now I haven't any time, so would you give me an envelope I'm told you've got in one of your drawers with a warrant card in it and let me get on catching the Suarez/Carstairs killer—that's all I'm here for.'

He said: 'I'd like to see you outside somewhere, on a piece of waste ground, I really would—anytime'd do.'

'Now don't get hurt in your pride, Superintendent,' I said, 'just give me the gear and I'll get out of here because it smells of rank in here—in fact it smells dead fucking rank.'

He gave me the envelope because he had to, but he handed it to me as if it were a pistol that he was inviting me to blow my head off with.

I opened it and there was a warrant card in it. I said to Jollo:
'Well, fancy that, I'm a copper again.'

He said: 'Worse luck, and may it not last, mazel tov.'

I said: 'Stack the commentary. By the way, do we still have a
Detective Sergeant Stevenson on the strength at A14?'

'Yes,' said Jollo, 'he's on a case just now; feller name of Roatta
over at Clapham had his head shot off about the same time as
your thing happened.'

'Roatta?' I said. 'Really? Well, that's one king-sized filter-tip
turd the world can now forget about. And you say Stevenson's
on it? Good, because if there's one detective capable of working
out of this building, it's him.'

I left. I raced for the lift to get down to the second floor where
A14 lived because I immediately wanted to start reading Suarez.
One of Charlie Bowman's promising young minions, one of these
teenage inspectors with the world on his shoulders and glasses
that Charlie liked recruiting for Serious Crimes got into the lift
at the same time as I did and started down with me; his razor
had left three bristles under his chin, but that was his business,
not mine.

'Hullo,' he said, 'so you're back again, are you?'

'Well, your keen detective's eyes must already be telling you
that I'm not absent,' I said.

'You've lost none of your charm, have you?' he said.

'I need all the charm I can get,' I said, 'because I don't know
about you, but the bodies I find have lost all theirs.' As the lift
slowed I said to him: 'You're an intellectual; one day why don't
you ask yourself why it is that not one tear ever leaks out under
those glasses of yours, and no troubled thought ever slithers about
in that thing that your Regent Street hat keeps the rain off?'

'Well, we're rather giving up the footwork; detective work's
more and more computerised nowadays,' he said seriously.

'Wait till you see your wife's death come up on the fucking

thing,' I said as the lift doors sighed open, 'and then speed over to find her with her head cut off, and a swastika smeared over your front door in her own shit, happy programmes, bye-bye.'

'You bastard,' he shouted.

'The truth is very painful,' I said. 'Didn't any of the thousands of villains you've interrogated ever tell you that, or haven't you ever met any?'

I got to 205 and kicked the horrible plastic chair into a position where I could sit on it without either wrecking my knee caps on the underside of the table or getting my balls crushed. Luckily for me I didn't care about the revolting green paint or the rabies posters, and it was a good thing I didn't care about the heating either, because there wasn't any; the heating was a special system which was designed to work flat out only in August. The top left-hand drawer of my desk had been turned into a kind of death row by seven of last year's flies; but except for them that piece of furniture was empty, so I decided to prove to everyone in the place, including myself, that I existed by picking up the phone. The phone sounded dead for quite a while, but after I had dialled zero nine and rapped its grey plastic head very hard on the wood-work several times I finally got a WPC with a bright little voice which said: 'Who is this, please?'

'I'll come down and introduce myself if you don't look out,' I said.

'Line 205 is not in use,' she said.

'Well, that must explain why we're both a couple of cunts talking down it then, mustn't it?' I said. 'Now pull your finger out with a loud pop, missis, get it functioning like five minutes ago was a hundred years too late and then I will give you per-mission to go even further and go totally and utterly mad by stopping all incoming calls while I read up on two murders, which, though you mightn't believe it, is the bizarre, rather sordid kind of work that goes on in this part of the building.' I added: 'And try not to waste my time, because with the current crime rate we never have any.'

'I was just doing my job.'

'I know,' I said, 'and that's what I'm complaining about.'

'Talking to you, I've decided I don't like working in the police,' she said bitterly.

'Do what I did then,' I said, 'leave it.'

She said: 'It's your filthy manners.'

'My manners came in with me from the street, love,' I said. 'It's dirty out there, now get chuffing.'

The Voice rang. 'Well?'

'I've found some stuff Suarez has written.'

'What do you make of it?'

'I'll tell you when I've read it,' I said, 'which I will the minute people stop pestering me.' As an afterthought I added: 'Sir.'

'Now you watch your tone,' the Voice said. 'I'm used to you, but I've just had Jollo in this office who isn't, and the way he went on about you I thought he was going to have a stroke.'

'I know a very good flower shop down the Fulham Road opposite St Stephen's,' I said. 'The lilies are quite cheap but they look really lovely at a funeral.' I added: 'I'll nail the man who killed Suarez and Carstairs and I'll do it fast, but there's a condition.'

'What's that?'

'All unsought-for help to stand absolutely clear.'

'Done,' said the Voice, and rang off.

# 4

Suarez.

I read:

> Once I was Dora Suarez, but even before I die I am not her
> any more; I have just become something appalling. Looking
> at myself naked in the mirror, I see that I have lost the right
> to call myself a person; what's left of me now is barely hu-
> man.

'Why's that?' I thought. I picked up the phone and dialled the
duty desk. I said: 'Is that autopsy report on Suarez and Carstairs
here yet?'

'No.'

I said: 'Why not?'

The sergeant said: 'There's a queue down at the morgue.'

'Then tell them to get it moving,' I said. The sergeant laughed.
'Don't laugh,' I said, 'or I'll run down and do no more but smash
your face in. I want it the minute it arrives, and that's all you
need to know.'

Suarez.

I am marked with a cross; I just have this pause between now
and my end. Here at Betty's I have this last short freedom; I
have no more real time. I accept that at thirty I am going to
die. I don't want to be parted from my body—what has happened to it is not its fault. But it says it wants to go.

I rang down again: I said: 'Come on—Carstairs, Suarez.'
'Nothing. Why don't you ring them yourself, Sarge?'
'Because I don't want to make any more enemies tonight.'
Suarez.

I don't know what I should have done if it hadn't been for
Betty. I was in Kensington by chance the day we met, having
left my suitcase at a girlfriend's not far off who had no room
for me because of her boyfriend being there—and besides, my
illness made her afraid—and I passed Betty going in the opposite direction along Empire Gate, and seeing that she was
having a hard struggle against the north wind with her shopping, I don't know why, but I stopped and gave her a hand
with it, meaning to go on south over the river afterwards to
see if I could find a cheap room down there somewhere with
people who weren't too nosey. But it ended up with Betty
saying, when we got to her street door, wouldn't I like to
come indoors with her for a moment and get in out of the
wind? I didn't want to be with any strangers, just on my
own—still, it was bitterly cold, so I followed her in the end
and found myself in this strange, dark flat crammed with
clocks, broken-down furniture from another age, and boxes
and cases stacked up to the kitchen ceiling. She went out
to the kitchen presently and made us a cup of tea. She brought
the tea and sat me down in the other chair opposite her
by the electric fire. The place was in a dreadful state and
smelled the way an old person's place does smell; but strangely,
I soon found that I didn't care. Besides, I was very tired; it
was one of my bad days.
    After about an hour she started asking me about myself,

something I usually don't like—only she didn't do it in a stupid, pressing way, but mixed up with stories of her own past,
taking my hand and stroking it absently while she talked. She
spoke softly, in a low Highland voice that reminded me of
fine rain; and later on she brought some whisky and a plate
of cakes to make it a social occasion. She had a quarter glass
herself, and before she went to bed in the kitchen under the
window sang snatches of Highland songs in Gaelic as though
she had forgotten that I was there:

> 'Take me to the house with many windows
> And I will stay with you forever. . . .'

She had the high, glorious voice of a young girl.

In the course of the evening I said: 'I really must be getting
on, Betty—I've found nowhere to sleep yet, and it's getting
dark.' Betty said: 'I wish you'd stay with me here, Dora; I've
been so lonely since Reg went.' And I said at once: 'I will,
Betty'—and that wasn't just because it suited me, or because
I felt ill and tired; at that moment I didn't really know why
I was so happy to stay, but I know now, of course, that it was
because she offered me peace.

I had long ago forgotten what it was like to be treated so
gently, so that in the following days, whenever she took my
hand and looked into my eyes, saying: 'Now you've your place
here, Dora, and it's such a wonderful thing for me that you're
here, you'll stay on awhile, won't you?' something jagged came
up into my throat. But I could not tell her much about myself,
with her aged eighty-six. All I said to her one night, after a
few whiskies, when she asked me: 'Where do you think you're
going to live in the end, sweet?' and I answered: 'Wherever I
can hide,' she took my hand and squeezed it hard, saying
calmly: 'Well, whatever you're hiding from, you know you
can always hide here'—without ever once going any further,
never wanting to know anything I couldn't tell her.

She's pure gold.

The other day, though, she got up from her armchair by
the electric fire, took me by the shoulders and held me away
from her a little so that she could focus me properly. She said:
'You know, I don't like the look of you, Dora, you don't look
right to me.' I wanted to cry and tell her everything, but I
didn't and just said: 'I'm perfectly all right, Betty.' She said:
'Dora, I've this bit of money, now I want you to take it and
go to the doctor's just for a checkup. You could go to my
doctor, Doctor Mathers; he's ever so kind, and his surgery's
only just round the corner.' But I said: 'No! No, no!' and only
stopped myself just in time from telling her that I was beyond
the help of doctors. All I said was: 'No, Betty, I really am all
right, you know, I swear it. I'm young.' She didn't believe
me, of course; but, seeing the kind of person she was, she just
turned and went into the kitchen for the whisky and the hard
little cakes she liked, and she never mentioned the subject
again. All I said to her during that period was: 'Betty, do you
believe that apart from you, somewhere beyond all the people
who only seem to be people, there truly are still some people
left, real people?' And she said: 'Ah, you darling pretty
woman, don't you know that my Reg, though he's been gone
so many years now, still comes in to see me quite often to
know if I'm all right? It's true he drank hard, Dora, but he
was always a gentleman—even in drink he was nearly always
collected and correct, and there could never have been any
other man in my life but him.' She was silent for a time,
staring at the floor, then she looked up at me and said: 'As I
think of it, have you no more luggage here than what you've
brought?' I started to cry and said: 'No, I've only my heart,
Betty, and that's heavy enough.' After she had comforted me
in her frail arms she said: 'For you know, Dora, I've all sorts
of clothes here, in the boxes in the kitchen, and though they're
old and out of style, I know, they're all handmade, for Regi-
nald was a major in the war, and so I had to dress correctly
for the officers' mess on ladies' night.'

But I told her I had all I needed. Later I said: 'Betty, don't you find it's funny how when someone isn't there with you, the least thing they've ever sent you, a postcard, a photograph, assumes an importance that you wouldn't think twice about if the person were there?' She said: 'The people who loved you never go away, Dora.' I said there was one case where I hoped she was wrong there, without going any further.

I said to myself: 'What case? Who was it?' But I could see already that Dora wasn't a woman to drop names. Staring at the horrible green wall of 205, I recalled the unseen presence that I had felt around me in the flat all the time I was there—a great pressure of grief close to me and weighing me down with hands, bodies, unable to reach mine, an aching desire to speak, a little sonata for which there had been no words until I found them in Dora's hidden box.

Suarez.

'I've never really loved anyone in my life like you loved Reg,' I told Betty, 'I never have had.' But Betty stroked my cheek and said: 'Oh yes you have. Because you've got me now. I'm here with you now and I always shall be.'

I said: 'Betty, don't the 1980's feel strange to you?' 'Oh no,' she said, 'for I live more in the past, and my memories are wonderful—imagine how fine it was the evening Reg first arrived in our village in the spring of 1940; he walked up from the way station looking so mighty grand in his uniform, posted to Argyllshire for a reason he must never name even to me, for fear that if I were caught by the enemy, I should be hurt. Oh, it was very exciting for me to know he was so important—girls half my age were mad with envy of me, and women were such romantics then. I can see now, Dora, how our eyes met as he turned to look at me as I passed him the first time he ever strode up our one street with his batman carrying his big officer's valise to the McGrath house where he was billeted, and how my heart sang at once, for I knew

I was in love with him, though I was never beautiful. Ah, but that didn't matter, Dora, girl, and wasn't the whole village amazed when the banns were called by the minister and we took each other in marriage, and myself already thought an old maid, since I was born in '04? I tell you, love is so beautiful; besides, there was a great deal of drink after we came away from the house with windows—even the minister tottered towards the evening in the front room—ah, that was one day we forgot the war.' 'Don't you ever feel that we're all of us just mirages, Betty?' I said. 'No, never,' she said. 'I'm a Scot and too hardheaded.' I said: 'I want to talk about something else, Betty—the rent. I can't go on staying here like this with nothing said or settled, but I have to tell you that I haven't any money right now.'

'You silly, darling girl,' she said: 'Don't you understand? Just stay here with me, and I'm forever repaid.'

Betty is very frail and I know that her heart hurts her all the time; she often groans in the night and I hear her immediately every time and go to her where she has her bed in the kitchen under the window. I fetch her her pills then take her to the bathroom and afterwards sit with her to talk on the side of her bed and soothe her, with an eiderdown over my shoulders till she sleeps again.

Yes, Betty is the only person who loves me, or ever has. I never thought that love would come to me in that way, through her. But there it is.

I laid Dora's book down. I went over to the steel window and stood looking out at Marks and Sparks opposite. Through Dora's words I heard voices now for the two women; I could hear them talking to each other, see them talking, even. Below me the wind suddenly raced along the grey pavement of Poland Street, whipping the rain round people's legs, shrieking through the top latch which never shut properly, then roaring out as a draught under the door.

Suarez.

No, it had never occurred to me that love would come to me through Betty. My former lovers paid for my face, thighs, hands, breasts and sex, then entered me. If I said anything for the sake of the ritual, they were shocked; for to them my lips existed as nothing but an encouragement to fuck me. One told me I was too beautiful to think, whereupon I turned my back on him and watched him in the mirror anxiously washing his prick in the bathroom. I accepted him in my arms when he cantered down the room towards me because I had to—a thin, hoarse man of sixty, rich, mean and gone in the hams. Sparse hairs curled without elegance round his crushed nipples, and in the morning, after a cold shower, I lay in bed watching him don a pair of pink-and-white striped knickers three times too large for him. When he was dressed, he left at once to catch his plane back to the Midlands; he was cold and didn't speak except to remind me as he shut the hotel-room door behind him that everything had been paid for. He had had his orgasm, but the closest I could get to mine was by bursting into tears. At dinner the night before in a medium-priced restaurant off Leicester Square he had said to me: 'I'm going to leave my wife for you, Dora!'

Going to? Going to?

Ha! Going, going! Gone!


'What will you do for money, Dora, for when you're short?' Betty said to me one night, at some nameless hour. 'For I've drawn my pension and there's a hundred pounds under my cushion here if it would help.'

'No, Betty,' I said, 'never. That's not how it works at all.'

It was very quiet in the flat that night; there was just the slow beat of the hall clock, the remote night traffic, and the two of us.

She said: 'It's only paper, after all.'

'No, Betty darling,' I said.

'But how will you manage if something happens to me?'

'Nothing will, Betty.'

But she had a sudden crisis then and there and clutched her
heart. I caught her, laid her down and covered her up warm;
she turned her face to me and said, crying: 'Don't leave me,
Dora!' I said: 'As if I would, heaven. Are you better? Do you
need your pills?'

'No pills,' she said slowly, smiling, only half-conscious, 'no
pills.'

Later she said: 'There's much that's dark in you, Dora,
much in you that I can't see; I love you and I worry for you.'

I said, 'You mustn't.'

'If only I could help you.'

'You've done everything for me,' I told her, 'far more than
you know, you've been an angel to me.'

She said: 'Dora, please don't leave me now.'

'I'll never do that,' I said. 'I can only be taken.'

'What do you mean?' she said.

'Never mind,' I said. 'It doesn't matter. Now you must
rest.'

She took my arm and stroked it till she fell asleep.


I picked up the phone and said: 'If that Suarez/Carstairs autopsy report isn't on my desk by the time I put this phone down,
there'll be a lot more bodies leaving for the morgue from this
actual building.'

'We've been on to them twice, we're doing our best.'

I said: 'It's not good enough. Ring them again and tell them
that I'm in charge of this case and that when I'm restless, I don't
bother with British Telecom, I arrive in person. They'll know
what you mean. Do it now and ring me back, you've got ten
minutes, I'm timing you.'

Suarez.


I've cleaned the cooker and the fridge out as best I can and
do most of our cooking now, then I bring it through to the
sitting room where I sleep and we sit in front of the TV,

which glitters silently because the tube suddenly went but its light's nice, so is the dim electric fire. Then we settle down and talk, sometimes we go on all night. One night Betty said: 'Haven't you any man in your life, Dora? Someone who loves you and could help you?'

If only she knew! I stiffened with terror when she said that and felt myself fading as they say ghosts do at morning, so that Betty said: 'You frighten me with that expression.'

'What expression?'

'In my village we used to say, she's walking in someone's shadow.'

'What shadow?'

That was what I wanted to know.

Another night Betty said, waking suddenly in her chair: 'Dora, are you there?'

'I'm always here.'

'Dora,' she said, 'what are you going to do?'

I had had a few whiskies and said, perhaps too sharply: 'What do you mean, Betty, do?'

'I meant, with the years you've got ahead of you.'

'What years ahead of me?' I said. I repeated it. 'What years?'

'You're fifty-six years younger than I am.'

I said: 'Betty, I'm much, much older already than you are, if you only knew.'

'Oh Dora,' she sighed, 'how terrible that would be if it were true, because Reg and I never had children, I didn't seem made for it, but sweet, I know you could have been mine.'

'I feel as though I were,' I said. 'I feel that at long last I've found harbour, so hold me close.' But she was getting sleepy again and soon after we had kissed each other good night she turned aside in her chair and rested on its worn-out arm, her hat crooked on her head, her spectacles clasped lightly on her knees.

I remember that night I dreamed I could shit again without

screaming in pain and then, having woken, fell asleep again and dreamed I was a bird in white; I opened my slender beak and it spoke tears. Then there was another event in the dream. Someone, a man, came running after me; but by then it was too late. It was over, and I was far away.

I stopped reading about Dora. A grey hand had fallen on me. I, too, felt dragged towards that grey arch through which Dora had disappeared; and blocks of me shifted about in my head; the weight of my ignorance pressed itself into me as new knowledge.
Suarez.
She had scribbled on a page apart:

Does a bird know why it's shot? Each time I look at my body in the mirror I realise that we have no hours left to ourselves or each other. There have been times lately, while Betty was asleep in her chair, where I have gone into the bathroom and looked at my naked body. I wanted to scream at it each time I looked at it and I did scream.
I know I am very sick because the hospital had explained my state. They told me that they had a bed and that I should be admitted, but I told them that though I knew I had to go, that wasn't the way I wanted to do it. However, here I am in great pain; I am in more pain than I can bear and he still menaces me and will find me; I must end it.

I had had enough, so I picked the phone up and got the morgue.
Some man the other end mumbled: 'Suarez? Who she then?'
I said: 'Today isn't the metaphysics course for you, sweetheart—so just do your job and get your nose into your dockets.'
'Oh God, more bleeding work,' he said. He went off. In the end he came back and said: '87471 and 2? You mean those women from Kensington? Christ, they haven't hardly been tagged yet.'
'Why not?' I said. 'You've had plenty of time, three hours.'

'Three hours?' he yelled. 'What do you think we are here, bleeding miracle workers?'

'You'd better turn yourself into a miracle for your own sake,' I said, 'otherwise I'll be over, and then there'll be a miracle fewer in the world; now I mean it.'

'Oh, come on, give us a chance, Sarge,' the man down at the morgue said. 'There's like a waiting list here, you know.' He sniggered. 'We've got all these quiet people keep turning up here the whole time.' He added: 'But at least they don't get on the blower screaming their head off the way you do.'

I said in a very low grey voice: 'Get off the line. Put someone with a normal brain on.'

'No point losing your rag,' he said cheekily, 'there's no one but me here, the mob's at lunch, I'm just minding the fridges, sorry.'

I said: 'I shall be over in thirty minutes, and if that report isn't waiting for me when I arrive, I shall tear someone's head off, probably yours. Come to that, what's your name anyway? Let's see what makes you tick.'

He finally grasped the major point, that I was serious. 'Veale.'

'You sound like third footman to Satan the night hell was invented,' I said. 'Now pull your finger out with a loud pop—I want that file, I want action, and I want the whole lot now, now, now, not sometime next Thursday week, you berk.'

'But where's the fire?' he bleated. 'They're not going any-where—I can't understand what the rush is.'

'Thank God you're not paid to understand what it is,' I said, 'but if you must know, the rush is so I can catch the bastard that did it—didn't you know that that's what detective sergeants are for?'

'All right, all right, friend,' he said, 'now calm down—anyone'd think they were Marilyn Monroe the way you're going on.'

'Compared to you they were,' I said, 'and don't ever tell me to calm down. Now get going while you've still got your ears on

your head, otherwise I'll likely find myself drawing twenty for
murder, and you can guess who the corpse'll be.'

'It means changing the order in the arrival files,' said Veale,
'and that's a terrible administrative problem, that is.'

'It's you that's the terrible problem,' I said, 'not just your files.'

'You people pull rank, you do,' Veale said bitterly. 'You coppers
really feel your bloody oats.'

'It must be spring coming on,' I said.

I knew there would be no action at the morgue till after lunch,
so I left the Factory and went over to see Frank Ballard; he only
lived ten minutes away from it by motor. I found him in his
wicker chair by his sitting-room window, lying back like a musi-
cian worn out after a concert.

He said: 'Hullo, you look bothered. Sit down, what's the matter?'

I said: 'I badly want to talk to you.'

'That's good, I'm here to be talked to,' he said. 'Does me good,
makes me feel useful.' He added: 'So they've taken you back at
the Factory; I knew they would.'

'Frank,' I said, 'I really care about this one, can I just talk to
you about it for a minute?'

'Carstairs/Suarez?'

'That's right.'

'I'm up to date,' he said.

I said: 'There seem to be features.'

'Features?'

'Suarez says herself she was very ill.'

'How do you know? Are you clairvoyant?'

'No. I searched the flat and found what she'd written.'

'Did she say what was the matter with her?'

'No.'

'It'll show up in the autopsy report.'

'I know it will,' I said, 'when I finally get my hands on the
bloody thing.'

'Meantime, how are you looking at it?'

'Right now through this Suarez exercise book she left. I only came on this morning and it's all I've got for now.' I added: 'In it she records some of the conversations she had with the old lady, Mrs Carstairs. She was frightened of someone, Frank.'

'Kevin Loftus was round just now and of course we started talking about it,' said Ballard.

'What did he have to say?'

'He said you were looking for a nut who had a grievance, and that the difference between a normal man and a nut was that a grievance with a nut stops being a grievance, it becomes life and death, mostly death—and I agree with him.'

'Yes, not bad,' I said, 'only where does it get us? He's a nut, all right, but he went gloved, so he's not a raver.'

Ballard said: 'How bad was it?'

I said: 'The lot. He wanked into her, drank her blood, shit on the floor. Here, look at the pictures.' I bit something back in my throat; it was grief.

Ballard saw that. He said: 'Axe murderer. You don't get many of them. Assuming he knew what he was doing, it makes too much mess.'

'Anyway, one thing's sure,' I said. 'We can't dig anything up on him. And yet I've a feeling it wasn't first time round for him either.'

Ballard put the pictures down and said: 'Motive. Anything at all occur to you?'

'From reading Suarez, I've an idea he may have loved her,' I said, and added: 'It may even have been mutual—in their idea of what that means, of course.'

'It wouldn't be the first time,' Ballard said. He thought for a while and said: 'Anything to suggest someone might have had a hold on her?'

'Well, I'm not sure,' I said, 'that's a very good question, Frank, and I just hope that the next card I turn up will give me part of the answer.'

Ballard said: 'He seems to be a good climber.'

'Oh yes,' I said, 'we're looking for a sporty type, like athletic.' I added: 'And how many young or youngish men with no form have we got like that living in the London area, always supposing that this is where he lives?'

'You could call it a couple of million,' Ballard said.

'That's right,' I said. 'Makes it easy, doesn't it?'

'You'll turn a corner and get on his track,' Ballard said, 'I know you.'

'I'll go on till I do.'

Ballard said: 'Well, thank God they didn't put a berk on it.' He added: 'You're really personally distressed over this, aren't you?'

'Yes,' I said. 'Somehow this is different.'

Ballard picked up one of the pictures of the bad side of Suarez's face and said: 'It's one of the most appalling sights I've ever seen, and I've seen all of it.' He added: 'And she must have been a pretty girl.'

'Yes,' I said. 'Is there anything you can think of that could help me at all, Frank? Shorten the track?'

'Two things,' he said. 'I think it may have been a pretty boy who couldn't screw her. Secondly, I don't know why, but where I get a tingle is with this Roatta that Stevenson's on, because that's three violent sitting-room murders less than three hours apart in time and barely a mile in space, and that's unusual even in the metropolitan area.'

'Yes, I like it,' I said, 'seeing I've got nothing else to go on, and I was going to have a word with Stevenson anyway. Besides, we get on very well, which helps.'

'Get that autopsy report. Talk to the pathologist.'

'That's where I'm going now.' I looked at the time and stood up. 'Christ, I must get going,' I said, 'they must have finished eating by now. Thanks, Frank—just talking to you about this has been ever such a help.'

'I'll have a go, too,' said Ballard. He tapped his head: 'From here.' It was hard for him being a detective inspector and para-lysed from the waist down. He said: 'Keep in touch.'

'I always do.'

'Crap,' said Ballard, 'you just come running to Mum when you bruise your knee. Don't worry, I'll ring you at Poland Street the minute I hear something.'

'Bye,' I said. I let myself out.

I came away from Frank's place and by chance found a small public garden by the river; I found a bench under a weeping ash and sat with Dora's book in my hand for a time, thinking about what I so far knew of her and her vanished life, that dark flower.

Sitting there, I felt stabbed by the sadness which had descended on me in this case. I could tell Ballard had seen it in me just now; it was the first time I had felt so deeply over any case, and I didn't know why.

I opened her cheap ruled book again.

Suarez.

Dora wrote in her short, angular hand:

> Until my illness forced me to think, I was neither intelligent nor stupid by nature but quite a passive girl. Of course I attracted men, I was young, and I enjoyed going out. Having fun stopped me thinking about the misery of my childhood. Betty's calling.

Later there was some writing to a school friend.

> Adele, don't you remember the evenings when I used to pass your dress shop on our corner when coming back from school?

Don't you remember how you used to invite me in to the
back of the shop for tea? Don't you remember how you said
to me: 'Courage, girl'—for she knew I had terrible problems
at home; she was one of the few people I told. 'Have you
ever known love?' I asked her once, 'because I never have,
not yet.' 'Only once,' you said, turning away. I don't know
why, but that was the moment when I thought to myself:
'Only rotten things will happen to me.'

On another page:

I have always needed people because I had no home. What I
had for a home was four rooms solid with violence—my father
beating up my mother, my mother fighting back with the
frying pan, my mother lying on the floor, blood on the floor,
never any money. I tell you, school was paradise, compared.
My father was Spanish, my mother Jewish from Poland. They
were both refugees.

On another page she described how she had listened to a poet
declaim his work in a crowded Soho pub one night when she was
there with a man, which was why she had copied down from
memory four lines of his that had struck her:

Tell how his gas was lost
His poor exhaust;
Remember he was fat but ran the race,
Was present in the war.

She said how after his recital he had gone round the pub for a
handout, and how she had given a pound.
On the next page she had tried to draw Betty Carstairs dozing
in her armchair, her head in its woollen hat lying back, her spec-

tacles in her hand. She had written underneath it, 'All my kisses, darling Betty, from your Dora.'

(Christ, I was in that flat with them at Empire Gate now. Peace. Their broken telly with its screen glimmered in the darkness of the sitting room at the foot of the two beds. The two women were talking together softly, Suarez knowing that this was the last night of her life; she was going to take it. Betty had just gone to the bathroom; the electric fire glowed. And then *snap!* Suddenly all the lights went on. Dora looked up from the picture in the magazine, perhaps—and there he was, swinging his hand axe. Terror! And then the end.)

Dora was beautifully dressed when she died. Besides her newly-washed hair, the frock she was wearing, the black high-heeled shoes we found near her feet which were curled up under her, everything she wore was brand-new. She was dressed for a special occasion. She was going out; as Dylan Thomas wrote, she was dressed to die.

She certainly had wonderful black hair. I saw it now, recalling how clean it had smelled, the part of it that was not matted with blood, from the scent of apples in the shampoo she had used. This little detail about her, her hair and the trouble she had taken with it, and with her clothes, the two bottles of wine that she had not even had time to drink before her murderer arrived, pierced me in the stomach like a physical wound, so that I wanted to clap my hand on the place.

What I felt was of no apparent importance to my enquiry whatever, and yet it was; for otherwise I could not have been so intent on finding the man.

For I had already read:

Saturday morning. I shall do it tonight, I've worked it all out. I'm not worried any more. Now that I'm at the last station, at the barrier with my ticket in my hand, I'm already in an-

other world, and there's even some kind of pleasure in arranging the details—in a way, it's almost as though I were going
on holiday; some part of me suddenly feels quite irresponsible!'

She wrote—later, evidently, because it was with a different pen:

Yes, it's certain I'll do it today, this evening, my mind's made
up. I said to Betty just yesterday: 'I suppose we have certain
rights to ourselves.'

I said to myself: 'When I find him, he'll have just five seconds
for his prayers, and then he'll be glad he's gone.' For I had already
learned by heart one passage she had written, poor darling:

So I shall die. I know how I shall do it—with the gas from
the cooker while Betty's out at the doctor's. I shall leave a
note on the front door, of course, explaining what I've done
so that she can get people to come and turn the gas off and
open the windows.

In writing that trailed down the page she added:

Betty will understand all right—in her heart of hearts she'll
know, she knows already.

She continued:

Since it's a grave matter, and the physical part of it difficult
to face, I have decided to turn my death into a party with
myself. First, I shall have a bath and wash my hair. Then I
shall dress up. I have bought a new dress and shoes, and two
bottles of wine to help me go, and I shall wear the scent I've
bought that normally I could never have afforded. I shall look
at the brochure on Hawaii, listen to music on the radio and
then tell myself as I go that my death having been my wed-

ding, I am leaving with my husband on our honeymoon to the Pacific. I have made the arrangements exactly because I have always found it soothing to make plans; it gives me courage, just as it helps me to write this; and so, with unearthly intentions, I go into a dark room as a dark bride.

I ran back to the Ford and started back to the Factory, driving too fast.

I got in to the Factory and said at the desk: 'Anything on that autopsy yet? Carstairs/Suarez?'

'They rang to say there were complications—out of the ordinary. It was the pathologist on the line, he said he was going to ring back.'

'What complications? What's out of the ordinary? When is he going to ring back? How long?'

'He didn't say.'

'Right,' I said.

Before I left for the morgue I went up to 205 and rang Tom Cryer at the *Recorder*. When the girl at the switchboard came on, I said immediately: 'Mr Cryer is not in conference with the news editor at the moment so can he ring you back—put him on straightaway, it's the Factory here.'

She was probably divorced with three children, dedicated to her job and in financial need—anyway, she must have been far too bright to stay on the switchboard for long because Cryer came on the line at once and I said: 'Well, there you are, take it or leave it, it's me here over at Poland Street—how's Angie and the kid?'

'Christ,' he said, 'don't tell me you're back at A14.'

'Why not?' I said. 'That's where I belong, isn't it? Look, can I see you?'

'What over?'

'Over a beer at the Navigator,' I said. 'But it'll have to be fast. Still, it's urgent I see you.'

He said: 'What are you on?'

'Carstairs/Suarez.'

'Christ,' Cryer said, 'that's the worst we've had for years, it's worse than Sutcliffe.'

'Mine's a Kronenbourg if you get there first,' I said, 'and get me a packet of Westminster filters, I've run out.'

'It's on the paper,' he said. 'Now just move your arse and get over here.'

Cryer and I sat at the counter of the Navigator in Little Titchfield Street on red plastic-topped stools like a couple of old tarts and I told him that this case was very bad and that one reason why it was very bad was that as yet I had no leads on the killer. I said: 'He's got to be found and caught.'

He said: 'Your people won't let us even go near the place, so why do we have to cooperate?'

'Because your job's to sell newspapers,' I said, 'and if you can't get near the place, that's because it's on my instructions, Tom— you know me.'

He said: 'What's in it for the paper?'

'I'm in it,' I said, 'and we've known each other awhile.'

'All I got was the usual crap,' Cryer grumbled. 'You know, the press would get an official handout; handout, my bollocks. Jollo and Charlie Bowman reading us the lesson on Sunday morning and wondering how the roast's doing, more like.'

I said: 'If you do me a favour, I can go better than that.'

'How much better?'

'Usual deal. *Recorder*'s there first, and only the *Recorder*. No other press.'

'What do I have to do?' Cryer said.

'Easy,' I said. 'Get your Pickwick nib out and get this down, are you listening? "Owner grandfather clock smashed Kensington Saturday seeks vandal responsible, reward interesting. Box number, *Recorder*'s phone number." That'll get all the grasses on heat.

Run it a week or till I tell you to leave off. Anything that comes through, bike it over to us fast. And the same goes,' I added, 'if you get any lead on this artist at all.'

'All right,' said Cryer, putting the message away, 'that sounds like jacks to open—I'll play.'

'Good,' I said, 'because without a little assistance from us from time to time, your crime page would look a bit on the empty side, wouldn't it, and that's what the public want to read about, not restoring thirteenth-century castles in Somerset.'

But Cryer said exactly what Ballard had said: 'This one is really bothering you, isn't it?'

I said: 'If you'd seen it, Tom.'

He said: 'There's a rumour going round our end that Suarez was very sick, is it true?'

'How do I know till I get some sense out of the morgue?' I said. 'But there's certainly something strange.'

'What?'

'It's in an exercise book.'

'Suarez's?'

'Yes.' I stood up. 'I must go, Tom—there may be something for me over at the Factory now. Let's keep in touch, big kiss for Angie, good night.'

After leaving Cryer I drove back to the Factory to see if the morgue had rung back, but in my head Dora and Betty were talking. Betty had nodded off in her chair; she had slid in it a little and her head had fallen in its woollen hat against the high back. Dora was saying:

'Betty, I don't want to wake you, but I've something I must say.'

'It's all right, I'm not asleep, just resting.'

'Betty,' Dora said, 'have you ever considered what it might feel like to be a horse?'

'A horse? No, dear, why a horse?'

'Betty,' Dora said, 'I remember once picking up a newspaper and reading a small ad quite by chance: "For sale. Young mare, Arab stock. £3000 o.n.o. Guaranteed docile." '

'I don't understand, Dora.'

Dora said: 'When an insecure man mounts a horse, his overriding instinct is to dominate it and prove he's the master. He thrashes it to make it obey. He behaves like this because he is frightened of the horse, Betty; the animal is much bigger and stronger than he is, and he thinks it could easily kill him, or at least throw him off, make him look and feel ridiculous. This can't be allowed to happen, of course, so he gets the whip out.'

'Dora, what are you trying to say?'

'What I'm trying to say is that the man hasn't understood that the horse lives in a different world to his, and that the horse has no need to be beaten into obedience; the horse accepts the master.'

'Dora!'

'Betty, I am the horse,' Dora said.

'Ah, darling,' Betty said, 'I see you have been most wrongly treated. Won't you go for help?'

'What help?' Dora said. 'I am just a horse.' She added:

I am dark, and have always had an obsession for dark hats. I used to go down Singleton Street at eighteen wearing black Levi's, smiling sharply at everyone. I wore my wide-brimmed hat tipped over my nose; inside myself I would be singing. I used to wear deep crimson scarves and say to myself, 'My name is Dora Suarez!'

I told Betty partly about when I was young when we were talking together this morning at about three.

# 5

As I went back into the Factory and was making for the stairs to go up to 205 I ran into Jollo again.

'Well?' he said. 'Nice to be back, is it?'

'Don't take the acid today,' I said, 'it isn't the day. I'm taking this very seriously, so listen.'

'All right,' Jollo said, 'I'm listening.'

'Suarez,' I said. 'That was her maiden name according to her DHSS papers. Has anyone checked to see if she had British nationality? It's just a detail.'

'Funny you should say that,' he said, 'because it was me that checked it, and the answer came in only twenty minutes ago.'

'And?'

'She was British,' Jollo said, 'born right here in London. It was her dad that was Spanish. Came over as a refugee in March '39 after some war they had down there and found work as a builder's labourer.'

'OK,' I said, 'and her mother?'

'British as you and me,' said Jollo, 'I don't think. Polish-Jewish from the East End, Whitechapel—you get all sorts, don't you?'

'I don't want your opinions,' I said, 'just facts.' I had my work cut out not to send him up to Harley Street to a heart quack's, but I kept calm and said: 'Don't any of you read her at all? Make out who she moved about with at all?'

'You expect us to keep a check on the entire population?'

'Now don't get high-flown,' I said. 'I was just asking if any of you knew anything about Suarez that could assist me in my enquiry, that's all.' I added: 'Any sarcasm being handed out, it'll be from my end, not yours.'

'I'll overlook the tone, Sergeant,' he said.

'That'll save no end of time,' I said. 'Well?'

He said: 'Well, she never did bird—but then a lot of people in this city who ought to never do, do they?'

'Now don't come on like a bishop or something,' I said, 'the holy tone doesn't go with your gear.' I added: 'Another thing. What about this autopsy report on Suarez and Carstairs?'

'These things take time, Sergeant.'

'I know they do,' I said. 'Only the problem with this one is that there most likely isn't any.' I went on: 'Look, don't be pathetic. Charlie Bowman and myself went and had a look at what this joker did to two women only just now, and I rather think we should get the spindles turning round here just that fraction faster before something else exciting happens with this cunt which'll get us all floundering around in another great flap. Look, there's your office just upstairs, so will you just give them a bell down at the morgue if there's anyone alive there and find out where that fucking report is, since we're on police business in this building, after all? Well? Will you or won't you? Because if not, I'm going down there on my jack, and there'll be breakage when I arrive, I warn you. But you're the superintendent, Jollo, and I'd rather you did it, darling, because rank always speaks louder than words.'

'All right, you insolent bastard,' he said.

I shouted after him: 'You've got five minutes, otherwise I'm on my way.'

He went on upstairs, while I went to 205. I'd hardly sat down on the edge of my desk when the phone rang. Jollo said: 'The report's here. It's coming straight up.'

'At last,' I said.

I took the envelope from the police clerk, signed for it and slit it open the minute he was gone. It felt strangely thin, and when I pulled out what was inside it, no wonder—for nothing came out of the envelope except one lonely piece of hospital paper signed by the chief pathologist, not the younger one I usually dealt with who was snide and chain-smoked Gauloise filters to cover his true anxiety. The message said merely: 'I have the Suarez report here, and I would appreciate it if you would come over and discuss it with me at once.'

I got the clerk back who had brought the message and said: 'What time did this document arrive?'

'I don't know,' he said. 'I'm not sure.' He added briskly: 'Not really my job, you know, Sarge.'

I said: 'What do you mean, you don't know? It's your business to know. So move your great boots and find out, you've got three minutes.'

'What's the problem?'

I told him: 'What you've given me is a very urgent message from the morgue. The time of its receipt here in this building should have been marked, look, here, and it hasn't been, see? Find out why that was, who was responsible and what time this envelope actually did arrive, and now you see what the problem is.'

'Tricky right now,' he said. 'I've got stuff running on the computer.'

'Well, I've got two murders running right now,' I said, 'and you don't care about the computer at all, Constable, what's running or not running on it, because the next computer that's going to concern you is the one that works out your sup ben, now get going or tune your guitar up, they say in front of the National Gallery's a good pitch in summertime.'

He trundled back presently and said: 'It came in by police bike and was timed here an hour and twenty-three minutes ago.'

'Your collective idleness could have cost somebody his life,' I said. 'What's your number? Turn around, let's have a look.'

'B381, Sarge.'

'So you're only in training,' I said. 'Well, don't count on a mortgage for a police flat yet, because you and the other berk who stuck this in a drawer and went off to lunch are both going to be on the mat, which will teach you to take the Factory seriously—you'll be able to watch it from where you're both on point duty, now fuck off.'

I rang the number I had been given in the message. When it answered, a voice I had already dealt with said: 'Who's that, we're just in the middle of changing shift here.'

'Well, mind you don't catch a chill in this bitter weather while you do it,' I said. 'And by the way, isn't your name Veale? It's got that tinny kind of ring to it.'

It said stiffly: 'Yes. I am Assistant Veale.'

'Well, prolong the experience while you've got a chance,' I said, 'because if Doctor Lansdown isn't on this line before you get off it, you're going to wind up in one of your own fridges; we've already had this conversation and I'm tired of it, now get him, move—tell him it's Unexplained Deaths and down to Carstairs/Suarez.'

The mentality of people like Veale wore my nerves red-hot because they were always the ones who told you that whoever you wanted to talk to was out; true or false, it was the negative little privilege that they reckoned went with their position—they were low on humility. Only I had already softened Veale up once and he didn't want the second dose I had ready for him, so Lansdown came on the line straightaway. He said: 'I understand why you were in a hurry for this report. How soon can you get down here?'

'Immediately,' I said, 'but I don't want to see anyone who answers to the name of Veale—it's for his sake, not mine.'

The pathologist said: 'That's all right, he was just replacing me while I was having a shit.'

I slammed the phone down. I sped out to the police car park where the Ford was, turning my collar up. It had started to pour with rain.

I drove over towards the City; I drove hard. As I drove I thought: 'This is far more than just a banal police enquiry into violent death; there's far more to Dora than that for me.' For I found that her death had affected me so deeply that by her defiled face I felt defiled myself. The sweet sadness in the new dress that she had bought and put on, the bottles of wine, the new shoes, the magazine open at the Pacific, her newly-washed hair, ready to go to death as she thought by her own will and of her own accord—she stayed with me, overpowering me; all I wanted to do was get her back as Betty Carstairs had wanted to. But Betty was too old, and I was too late.

Alone, jammed in what she considered a fatal position, without ever bothering Betty, who was old and sick, with enormous, solitary courage she planned and took her first, faltering steps into the dark, only to be cut down and fall the rest of the way in her own blood at the hands of this cunt. I thought as I drove that even though I was too late to save her, if I could solve her death, I might make some contribution to the coming of a time when such a horror would no longer be possible, a time when society would no longer throw up monsters. I had long understood that every effort was worth that effort, but I had never understood it as clearly as I did now.

I whispered in the car as I drove to the morgue: 'Join me by the hand, all of you, living or dead, and consider for one moment of your generosity, poor Dora Suarez, who should never have been slain by an axe at thirty.'

Disjointedly, phrases that she had written recurred to me: 'That in some other world I may at last be able to shit again without screaming in agony. But of course I can't tell Betty that. I can't tell anybody that.'

And then: 'One night lately I fell asleep with Betty in my arms and dreamed I was a bird, and that when I opened my beak, it spoke tears and the whole world heard them.'

I was coming up to the long facade of the hospital where the morgue was now. I drove past the main gate and on till I got to a narrow unmarked entrance in red brick that was just wide enough to accept an ambulance. Like death itself, the gateway was tactful and half-concealed.

I parked in the space, whirling with dust and waste paper, reserved for staff, and got out into the bright London wind, my trousers clinging damply to my legs and the cold reminding me of everything I had ever wanted to forget.

# 6

I went up through the morgue door by three shallow steps in the wet spring wind, feeling the concrete through the soles of my shoes, and was immediately in the atmosphere of that frozen and terrible place while I was still only at the desk. Since I had no manners, I didn't bother with any but just went up to the clerk at the desk and slapped my card down, saying, 'Police, A14.'

The man at the desk said: 'What's it down to?' and I answered: 'You can think yourself lucky it's not you, it's 87471 and 2 Carstairs/Suarez, and I'm pushed, so can we get on with it?' He was going to start moaning but I pointed my forefinger at his head in a gesture for him not to bother, so he jabbed his thumb irritably towards the lift the other side of the empty hall. I walked off across the fake marble through the special odour hospitals have and came up to the duty porter, a bald, bearded boy swabbing away at the tiles with a mop tied into a rag; he also had a green plastic bucket for company, which he brought up beside him with his foot from time to time. Mop, bucket and man looked weary under the state-paid neon lights. I said: 'This service lift working?'

'Yeah,' he said, 'don't take no notice where it says out of order, it's repaired now. I'm going for a break myself,' he added, thumbing the lift button. 'Which floor, canteen?'

'No, the one under the food,' I said. 'The morgue.'

'You want the basement then,' he said, 'and well, there, I'm sorry for you; sad down there, isn't it?' I didn't answer, so he said: 'Don't worry, it's pretty reasonable your being depressed going down there, I'll take you down and see myself all right after. OK, here we go.'

The bell rang on the down arrow and the doors hissed open. As we got in he said: 'You haven't got a smoke on you by any chance?'

I gave him my half-full packet of Westminsters and said: 'Take the lot. It's all right, I've got another.'

'Nice one,' he said, lighting up, 'Christ, this'll do me all the way back to Manpower. Anyway, well, here you are.' The lift stopped with a sighing bump. He saw me out and pressed the button to go back up to the canteen for tea and tabnabs. As the door was closing in his face he added: 'So long, mate, mind how you go now, take care.'

The morgue was an area so vast that its tiled walls, the colour of tired ice, looked grey even under the sunlight that filtered as yellow water through the opaque roof. I breathed formaldehyde; the place was deserted except for two assistants far down the place, just boys, both shod in tired blue Dot Martins, who were leaning against a surface enjoying a smoke.

I said in a general way: 'Doctor Lansdown in?'

'No. Out.'

'Get him in.'

'What makes you so special?'

'The taxpayer,' I said, 'I'm a police officer.'

'You got an appointment with the doctor?'

I said: 'You must be brand-new on this earth. The police don't need appointments. We make them and folk keep them.'

'I don't know about any of that,' the one in front said. His face was white, freckled, and framed in pale orange curls. 'Your best plan is go and see Mr Veale in Room G4, it's just down the corridor. He'll fix you up.'

'There's a danger it might all go the other way,' I said, 'if it was Mr Veale.'

'Why's that, then?'

I said: 'He mightn't have made his will.' I pointed to a phone in a corner and said: 'Does that work?'

'Don't know.'

'Let's try it anyway,' I said. A voice I was getting to know well came on and I said: 'I am about ten yards away from you, Veale, and even fewer seconds, now get Doctor Lansdown in here or say your last prayer, I'm in the morgue. Either the doctor comes to see me or else I come to see you, and you really don't need that, Veale.' A nasal rattle started up the other end; I put the phone down on it.

Soon we heard footsteps in the long corridor I had come in by. I turned to the others and said: 'See? It's easy.'

But they had faded.

A man in his fifties wearing an open white coat over an expensive suit appeared and walked up to me. I said: 'Doctor Lansdown?'

He looked very fit, tired and stricken. He said: 'Carstairs/Suarez?'

'That's right.'

He said: 'It's Suarez. Have you examined her?'

'As she was found. I'm in charge of the case. Why?'

He said: 'Are your nerves good?'

'I've seen most things. Why?'

'You're going to have to look at something you may not have seen,' the pathologist said, 'that's why. I'm just saying that it's very important that whatever you see now, you must control yourself and remain calm.' He added: 'It won't be easy.'

I said: 'If what you have to show me could help me find her killer,' I said, 'then I guarantee I'll remain calm.'

Lansdown said: 'Poor child. It might.' He added: 'I've examined the dead here for twenty-two years, and I found it difficult
to stay calm over her.' He looked me in the eyes. 'That's what's
delayed my report—there were checks I had to make.' He turned
away from me and looked suddenly like a cheap curtain when the
rod across its window breaks. He said: 'Did you think you had
seen all of Suarez when you saw her?'

I said: 'What more is there?'

He said: 'Did you touch her?'

I couldn't tell him how I had kissed her dead hair that still
smelled of apples. I said: 'No.'

He said: 'She was dressed when you saw her?'

'Of course.'

'You didn't interfere with her clothing?'

I said: 'Doctor Lansdown, as a police officer I was there to
examine the position of the bodies and to examine the flat.'

He said: 'I'm afraid you've seen nothing yet, then. Nothing of
87471 at all.'

There was a stool beside a vacant bench; Lansdown pointed to
it and said: 'Why don't you sit down?'

I said: 'Christ no. I'm not the kind that needs to sit
down.'

'It was to try and prepare you,' he said. 'I've seen death here
every day for twenty years—but I've never seen anything worse
than this.'

I said: 'I've seen violent death as often as you have.'

'I know, but until you've seen Suarez you can't imagine what
she went through.' He added: 'Don't tell me she hasn't marked
you, too.' Then he said, turning away: 'I'll just get Wiecienski,
we work together. His name's Andrew. He's Polish, the rest of
the people here are just a farce.'

He went to the door and called out: 'Wiecienski! Are you
there?'

A distant voice said yes, he was there.

The pathologist shouted: 'Bring the Suarez file with you, Andrew—87471.'

The voice said in accented English: 'Who've you got with you?'

'Someone who apparently wants to see some justice done around the place.'

'What?' said the voice. 'I didn't know there were any of them left.'

Wiecienski came in and put the file marked Suarez D-87471 on the edge of a desk by the door. He was a heavy man of about fifty, with blond hair that looked as if it had been rained on. The pathologist said: 'Bring her over, Andrew. Bring her out covered so that at first the officer here can see only what he saw of her before.'

She arrived on a chrome trolley, wheeled slowly over by Wiecienski. She was clean, bloodless and frozen; her blind eyes, black under their heavy lids, shone brilliantly up into the hard light that Wiecienski had switched on over her. She lay half-turned on her side like goods being delivered at an exclusive address on ice; and the unmarked side of her dark head that showed above the towel, lying on its cheek, reminded me of a girl lying stiffly asleep, as long as you did not look too closely—her lips parted on a dream word. The pathologist turned to me and said: 'I'm going to take the towel away now.'

I said: 'Do it.'

The doctor took the towel very softly by its two corners from under Dora's chin and in silence folded it down as far as her shins—and when that gesture revealed the rest of Dora's body, whose state had been concealed from me in the flat by her dress, my stomach came up to the front of my mouth and I thought, 'Christ, I'm going to spew,' but I just controlled it. 'All right,' I said. After a moment I leaned over the body again and this time found that I could look at it.

'Andrew,' the pathologist said, 'will you just help me to turn her?' As they were doing it the pathologist said: 'I want you to see her anus.'

When they had it displayed, I said: 'What is that abominable thing Dora has there, like a mushroom?'

The doctor said: 'That's a development of herpes simplex, orchestrated with mucocutaneous warts.'

I looked. Some of the mushroom had burst. I said: 'How did she manage to defecate through that?'

He said: 'It was an intolerable agony for her, made worse by the fact that as she crouched on the loo she must have looked at her thighs and seen these, and these, and these, see? Look, here, here and here.'

I looked at the dark, disfiguring plaques on her upper thighs and said to Lansdown: 'What is it?'

'It's classic Karposi's sarcoma. Why, haven't you ever had to deal with a case of AIDS before?'

I said: 'How did she get into this state?'

He said: 'That's what I'm trying to find out. That's why this report on her's delayed. I'm a pathologist, not an AIDS specialist, so I got on to Westminster where they've got a specialist team; they came over, examined her, took samples, and I'm waiting. Don't rush them,' he added. 'Particularly as it's a case of murder they're doing their best, but it takes time.'

'All right,' I said, 'yet you realise that from my point of view I've got to find the killer.'

'I know,' he said.

'So that the longer your report takes, the further away he'll get. Could you ring Westminster?'

'Look, it's arranged,' said Lansdown. 'I have a permanent line open here—if I'm out, Wiecienski's in and vice versa, and the second they've got anything, they'll be on. The head of the team they sent over was Johnson. He was in charge of the Suarez examination and there aren't six men in this country who know more about AIDS than he does.'

'Did he say anything?' I said. 'Anything at all? Because what's beginning to interest me more and more is how she caught this.'

'After an hour he said he couldn't understand how her lower intestine had got into the state it is. He told me: "It's the vehicle by which the virus was introduced into her that I can't make out—it wasn't the male organ." After he had looked into her lower stomach anally and then got film of it he said to me: "The colon is abnormally dilated and appears to have been scraped raw and eaten in places. But I shall have to analyse the film, of course." Then he turned to me suddenly and said: "To put it vulgarly, what was left of her colon wouldn't make a paper handkerchief worth sneezing into." '

'In your opinion, was she correct in what she wrote, in the book of hers that I found, that she was dying anyway?' I said.

'Oh yes,' said Lansdown. 'Look at her—here, here and here.' He took up a pair of forceps and curled her upper lip back from the gum. 'You see this gingevitis, the teeth exposed to the roots? Hairy leukoplakia on the side of the tongue here? And here? That's a proliferation of the Epstein-Barr virus. Oral thrush, aphthous growths right at the rear of the cavity, epiglottis generally infected—these are secondary infections, but they often spread downwards into the lungs, usually presenting as some relatively untreatable, because rare, form of pneumonia, pneumocystis carinii, toxoplasma, or pneumococcal lobar.' He added: 'While you can stabilise some of these infections temporarily, there is no guarantee that they won't recur or manifest themselves differently in other parts of the body—advanced AIDS, in our present state of knowledge, is irreversible and the prognosis in the case of Suarez, negative.'

'How long would she have had to live?' I said.

'Anywhere between three months and three years,' said Lansdown, 'but Johnson's opinion was from six to twelve months.'

'Well,' I said, 'anyway she had made up her mind to kill herself.'

'I can understand that,' said Lansdown.

'Yes,' I said, 'only then in rushes your man and saves her the trouble by taking an axe to her the night she'd decided to do it.'

The phone rang and Lansdown went over to it. He listened and said: 'There's a police officer upstairs in the main hall, wants to know if he can come down.'

'He give a name?'

'It's a Detective Sergeant Stevenson.'

I took the phone and said: 'I don't know why you're here.'

He said: 'I think I might.'

'Come down anyway,' I said. 'Someone'll show you the way.'

'I know the way.'

'Avoid a man called Veale,' I said.

While I was waiting for Stevenson I walked away from the others to a tall window and looked out over London. Words of Dora's poured through me:

> I am too fragile; I shall never find the courage to free myself— I'm blocked, I'm dying, I can't move. I saw him last night on the waste ground behind his place where we meet now and I told him this; he turned on me like a viper and said, 'I'll kill you, you bitch.' He took me by the wrist so hard I thought he was going to break it. He said: 'I can't yet,' then he threw me on the ground and just trotted off, shaking his hair out of his eyes.

I thought, 'Yes, but who the hell was he? Where was this piece of waste ground? What couldn't he do yet?' I was certain she was talking about her killer—but Dora never named places, never once named people.

There had then been a page after that on which, marking it with a star, she had added in her swift, angular writing:

> Some hand will come for me, I know it will. Meanwhile, the last battle is in the sitting room

—and as I read I felt I could see, now that I knew that she was dying of AIDS, how, cornered, she had both found her mind and lost it in the terror of her approaching end.

They say that in the old war at the beginning of the century men going up to the front found their best friends at the last moment, just as Betty and I found each other.

'Hush now, Dora,' I said, going back to her body and stroking her cheek, 'hush, rest now.'

There was a knock on the door and Wiecienski opened it. A voice said: 'Sergeant Stevenson.'

I led him across to where the others stood by the body.

He looked down at her and said: 'Suarez?'

I said: 'Yes.' I said: 'You're a mate of mine and I just wanted you to look at her, as you're here.'

He stood looking down at her; he didn't say anything.

I bent down and pulled out a small, icy box from under the trolley wheels that had accompanied the body. Without opening it, but placing my hand on it, I said to Stevenson: 'In this box there is a part of Suarez's left breast and most of her right arm. But I have forgotten that she is not complete; to me she is complete, and I am going to catch this man. The world isn't big enough for him to escape me.'

Stevenson said: 'It depends, but I think we might—you know I'm on this Roatta thing.'

I said: 'Yes, let's talk about it when we leave here.'

He said: 'I came over here because I wanted to be sure of catching you.'

I said: 'Yes, all right.'

'Let's get off back to the Factory when you're ready,' said Stevenson, 'and have a talk—see if we can't connect up a few things. Might be nothing in it, but you see how the times click, and villains have wheels. I see no reason yet why he mightn't have carried straight on after Carstairs and Suarez and done Roatta, do you?'

'I'm glad to hear you say it,' I said, 'because it's what I think of as a possible, too, if we could find a link that tied Suarez and Roatta together. The old lady's not a problem—for me she was killed because she butted in at the wrong moment and saw too much. Anyway it's a starting point.' I added: 'Also I've got the press on it. Cryer.'

'Yes, why not stir the sauce,' said Stevenson, 'certainly. Villains and maniacs buy a newspaper same as the next man.' He added: 'Not that that makes them human.'

Wiecienski shuddered in the cold room. Without looking at anyone, he said: 'Get him.'

I suddenly wanted to be back to the Factory. I looked at the time; it was ten to one in the morning, but I wasn't tired. I said to Lansdown: 'We've got to leave. Thanks very much. We've learned a lot.' I thought, 'So she had terminal AIDS.' It was all I could think about. So that was at least one of the things she could never tell Betty Carstairs—but talking to Lansdown, I tried to sound as if I were just talking about the weather.

Lansdown was saying: 'I'll keep you fully in touch.'

'Yes, thank you,' I said. 'One thing—if you could try and let me know when the funeral is.'

'Carstairs will probably be buried next Saturday,' Lansdown said. 'With public funerals it's usually on a Saturday afternoon— but Suarez is going to take longer, depending on the Westminster, our report, the coroner, yourselves.' He said to Wiecienski: 'You can take her back now, Andrew.'

Wiecienski said: 'I'll take care of her,' and he drew the towel over her.

Time put a dead little question into a silence that fell as he did so, marred only by the squeak of the rubber wheels; and then the full horror of Suarez's death must have struck all of us in that high room smoking with ice simultaneously, because we all turned and looked at each other, speechless, and Wiecienski looked back at us over his shoulder once with red eyes as he took her back.

Stevenson had been dropped off at the morgue by a passing squad car, so to get back to the Factory we took my Ford, and to take my mind off Carstairs/Suarez for a few minutes, I started talking to him about my recall to A14—I was glad to have a straight man to talk to. I said: 'It was surprising; the Voice rang me, and I was told what I'd never been told at the time of the internal enquiry over the Mardy case—that the decision of the disciplinary board was that I be suspended from the police force, you know, the door shut but not locked, so that you stand around with your head under your arm until they suddenly come on the line and say you can have your head back on your shoulders again now if you want, we've a job for you and you're reinstated, only don't fuck us about this time. Yes, well, then I see Jollo, and when I've got him tuned in, it turns out they've no one over at A14 to put on Carstairs/Suarez, you being busy over Roatta. I said, you can't just fire and rehire people like that and they said why not, you like police work don't you and I said yes. Then they reminded me that I was a very dedicated officer, which I had been in danger of forgetting, and Jollo and the Voice started up again with their dreary old music—why is it we all hate you so much at times, Sergeant, why are you always a loner, always so fucking difficult. The only way I can solve my cases is by being myself, I said—I don't think they got it, though. Jollo said, your tongue's too sharp, why don't you try keeping it in your pocket? It would cut the pocket, I said, I'd rather nail a villain with it. And it's true I'm a loner, I added, though I've one or two mates—but that's because I don't want a whole load of zealous cunts looking for promotion tumbling all over me when I'm on a matter. You know me, Stevenson, I always warn them first, like politely—nothing at all today, thanks, fuck off, always leave me alone when I'm work-ing—because that way I can hear a murderer, feel him, hunt him

my own way; that's what I'm made to do. You're really too old
to stay a sergeant, you know, Jollo said, you're forty-five. I said,
if you kick me upstairs, I go straight out at the front door again—
that's final and I want a divorce, as they say on page three of the
linens, so why don't you just let me get on with it? Because if
everyone behaved the way you do, Jollo said, what kind of a
police force would we have? Why not reverse the question, I said,
and try answering that one? After all, I said to them, look at my
private life. That's quickly and easily done—it's me. What I had
going for me on the family front before, well, that blew itself to
bits, as you well know, and it's not because you're a loner that
you're a bad detective; besides, the hours of work don't bother
me at all, and that's all I think you need to understand, Mr Jollo.
I told him well, look, anyway, you know me—if you put me onto
these two women's deaths they'll become the whole human race
for me till I catch the individual, and I will. I'm always the same;
I'm always on the side of the victim; I never change. But if you
give me a case, Mr Jollo, it's my case and nobody else's. It's my
nature; it's like putting a mongoose to a snake. All right, all right,
Jollo said, just get on with Carstairs/Suarez, and I said, that's
what I'm patiently waiting to do when you've finished talking. So
then afterwards the Voice, which had been told of this conversation with Jollo, rang me and said I had this really lyrical side to
my nature and I said there's nothing very lyrical about an A14
death.

'I've got my contacts and I've got my territory, that's the London metropolitan area; I know it the way a blind man knows
each wall he taps on when he goes down his front steps into the
street to turn right to reach the shops. I've got my grasses, all
like snide whores, all with the mentality of garbage pickers—ready
to sieve through any shit in the hope there's a coin in it somewhere. I've got my drunks, my half-pardoned villains waiting to
come up for trial and anxious to trade if it'll mean a year off their
sentence or even reduced to community service in exceptional

cases. I've the press, I see a feller or two over a drink across at the Clipper or the Yorkshire Grey and I'm set to go; I'm permanently set to go. All I need to get to work is the minimum that any police officer needs—a warrant card, which is authority to go in, and access to police computers and information on file.'

I parked in the Factory lot and said: 'I've been blagging on.'

Stevenson said: 'My eardrums aren't bruised.'

'All right,' I said, 'then in that case let's drive the lift up to the second floor.'

'I'm very hard into Roatta's past,' Stevenson said as we went up in the lift, which was empty, 'very hard.'

'It cheers me up to hear you say that,' I said, 'because once you start digging into that load of shit, there's most certainly plenty of it.'

'I tell you, it's the close timing of Roatta's death with yours that fascinates me,' Stevenson said.

I said: 'It interests me a great deal, too.'

'By the way,' he said, 'have you heard of a club called the Parallel Club?'

I said: 'Yes, that's up near Carnaby Street. Used to be called the Night Off, then there was heavy bother and it burned.'

'Roatta had it done,' said Stevenson. 'The old management weren't paying him off enough, so it was smashed up with the first warning, and then second time round, up it went.'

'Rough.'

'Don't go crying your eyes out,' Stevenson said.

I said: 'It's that place the yuppies go to for extra sex, and so what else about it?'

'Roatta's about it,' said Stevenson. 'He was co-owner with Giancarlo Robacci.'

The lift stopped on our floor and we got out. 'Well, I've been away,' I said, 'I didn't know that.' I added: 'But we all know about Robacci.'

'Now there's a man I'd like to clobber,' said Stevenson, 'but the trouble is that he's Bolivian these days. Failing that, I've twice tried to get him deported, but I don't know why—I just couldn't pull the trick.'

'Well, fancy that,' I said.

We went into his office. I turned a chair round and sat with my arms crossed along its back. I said: 'There are a lot of Italians popping up in this hand, aren't there? Had you noticed? Some of them alive, some of them less so.'

'Well, we're the West End here, aren't we?' he said. He was restless, tapping his nails on the desk.

'What's the matter?' I said. 'You suddenly decided to take up the piano?'

'This morning I paid a man cash for a photograph and it isn't here when he said it would be. I paid a ton for the fucking thing. It isn't an old master; still, if it isn't here in five minutes, I'll tear the cunt's head off for him.'

'They ought to make you public-relations officer,' I said. I added: 'What made it so interesting that it was worth a ton of public money?'

'It's to do with a party Roatta threw at the Parallel for his birthday a month back,' said Stevenson, 'but why don't you wait and see it, too? If it arrives.'

'Yes, I will,' I said. 'Anything go on at the Parallel besides sing, strip and get pissed out of your brain on the ground floor?'

'There's an upstairs.'

'What makes that exciting?'

'Roatta was a blackmailer,' said Stevenson, 'and Robacci's another. Only they weren't into reputations—who gives a fuck about them these days? No, they were into a brand-new scam, only I haven't been able to find out what it is, and that's not for want of trying—nobody's talking.'

A WPC came in with an A4-sized envelope. She handed it to Stevenson and said: 'Sign.'

Stevenson said: 'How did this arrive?'

'Bike,' she said, but Stevenson was slitting the envelope open. He slipped out a blown-up glossy photograph in black-and-white, that was all I could see, and bent over it. When he had finished, he spun the picture round so that it was right way up to me. 'Just as a one-off,' he said, 'anybody in this elegant company ring a bell with you?'

I looked. In the photograph, among the tables, there was a girl singing, holding a microphone.

I said: 'That's Suarez.'

Stevenson said that he thought there was a far-out chance that it might be.

There were a great many other interesting features in the photograph, but in that second I only had time for hers.

# 7

I went into 205 for a minute and there was a letter on my desk, come by ordinary mail. I looked to see where it had been posted: Dulwich. It looked like a nasty letter, and I felt just by looking at it that the only prints on the envelope would be the postman's. It lay in front of me in a Menzies envelope with dirt marks on it and the address was written with a ballpoint in sprawling block capitals. Even so, I rang down for a fingerprint man to come and take it all away—you never knew.

I opened the letter using a knife and a Kleenex. Inside was a sheet of paper with gold-scrolled edges. The letter, too, was all written in block caps. It read: 'Hello cunt. The linen says your the bastard that's put a reward out for a geezer that smashed a clock. I ever meet up with you you nosey git and you won't need to know what the time is.' I put my Westminster down and smelled the letter. It smelled faintly; the only smell I could associate with it was dirty clothes. I looked at the writing; the strokes were broken and cracked, as if they had been written on a rough surface. Then the fingerprint man arrived and took it expertly away.

I went back into Stevenson's office. He said: 'Anything interesting?'

106

I said: 'No, just fan mail.' Even though the letter was from the killer, it was of no immediate or direct use to me. Still, if the ad had helped upset his balance wheel, it hadn't been wasted.

Stevenson said: 'Why don't you and I just have a look at this photograph again? The faces in the audience?'

I went round and looked at it over his shoulder. 'Christ,' I said, 'you've got some familiar ones here—it's like a villains' "This Is Your Life." '

'It was happy hour, wasn't it?' Stevenson said.

'Yes,' I said. 'For some.' I ignored the faked uproarious bonhomie of the faces at the tables with their cold eyes; I concentrated on only two. I looked long and hard at Suarez with the mike; her lips were parted much as I had found them. She was evidently singing, her eyes shut; nobody was paying any attention to her. Then I put my thumbnail down on a man with his back to the camera; he was going out under a lit sign that said EXIT. It was dark in that corner of the club and the camera must have caught him by accident. He was moving a little faster than the film, which blurred him, but he was black-haired, maybe in his thirties, on the short side, wearing baggy sports trousers and a dark shirt. I said: 'Have you any idea who that is? That's no waiter or barman, he looks sort of functional.'

Stevenson studied him and said: 'Never seen him before, and the fact he's the wrong way round doesn't help. Maybe a bouncer.'

'Maybe,' I said, 'only bouncers at the Parallel like to dress up.' I put the photograph down. I said: 'Where did you get it?'

'From a hostess who had her clothing set on fire by three punters because she wouldn't cooperate the way they wanted her to,' said Stevenson, 'and I'm not joking.'

'Civilised blot on the map, London is, isn't it?' I said. I added: 'Well, I don't know what you think, but I reckon your photograph makes this both our case.'

He said: 'I thought you didn't like working with other people.'

'Depends who they are,' I said, 'and we'll wipe the whole of this lot up much faster if we go about it two-handed.'

He said: 'You fancy a trot round to the Parallel?'

'Yes, I very much do,' I said. 'Right now, why not?'

'Will we get a W?' he said. 'I think so, don't you?'

'Oh yes, most definitely,' I said, 'a warrant to go right through the pad from tit to arsehole, I think that might really come in most useful.'

'I'll just see to that while you comb your hair then,' he said, 'and we're on our way.'

I said: 'You may have problems getting it.'

'I don't think so really,' he said. 'I think you'll be surprised. I think they're beginning to have problems over Carstairs/Suarez up on the fourth floor. Big problems.'

'What sort of problems?'

'Word gets around, doesn't it?' said Stevenson.

'Well, that's exactly what words are for,' I said. 'It's good, I like it.'


It was obvious when we got to the Parallel Club that Stevenson and I didn't look at all the same as the other people who were going in and out, but we didn't care—we weren't going to hang about on the steps because of that. The boulder-sized doorman in a cherry-coloured overcoat, topper and buttons that could have done with a dash of Brasso moved over and said: 'Where do you think you're going?'

'In,' I said. I showed him my warrant card and said: 'We're members of an affiliated club, see, so it would be a pity if you upset our night's fun.'

The doorman didn't quite know what to do about that, so he very sensibly did nothing, anyway for the time being, except go for a blower in the corner. Once well inside the gaff, the next person I caught sight of was the hats and coats girl. It didn't take me long to work out that she knew, or anyway as deep inside herself as she knew how to go, that she wasn't nearly as pretty as she thought she was, and spent as much of her free time as possible making sure everyone got a good hammering for it, especially men: between her thin lips there was about as much compassion as a cash-point machine gobbling up an expired credit card.

There was plenty of action in the bar, and some slow blue revolving on the lit-up plastic dance floor, too; but in general the bottles hurried about the place a good deal faster than the customers did. Another well-stuffed fun seeker who looked as if he were quick on his feet if he had to be came over to us and said: 'Who was it you said you were again?'

'Correct the tone, son,' said Stevenson. 'You can see we're police officers, so fuck off and wheel some brains on or I'll have you on a one-way single.' A passing punter who looked as if he had caught socialism in the bar and then brought it up in the scented jacks wavered past us on his way over to an Indian girl naked except for gold slippers and a fur coat, who obviously, from her choked expression, looked as if she felt she could have scored higher. The punter, who was young, with a very high, fairy-tale bald head, said to Stevenson: 'Manners!'

Stevenson said: 'I'm on my manor, it's called the Factory. Are you on yours?'

'My father owns half this street!'

'Don't bet on it,' Stevenson said.

We were alone for a time in the cold pool of silence that coppers create round themselves. Looking through into the dance area further back, I watched a black girl moving among the tables with a microphone just as Suarez had done. I caught a couple of lines: *I'm eighteen years into my fever! I'm eighteen years into my mind!*

A tall young man who might have carried it off as a post graduate from a smart university if he hadn't been so obviously knifed in the face came up and said: 'Now, gentlemen, I'm the assistant manager, what is all this about? Can I help you? You can see you're emptying the place.'

I noticed that people were in fact starting to leave with an unhurried, yet rippling urgency.

'It's obvious what it's about,' said Stevenson loudly. 'It's about a death, isn't it?'

The undulations of the quitting punters imperceptibly speeded up.

I said: 'Who's in charge? Come on, darling, we haven't got all night.'

'Mr Robacci just happens to be in.'

'Bring him,' said Stevenson. 'Now go on, go mad, do it now.'

'Perhaps you'd care to come into the office.'

Stevenson said: 'No. We're staying here.'

I had been looking keenly at the post graduate for some time and said suddenly: 'I've placed you now. You were busted as front man for a stolen car ring in '85, drew three and did eighteen months at Ford Open. And then you did community work gardening in St James's Park for kiting, didn't you? You were lucky that time, weren't you? Well, my life, so it's old Arthur "Hullo All, I'm Dealing' Apsley-Kingsford all over again come back as a new person!'' I shook my head. 'I hope for your sake you know nothing about this Roatta death, but I'm not fucking praying for you.'

The young man was sweating hard now and I said: 'Go and get Robacci before I manacle you to the nearest radiator. Now move.'

Now it was the head doorman's turn to see that the all-time dealer was getting out of his depth and that events were taking a wrong-o; besides, he was fed up at having been pushed onto the sidelines, so now he came back out onto the field to make his breath felt a bit. He said to Stevenson: 'So you're both out of the Factory, are you? What? Serious Crimes? I don't make you, I don't know you.'

'No,' said Stevenson, 'We're from A14.'

'What's that?'

'I hope you never find out,' said Stevenson. 'It's Unexplained Deaths, and I've got some very bad news for all of you—we have a warrant to search this premises till it's stark bollock naked and that includes the whole building, not just the downstairs here, and what are you going to do about it?'

The doorman said: 'I expect there'll be a few phone calls, I don't know.'

'Forget it,' said Stevenson. 'People may or may not come round for an envelope on the fifteenth, but here we are on the twenty-eighth—we're a completely different mob, see, and you're all fucked sunny-side, sweetheart.' He added: 'So take good advice, obliterate, stay quiet and wise, and who knows, you might wind up doing no more than a year hard. But start being clever and you can make that five, flower.'

The doorman started to say: 'It's not the night really for you to—'

'No, I know,' I said, 'but you're not paid to break a mainspring, you leave all that to us, we're the specialists.'

'That's right,' said Stevenson seriously, 'you'd really be better off.'

'Yes, but your improved circumstances don't prevent you from answering a question or three,' I said. I went right up close to him, pushed his topper gently back on his head and laid both my hands on his shoulders. 'Now,' I said quietly, staring into his bobbing eyes, 'when did you last see a girl here called Dora Suarez?'

'And don't be pathetic and bleat who,' said Stevenson. He handed me a copy of the photograph we had been looking at in 202. I took it and spread it under the doorman's nose.

'That girl,' I said. 'The girl there singing the night of Roatta's birthday party.' I added: 'His last.'

'She used to sing here.'

'We know she did,' I said patiently. 'You've just seen photographic proof that we know it. But she won't be singing here any more, will she?'

'I suppose not.'

'And why's that?'

'Well, I've heard she's dead,' said the doorman.

'You heard right,' I said, 'the same as everyone else in this country—and what do you think she died of?'

'I read in the paper that she was killed by a man with an axe.'

'True enough,' I said, 'as far as it goes, friend. But not quite far enough—she was one of those fortunately rare people who was killed twice over.'

(In my mind Dora was still writing at me from her exercise book: 'If you want us to live we shall all live—and if not, not. But get justice for us, that had none.')

'I don't understand,' the doorman said. His thick boxer's chin was beginning to wobble, and I watched his eyes sliding around looking for help; he had had about enough.

'The other way she was dying was from AIDS,' I said, 'and since you're the strength here, what do you know about that? Could you have infected her? Are you seropositive, you fat git?'

'Look, I'm just the doorman,' he whispered.

'Someone has to open the door and let the people into hell, don't they?' I said. 'Do you do well on tips? From "my father owns half the street" and all that mob? And then do you take it out on the staff girlies, the bar-girls, singers and that on the side? A few hot, wet little fucks otherwise you could make things hard? I bet you just do,' I said, 'you've got just the face for it, you lovely big bouncer, you great bundle of what nobody ordered.'

'I don't know anything!' he mumbled. 'Nothing!'

'We'll find out what you know and what you don't know,' I said, 'over at the Factory, leave it to us. Without us laying a finger on you, we'll have you telling us things that you didn't know yourself.'

'Doorman?' said Stevenson softly. 'That's just like really a very kind of temporary job; I think you're going to find yourself very soon on a much longer-term contract, satisfying work that could last for years, sweeping dust into a shovel with a handbrush every day along a very long gritty corridor made of cement. Lovely country air, too, not like these stuffy West End places. It's in a town called Maidstone and it's really really nice, do you a world of good.' He felt the doorman's gold-braided collar absently, picking a piece of fluff off it in a tender manner. Its wearer swallowed dryly.

'Now look,' said the doorman, 'if I was to tell you—'

I said: 'Did Suarez have a boyfriend at all who hung around here in this place? And don't tell me you're just the doorman all over again, because that isn't the right answer at all.'

'Look, Christ,' said the doorman, 'I never noticed her with anyone in particular—anyway, she wasn't the kind of girl to talk about it if she had.'

'All right,' I said, 'but now mind how you reply, because these are three really heavy deaths, what this officer and myself are on.'

'That's right,' said Stevenson, 'and what was your name again?'

I said: 'No need to ask, I read him—the name's Margoulis, Johnny, and I make him in the Scrubs one year down to petty thieving, two in Maidstone, which he went down for because he tried to flog the gear he'd nicked from the folks he'd thieved it from. Brilliant, that's right, isn't it, Johnny, and so when's the big match then, like five to seven down at Canterbury, charmer?'

'What's past is past,' the doorman said.

'It may be over,' I said, 'but what's over still leaves traces, Johnny—like in our records, see what I mean.' I said in a serious tone: 'Now you've zero interest fucking us about, Johnny, so start telling about Suarez and if and when she met up with anyone more or less regularly in here. Come on, now, be a big boy. You're just a fat prick and a low gossip for your own interest, you think garbage level just like any grass—and for my money you're yellow like all grasses, for all your big build.'

The doorman was just starting to say maybe we could meet and like discuss it elsewhere when at that point a very fat man in dark glasses who looked as if he and his dinner jacket had been boiled as a single dish appeared and said: 'Good evening, I'm Robacci, the owner here.'

Stevenson said: 'Yes, we've already had the pleasure.'

Robacci said: 'Bother here?'

'That's right,' said Stevenson, 'in the circles you move, bother's the other word for the law.'

'You've emptied my place, you two,' said Robacci, 'you realise that.'

'We'd have done it before,' I said, 'only we were busy.'

'You've really spoiled my evening,' Robacci said, 'and my takings, and I was doing so well.'

'You should have gone back to Bolivia, then, shouldn't you, love?' Stevenson said. 'I already told you twice.'

'I could catch the ten o'clock plane in the morning if I liked,' Robacci said.

'That mightn't be quite so easy now,' Stevenson said. 'You wouldn't listen to a warning, would you, you cheeky little man? If you're clean on Roatta, you can go—it'll take a wearisome time to establish that, though. On the other hand, if it shows that you're not clean, forget the splendour of the Andes and start emptying pisspots at the Scrubs, OK?'

'Let's get to the point, shall we?' Robacci said. 'How much this time? I suppose you've been sent over from the top floor.'

'You're not reading me at all,' Stevenson said. 'I've never done a stint with the Bolivian police, but I daresay you need to know a few people in it, I don't know, don't care. The difference here is that you're in London, and it's us over at the Factory that run the manor and that includes you as long as you're on it, sweetheart, and we don't know you at all, and what's even worse luck for you, we don't want to.'

'It's what the unions call working to rule,' I said, 'or in plain English, no deal, do you read?'

'Christ,' Robacci said.

'He usually takes the weekend off,' said Stevenson, 'and he certainly wasn't on tap last Saturday night, Sunday morning, when there were three particularly disgusting murders committed in the space of less than three hours—your co-owner, Felix Roatta, was one of the victims.'

'I know that,' said Robacci. 'We all know it and deplore it. But Felix—he and I were just financially interested in the club together; otherwise he did his own thing, you know.'

'What I know,' said Stevenson, producing them, 'is that I've two documents in my hand here, and if you go wrong on either of them, you're likely to wind up doing twenty years in a British jail. You're already not young, and by the time you come out you'll just be a wispy little old man on two sticks and a prayer.'

'I wish we could just go into my office at the side over there where we could be private and discuss a little serious money for you to drop all this,' said Robacci. He did not look healthy as he spoke. 'There must be a rate for it.'

'No, there isn't,' said Stevenson. 'Two junior officers put in charge of an explosive case like this one, they can't afford to go wrong over it, and we're not going to.'

'So let's not talk about money at all,' I said. 'Let's talk about Roatta and Dora Suarez.'

'Yes,' said Stevenson. 'This first document I have here is a magistrate's warrant to search these entire premises.'

'Look, some of the building belongs on the Parallel lease,' said Robacci, 'some of it doesn't.'

'We don't care,' said Stevenson. 'This document empowers us to rip the lot out, flats, clubs, mice, vice, uncle tom cobley and all, read it.'

I said to Stevenson: 'Now show him the other one, why not?'

Robacci said: 'Before you do, I want to tell you something. Do you know who I mean by Chief Inspector Bowman from Serious Crimes, works out of your house?'

'Yes, extremely well,' I said, 'Mr Bowman's a glutton for other people's punishment. Why? Did you want to see him? It could be arranged straightaway.'

'I should drop that if I were you,' Stevenson said, 'for your own sake. A copper's like anyone else—treat you fine if you're his side of the counter, smash you one in the face if you're on the other, and that's life for you, isn't it?'

I said: 'Or is it that you're alleging improper conduct on the part of a police officer? In which case you are in conversation with two police officers, so bring a charge, why don't you?'

'Christ no,' Robacci said, 'are you mad?' He dropped it.

'Right now,' I said to Stevenson, 'show him the other document. Let's see him respond to a face or four in his own club.'

Stevenson showed Robacci the picture and said: 'OK, now. Now we're here in the Parallel with this photo, aren't we? What night was that, then?'

'No need to stammer over it, Robacci,' I said. 'We're in the middle of Roatta's last birthday party here, aren't we?'

He had to say yes.

'The girl singing,' I said. 'The dark girl with the mike there.'

'Don't know her.'

I said: 'Repeat that, but take all your time, because your answer could affect your long-term future.'

'I might have seen her.'

'Don't tell me people sing in your club in front of your customers without your knowing who the fucking hell they are,' I said.

'They came and went,' Robacci said, 'you know. Felix looked after that end.'

'This is the face of one that went,' I said, 'and the payment for that is going to be weighty.' I said: 'So wring your brains out and put a name to her before you lose your own—because I'll bury you in the British prison system till the end of time if you don't; the Factory always finds a way.'

There was a long silence until I said: 'Silence is not always golden, Robacci, and I'm getting restless.'

Robacci said: 'Felix could have perhaps told you.'

'Well, he can't now,' I said, 'so you're going to have to. After all, you were co-owners in this shithole.'

Stevenson said to me: 'Look at his face, you can tell he knew her.'

I turned to Robacci and said: 'When did you screw her last, you fat bag of piss?'

Robacci turned white and said: 'I never did that.'

'Oh really?' I said. 'Why not? Not pretty enough for you?'

Robacci said: 'It wasn't that.'

'No,' I said, 'I know it wasn't.' I said to Stevenson: 'We'll put this one on board.'

Robacci said: 'What do you mean, put me on board?'

I said: 'It means a single to the Factory, and there we're going to press on the pod till you spring the peas.'

He said: 'You lay a hand on me—'

'It doesn't work like that,' I said, 'it doesn't need to.' I said to Robacci, putting the photograph to him again: 'And this man, here, yes, this one, the one running out of that door fast in the corner there by the dance floor under the exit light, who's he?'

Robacci said nothing.

I said to Stevenson: 'When people give you a spiel, they're lying. When they say nothing, they know. It's like that, isn't it?'

'That's right,' said Stevenson, 'anyway in my experience.'

Robacci said: 'What are you holding me on?'

I said: 'Anything that'll hold you for twenty-four hours—

because we'll break this in twenty-four hours. Papers not in order, tax enquiry, known to frequent criminals, Christ, I can think up thirty reasons.'

'I'll speak to my consulate!' he screamed.

'It's a funny thing,' I said, 'but diplomacy is one of those few areas where Bolivia is rather slow on the draw—bad luck, darling.' I said to Stevenson: 'Ring a squad car and get it to roll round and drop this lot off at Poland Street, will you?'

Robacci said: 'You can't mean it.'

I said: 'Well, I said it, didn't I?'

'Yes.'

'Well, then, if I said it, I meant it.' I called over to Stevenson, who was on the phone: 'When you're finished there, let's really get going and take this fucking place apart.' I said to Robacci: 'You got the keys? I want all the keys. Because we can kick your doors down, but you can't kick ours down. Villains all know that, it's iron rule number one.'

He said: 'I don't know if I've got them all.'

'Well,' I said, 'you'd better have them on you tonight the same as you do every other night, including the ones to the upstairs at the back there going on past the toilets where there's a door that says top members only, if you ever want your own cell unlocked again. Otherwise we melt our key down, which means you melt with it, OK?' I added: 'You still say you only knew Suarez by sight, before you leave here? The man running out of the back, the sporty-looking type? Don't be too immediate in your answers—take your time for the last time.'

'I'm telling you what I told you,' Robacci said.

'He's terrified,' said Stevenson, who had come back from the phone, 'and frightened men tell the best lies of all and stick to them like shit to a blanket.'

I held my hand out to Robacci, 'The keys,' I said. 'I don't want to have to go to the Factory for them once they've stripped you there.'

Robacci gave me the keys.

The squad car arrived outside. I said to the sergeant: 'This one, a quickie to the Factory. Hold him for A14, 202, 205, we'll be over in an hour or less.'

'What's the charge?'

'Sus,' I said.

Actually, there was another bit on the side here before we went in and searched the upstairs of the Parallel. We did three of us go into Robacci's office, but we didn't take Robacci, we took the doorman. Doormen depend on tips, taxi drops and a bob or two from phone numbers, sexual contacts because they're very low paid; so even if they're not naturally inclined to it, they have to see too much—they like are forced to eat with their eyes. Robacci once split off down to the Factory in the squad car, the doorman had no further line of defence and he knew it.

Stevenson said: 'Now we're not going to be unkind because unkindness in this Christian world of ours I find doesn't pay off—Johnny, isn't it?—only don't be too definite with your answers straightaway, off-the-cuff like that as you did earlier on in the evening when I put you a question, else I might just forget my principles and start to sin, which means there could be like an accident affecting you, not me, which could make you look like a very old, tired and worn-out-looking squash ball that had bounced off too many walls, so that you ended in hospital.' He smiled. 'Did you know by the way, Johnny, that squash is one of the police's favourite games on its day off? Good, well, we've got a court over at the Factory in the basement, between the computers and the canteen.'

The doorman didn't say anything.

Stevenson said: 'Yes, I do love a good game of squash.' He leaned eagerly forward to the doorman and said: 'Now I'm not a man of violence, and to prove it, here I am lighting a Westminster filter. On the other hand, this officer and myself have three revolting murders to solve, which means putting an arm on the man, in no time flat, so it's the old time and motion study, isn't it? The clock against results. Isn't it?'

The doorman said he supposed it was.

Stevenson said: 'It is.' He took the doorman gently by the elbow and felt the joint. 'That's where it always gets broken,' he said to the listener. 'It's always the same place. It's dreadfully painful, and takes years to heal—in fact there are some doctors who say it never really does. Now you've got considerable form, Johnny, but that's no crime—I daresay that if the Lord God were looking down at the three of us in this office right now, he'd say we'd all got form. Only the thing here is that you've seen things go on in this place that we haven't, so don't you think you'd better spare us a word?'

'Yes, look, Johnny,' I said, 'we're trying to start off being kind with you about this for the moment but it's not really our style on an urgent enquiry, and there are a hundred questions outstanding on these three deaths and we don't like that at all, of course. So never mind Roatta for the moment, we'll get back to him— let's just start off with this poor girl Dora Suarez who was chopped to death in South Ken.'

'I tell you I hardly knew her.'

'Steady, steady now,' I said, 'you're gambolling away in front of yourself again, Johnny, you're just like a kiddie with a little football Saturday afternoon in Battersea Park, the way you play about, you're not being serious, darling.'

The doorman said: 'Dozens of scrubbers get in here, so what?'

'I see you've got a problem,' Stevenson said.

'Oh yes?' said the doorman.

'It's not only your blackheads that are working against you this time,' said Stevenson, 'it's more that you're not really cooperating with us yet. Mind,' he added, 'it's your problem, not ours. Only, where your boot pinches is, where we've got one problem you've got three or four, which normally add up to as many years in a shady room, OK? Might be Canterbury, and then again it might not, depending.'

The doorman said: 'All I can tell you is, Suarez was in the club, she was out, she was either in or out, she was in and out, sometimes she sang here, sometimes she didn't, sometimes she was with some feller, sometimes she wasn't, and that's all I can say.'

'Well, then, I'm grieved for you, Johnny,' I said, 'Because not enough in your case simply isn't sufficient, and it is beginning to look to me as if you were deliberately preparing yourself to spend a long, wearisome time in our company. The food in the Factory's appalling at the moment and the heating's off again, but you'll get used to it, they all do. Mark you, once we've got you across to Brixton on remand you'll find things are worse still, but in the meantime I expect you know all about what a second-class single to the Factory means—and I mean a fucking single.'

'But why are you grilling me?' shouted the doorman. 'Why me? I'm just the doorman!'

'But that's just it,' I said. 'It's because you are the doorman, love-song. You see everyone that comes in and goes out through these club doors, so you're the liar that conceals more truth than the others on the scene and you must be well paid not to spill it, which also intrigues me, otherwise you'd have done it by now.'

Stevenson said: 'What goes on upstairs here?'

'Upstairs?' said the doorman. 'What upstairs?'

'You realise we've got a W to take these whole premises apart,' said Stevenson. 'Now, the bother you're already in, you perjure yourself in front of two police officers and you'd best make your will, I'm telling you flat, Johnny.'

'Now let's play it again,' I said. 'The upstairs.'

The doorman's face was both white and grey now; it looked ridiculous against the cherry-coloured coat. 'I know there's an upstairs,' he said, 'but what goes on up there I don't know, I swear to God.'

'Make us a list of everyone you saw going up and down those

stairs and turn evidence,' Stevenson urged him, 'and we'll make life easier for you, Johnny; otherwise it's going to be hard oh so hard.'

I said: 'Did you see Suarez go up and down?' I added: 'You'd better tell me if you did—you lie to me now, and it's a lie that'll cost you five years inside to the day.'

'Yes, I saw her.'

'Often?'

'Fairly often.'

'With a man?'

'Yes.'

'Always with a man?'

'Yes.'

'Always the same man?'

'No.'

I said, taking the photograph from Stevenson and showing the doorman the blurred figure running out of the emergency door: 'Ever with this man?'

'Can't see his face, can I?'

'I hope you're beginning to tell us everything you know,' said Stevenson. 'The games upstairs again?'

'I've never been up there,' said the doorman. 'I don't know what they do in the top members' place.'

'But you know who went up and came down,' I said. 'Now the point is, have we bought you or not? I know you're well paid to belt up, but you can't spend your dollars in jail, there's no Harrods at Maidstone.'

'Anyway,' said Stevenson, 'your chief's inside with us down the street, Johnny—you've no baseline now, you're lost.'

'I want to know about that sporty-looking man running out of the door there,' I said, 'there in the photograph. He's a man I feel I want to get to know.'

'I can't help,' the doorman said.

'Not even against your liberty?'

'I can't tell you anything,' said the doorman. 'I can't tell you what I don't know.'

'All right,' said Stevenson, turning to me, 'I see we're wasting our time here, so let's get what's left of this lying git motored over to the Factory so he can play his luck down there with Robacci.' He said to the fat exhausted figure lying back in his chair under his top hat with the gold cockade in it: 'Now you know what it's like in the Factory, don't you, Johnny? You know how it works, people must have told you. Folk that've been through the grill with us, three teams of three under the lights, no time limit, sky's the limit, forty-eight hours is too long—Bowman, Rupt, Fox, that's team one; then Drucker and ourselves; then Goldman, Draper and Steele, the same questions over and over—even the few folk that come out the other side never seem to quite get their health back, they're just not the same as when they went in; what you're getting from us is just openers to see if your story stands up, and I think it doesn't, sweetheart, which makes it a soaking wet day where you're standing. You won't play with us, so you're in for the long haul, Johnny—ask your poor weakling solicitor when he does finally get permission to come in and talk to what's left of you, and he'll tell you that even if the judge is in a good mood and got his rocks off with his secretary last night, you're still looking at between seven and twenty years deadly nightshade, and that's why it's called the Factory.'

'You've always got the other choice, of course,' I said.

'What's that?' the doorman muttered.

'You could top yourself,' said Stevenson, 'and I think I would if I were you. We'll leave you one shoe lace, it's probably your best way out.'

'Your bosses can't help you,' I said, 'they're dead or nicked.'

'I'm just the doorman,' he said again.

'I know,' I said, 'and you were buried under it because you hadn't the brains to go upstairs.'

The doorman said: 'I can't tell you what I think goes on up there.'

'Why not?' I said. 'Are you struck dumb?'

'That's it,' said Stevenson. 'He hasn't the brains to tell us.'

'Let him speak instead then,' I said, 'if he wants to.' I said to the doorman: 'We are investigating a filthy matter with which you are to some extent involved as an employee of this club; for humane reasons you ought to help us to catch the man that did it, forget the rest.'

'Humane?' said the doorman. 'What does that word mean?'

I said: 'Have you ever seen the body of a woman axed to death?'

He reflected a bit and said: 'No, just two shot, but that was down to cards and then a bit of the other, so what then?'

'Nothing.' I turned to Stevenson and said: 'You remember the old song? *"Said one old dear. You'll get nothing here."* '

'Right then,' said Stevenson, getting up, 'let's weigh him off. There's nothing more to be got out of this dreary, battered-looking individual. He either won't talk or he can't, and the pips we've squeezed out of him are beginning to make my bleeding ears squeak.'

Stevenson and I decided to leave the upstairs of the club for the time being: we opted to go back to the Factory and get some more sense out of the pair we had in the cells; we posted a uniformed officer at the door of the club; we left him looking rather sad, framed against soaking old posters either side of the dark door of the Parallel Club and its dank steps: MIGHTY NIGHT IS OUR NIGHT, SAT FEB 2, ALL TO BRENT CROSS, MUSIC FOR LIBER-ATORS!

Etcetera.

When we had got our pair brought up from the cells, Robacci came in saying: 'You didn't even give me a chance to sleep!'

I said: 'That's not standard practice at the Factory. We need you, we need you, could be day or night. Detainees work the same hours as the police here, we none of us need to know what time it is.'

Robacci said: 'Look, what about my Rolls? She's wired to a yellow line, could we act about that?'

I said: 'When you collect the heap in twenty years' time, it'll be in a museum and there'll be a big fine to pay, won't there, now belt up.'

When we were all four settled down, Stevenson said: 'All right now.' He split open a packet of Westminster light filters and lit one with a match which landed on the doorman's trousers, burning a small hole in them. He inhaled, then blew the smoke out absently into Robacci's face.

Robacci said: 'That's disgusting,' and Stevenson said: 'Sorry, this is a smoking compartment, darling, can't you read?'

Robacci said: 'What is the purpose of this meeting?'

'Nothing in particular,' said Stevenson. 'The club's locked and sealed, and this officer and myself will be searching it during what's left of the night.'

I said: 'What's interesting to us, of course, is the difference between what you two tell us now and what we find when we pick through the shit-heap.'

Stevenson said: 'For your sakes, there had better not be much fucking difference, or neither of you are worth a light, I tell you for nothing.' He blew more smoke around the already fogged room. Robacci started to cough, but I knew how Stevenson chain-smoked the minute he was working and interested. He said: 'Now come on, we can't go on pretending forever; the four of us in this room can solve three deaths, and as far as I'm concerned we're going to sit here till we do. The reason for this officer's presence is on account of this photograph, which you've already seen, showing that his victim, Miss Suarez, was singing in the presence of Felix Roatta and yourself at your club—that makes it a joint enquiry for us. Now both Suarez, Roatta and the old widow, Mrs

Carstairs, with whom Suarez was living the night they died, were all killed in a terrifying, inhuman and brutal manner, while I myself am concerned with the shooting of your ex-employer, Felix Roatta. Now, because of this photograph, we both of us feel we have really good reason to believe that these three deaths are connected—and not simply because they occurred on the same night, Roatta's death only an hour or so after the deaths of the two women, but because of the photograph.'

Robacci said: 'Where did you get that picture?'

Stevenson said: 'You might have been one of them who set her alight. Do you remember a girl who was set on fire by three men in your own club?'

'Well, come on,' I said, 'answer the question, you either know about it or you don't.'

But Robacci said nothing. I turned to Stevenson and said: 'Draw your own conclusions.'

Stevenson said: 'I am.'

'You understand,' I said, 'that we are here for no other reason but to get justice for Miss Suarez, Mrs Carstairs and Felix Roatta, and that we will get it.'

Robacci said: 'I've never had to do with you before.'

Stevenson said: 'The girl who took this picture brought it to me and showed me her legs where they had burned, and that's why you've become interesting to A14.'

I said: 'It was this girl's legs, but it was Suarez's life.'

I said: 'Unexplained Deaths is objective; even if we're middle-aged men, we're junior officers by our own choice and can't be bought by any side.'

'I've had enough of this,' said Stevenson. He went out into the passage, caught sight of the duty constable and said: 'Hey, Officer! Buckle these two up again and take them back down where they belong.'

The officer said: 'Right, come on then, you two, on your feet, tickle yourselves, now move.'

Robacci shouted: 'I can tell you there are going to be come-
backs over this!'

'Yes,' I said, 'it'll come back from the DPP's office, meantime
you're both in front of the magistrate at nine in the morning and
go over to Brixton on remand till the killer's put to you and you
go on trial.' I said to the officer: 'Take them down, we're busy.'

We did have trouble with the search warrant; there was like a
delay over it. It got so bad that finally I rang an internal number
and said: 'I want that warrant for the Parallel Club now, not in
ten days' time.'

'That's impossible. Do you know what time it is?'

'No, I don't,' I told the clerk, 'all I know is that it's dark, and
who cares? You're on duty, aren't you, same as me.'

'Why should you want to search the Parallel Club anyway?'
the voice complained. 'What's the Parallel Club got to do with
you? That's the Roatta case, that's down to Sergeant Stevenson,
it says here.'

'Listen, sport,' I said, 'are you a clerk or a fucking copper,
make up your mind.'

'I'm administration, you know that.'

'Then stop trying to do my work for me,' I said. 'You're not
up to it and I don't need it, though of course what a sweet
kind thought. Now fuck off and get me that warrant because
you're going to wear your few brains right away to nothing if
you let go of your calculator like this. Now get that W biked
round to 205 now—otherwise you're going to need blood-proof
pyjamas.'

'What are you and Stevenson doing?'

'Something that would make you shit in your galoshes if I told
you,' I said, 'so just stick to your work and get that warrant made
out before I come down in person for it, love.'

'It'll take an hour at least.'

'Look,' I said, 'the killer doesn't care. As far as the killer's concerned, with your attitude you suit him fine, sweetheart, and Christmas Day would suit him better still.'

I got off the phone, put my elbows on the desk and my face in my hands; I suddenly felt appalled, helpless. What few sweet things, such few people as I had ever known and trusted, this handful of promising elements that I had learned unconsciously to depend on, were now like something poisoned that I had just eaten, sickening me—now such love as I knew reversed itself into an agony that spread to my fingertips, to my gut, my brain. Like Dora herself, and Betty, I, too, was battering my face against the blocked-out concrete collective face of what administrators describe as society, behind whose lethargic unhurried paperwork lay the horrors of Empire Gate, and then I knew again what I was always in danger of forgetting—what it was to look at yourself as a structure in itself, totally isolated, coming from nowhere, going nowhere; then I experienced once again what it was to reel and fall. Someone had left the day's newspaper lying nearby; the copy had been well read and thumbed in a pub and the headline hung over the edge of the table like a greasy tongue drooping over a lip, printing in block capitals what paper could not speak: KEN-SINGTON AXE HORROR.

'Oh Dora,' I said aloud, 'you feel so far away now.'

Yet it was absurd that Dora should be so far off. 'It's our fault, Dora,' I said upwards into the stale air of the empty office. For she had scribbled in the little time left to her:

I know one thing—I must never breathe a single word of my fear. I'm no longer a woman—I'm just a discoloured mass of pain. The state of my body poses all the great questions that matter to the two of us, and in begging me to liberate it, now that it's no longer capable of living with me, it's telling me, in its own way, 'This is the worst of good-byes for us two,' and I told it that because of your state, which is also my state, our state, because the cards fell wrongly for us, we are at that point of disorder where existence is no longer possible, for the more order you try to put into your life beyond a certain point, the more you fall ill, despair, and peel away. For what is knowledge for, if not getting ready for death?

Oh, Dora wrote, Dora said, Dora was!
Oh, Dora, Dora, Dora!

I picked the phone up and dialled. When a girl's voice answered and said Records, I said: 'Cheryl, is that still you?'

'I hope so,' she said. 'Anyway it's nobody else, and don't I know your voice?'

'Well,' I said, 'anyway you used to. You, me and Brenda used to have a few beers over at the Dog and Duck.'

She said: 'Christ, it's not possible. I'm even hearing that you're on Carstairs/Suarez.'

'That's just it,' I said. 'That's why it's tight, there's a rush on. Is Barry there?'

'You're dead in luck—he was just leaving, I'll put him on.'

I said: 'Barry?'

He said: 'Ah, this terrific, A14 strikes again.'

I said: 'Barry, it isn't terrific, it's Carstairs/Suarez—that's all they've called me back for. I'm not young, but this is something that makes me feel old, Barry, old. Listen, they bring you down any prints from Empire Gate?'

'Prints?' he said. 'Shoe prints, and he'll have burned them by now.'

'Barry,' I said, 'I've got to have something. Anything on this operator. I'm on this with Stevenson partly, because we reckon that my two and Roatta are connected.'

'Why's that?'

'The Parallel Club. Stevenson's got a photo of Suarez singing there the night of Roatta's birthday.'

Barry said: 'Have you got any description of a suspect at all?'

'A short, dark-haired man running out through an exit door as the flash came on, back turned to it.'

'Useful.'

'Useful like fuck all,' I said. 'You've got Suarez's face down where you are?'

'What's the good of that, though?' he said. 'There's nothing known, I can't match it.'

'I realise that,' I said. 'But what I also want you to realise is that the murder of these two women is one of the most shocking things we've had even on this manor for a very long time, I'm just marking your card.'

'Give me anything you find,' he said. 'Give me something I can bite on, then we can get going.'

'Yes, OK,' I said, ' 'night, Barry.'

' 'Night.'


I said to Stevenson: 'Right, now we've got those two sweethearts barred up, let's get back to the Parallel and take it apart.'

He said: 'You should have taken the uniformed man off the door.'

I said: 'I did. Why? Do you feel there might be folk there?'

'Why not?' said Stevenson. 'We're them. We're worried. The pot's boiled over.'

'That's right,' I said. 'That's what I think, too.' We took the keys and went into the club, which was lit—just the bar. Inside we found a man in a black suit; he was a size too large for his underwear, which constricted him and made him gasp from time to time.

''Evening,' said the fat man.

'Cut the acid,' I said, because he was in the photograph. 'Been to any good birthday parties since Felix Roatta's?'

He said: 'I make them when I can.'

'I don't think we know each other,' I said.

'No, it's funny, that,' said the fat man, 'Oughtn't I to know you, the way you're making yourselves at home in this place?'

'I don't know yet, do I?' I said. 'But I should say that if I were in your place, probably not.' Without turning away from us, the fat man called out: 'Giorgio!'

A thin man with the squat white face of a killer appeared. 'Yes, Mr Scalo?'

Scalo said: 'Take these two people apart, will you? Ask them how they came by their set of keys to in here.'

'Now don't let's go acting hasty,' Stevenson said. 'Let me just put you an easy question. Where are you in from?'

'I'm in from Rome,' said Scalo. 'I'm in from there pretty often.'

'We're round here quite often ourselves,' Stevenson said.

'What wind blows you in, then?'

'The sail's called a search warrant,' said Stevenson. 'We don't come from as far off as you do, just from over the road at the Factory, and when we come in, it's for business.' He produced the warrant, reached over and trailed the edge of it gently across the tip of Scalo's nose.

'OK, OK,' said Scalo. 'Giorgio, forget the games for now— instead, make like a bottle tinkle with some ice, why don't you?'

I said to Giorgio: 'Forget the bottle. Take that gun out of your right-side coat pocket and put it on the bar there now. Do it now.'

The man said: 'You threatening me?'

I said: 'Yes.' Stevenson kicked him one in the knees, one in the fun-bag. The man fell, knelt and crouched as though in a state of prayer, holding himself together with his hands to his crotch. I kicked him in the back of the head, got the gun out and threw it to Stevenson. I said to him: 'Let's put that somewhere safe.' The man was crying. I went over him but found no more than a wallet full of credit cards. 'Bent credit cards,' I said to Stevenson.

'They're not bent,' said Scalo.

'If I say they're bent, they're bent,' I said. 'That's how it works here in the West End. You ought to drop in from Rome more often and take some lessons, flower.'

'Look, for Christ's sake,' said Scalo, 'what the Christ's going on here?'

'That's what we're going to find out,' I said, 'that's what the paperwork's for.'

'I just got off the plane at Heathrow,' said Scalo.

'We all make mistakes,' said Stevenson. 'You should most likely have stayed on it—anyway you're going to wish you had, my crystal ball tells me that.'

I said to Scalo: 'You fit in where in this place?'

'No secret,' he said. 'I finance it.'

'A sleeping cherub,' said Stevenson, 'is that it?'

Scalo said: 'I drop in to see how business is doing and look at the shit I get.'

'Two things,' said Stevenson, 'if I have to mark your card. Drop the armed-guard habit in London next time, darling; it just gives us another holding charge. Two, don't count on being back for mass by tomorrow night.'

I said: 'Now you're going to ask us what we're doing here.' I added: 'And you can. It's all legal.'

Stevenson said: 'You'd two partners, both of them into a scam.'

'One of them,' I said, 'Felix Roatta, sprayed a wall thorough with the top of his head, thus inventing a brand-new wallpaper; the other, Giancarlo Robacci, is over with us having a rest at the Factory, Cell 3.'

Stevenson said to Scalo: 'It's your unlucky night.'

Scalo said: 'I don't know what you expect to find here.'

Stevenson said: 'Not you, anyway.' He went over to the phone and dialled the Factory. He said: 'Bring up a car, yes, it's to the Parallel again, regular minicab service, isn't it? You've one with a wing down for St Stephen's, the other wherever you've a spare cell in the building. Its name's Scalo. Ice it, we've a search on, then we'll be over with a few questions—yes, straightaway, nice one, bye.'

Scalo said: 'You're never going to nick me.'

Stevenson said: 'What do you mean? That was it, they're on their way, hot-throb.'

I said: 'What we expect to find is some evidence concerning three revolting murders, and that's what you came over to deal with, sweetheart—the phone works all the way from here to Rome.'

'You see what it is,' Stevenson said to Scalo kindly, 'we can't really get to work unscrewing this place properly when there are other folk about; you're like jamming the vibes.'

I said to Scalo: 'You any idea what we're going to find in this place?'

Scalo looked blank: 'None whatever.'

'That's it,' I said encouragingly. 'Your counsel won't get you off, but you carry on like that and you'll be giving him a helping hand; he might even get fond of you.'

There was a bang on the door; it was the squad car, I said to the two officers: 'Weigh this lot off.' I said to Scalo as they brought the cuffs out: 'Spend time till we get round to you trying to learn to be interesting.' I said to the police driver: 'Ask them to give him a bit of knitwear that fits him, by the way, will you? He's strangling himself in that gear and we don't want a death on our hands.'

Scalo said: 'Look, just a minute. Listen, do I have to go in?'

'I don't see why not,' I said, 'or are you going to try and make yourself interesting? Better hurry if you are.'

'I've got a lot of business on.'

'I can see that,' I said, 'and I'm quite sorry for the punters.'

Scalo said: 'What I mean is, I really haven't the time to waste, going over to your place, so why can't we talk?' He gazed at the Rolex watch on his wrist, turning it towards him till it glowed under the single spot. 'Nice watches these,' he said.

'They're not really all that waterproof,' I said, 'and I find the kind of people that wear them far more exciting.'

Scalo said: 'I mean, I really wouldn't mind if we had a discussion.'

'That depends what you've got to say, Mr Scalo,' I said, and Stevenson said: 'In any case, whatever you say, it'll take time; you'll have to ride down, make a statement, reread it and sign it—you probably know what police procedure is.'

'Especially at the Factory,' I said.

He looked at each of us and said: 'Personally, I find three's not a crowd.'

Stevenson said: 'That's lucky, isn't it?'

Scalo said: 'But your men here.'

Stevenson said: 'They stay, sorry about that.'

Scalo said: 'Pity we couldn't have been more private.'

'Ah, well there you are,' I said, 'we can't always have the sunshine, can we?'

'Anyway,' said Scalo, 'here's one time when three's not a crowd.'

'Depends a good deal on which three,' I said. 'We're the live three, the bright three. The other three are the dead three—Carstairs, Roatta and Suarez.'

'I don't suppose you've ever bothered about death much, Mr Scalo,' Stevenson said, 'I expect that with those clothes you've got on and the watch you're wearing, you'd far rather dance than die.'

'I have thought about death, of course,' said Scalo, watching us. 'I'm a Catholic.'

'Well, I'm glad you take death as seriously as we do,' said Stevenson, 'since this officer and myself are investigating these three particularly disgusting ones, and we are now going to take this place apart.'

'That's not how these things are generally arranged,' said Scalo.

'There you're dead right,' I said. 'They're arranged at our little family hotel round the corner. It's called the Factory, and that is where you are now going, my fat old darling. It's better than a Swiss spa for losing weight; people slim quicker with us than they do even on a thinning biscuit.'

'Look,' Scalo said, 'frankly, how much to drop all this? Say ten long ones? I've got it on me. Get rid of your men and we can spiel.'

'That's not how it works at all,' I said. 'This one has gone way, way over the top.'

'You won't find anything,' Scalo said.

'Your problem might just possibly be that you don't know what we're looking for,' Stevenson said, 'in which case I bleed for you. On the other hand, you fucking well do know what we're looking for, in which case you must have made your will. Now, you are going off to the Factory and we are going upstairs and around and about, as we do have a search warrant, and such keys as we have not already got we will just kick the doors down, and such damage as we may do to the property will be made good to you at a later date maybe—all right?'

'Look,' Scalo shouted, 'you can't walk all over a private citizen like that as if he was just dog shit.'

'The paper I've got in my hand here says we can,' said Stevenson. 'I've been kind and read it out to you, haven't I?'

He said: 'I've got some murderous lawyers.'

I said: 'Yes, I've heard they come on extremely heavy when it's a question of fees—we've all got to scam.'

Scalo said: 'Are you like trying to take the piss?'

'Yes,' said Stevenson simply.

I looked down the bar into the shadows at the back of the place beside the door where the man had been photographed running out and I said to Stevenson: 'I want to get up those stairs.'

'Your warrant only covers the public premises!' Scalo shouted.

'The day you join the police force,' Stevenson said, 'an instructor will explain to you what a search warrant covers. What it covers will totally stagger you, darling—it covers exactly what this officer and myself decide we want it to cover.' He said to the police driver: 'Scrape this little twat of a gunman here up off the floor, he's making a mess.' He said to Scalo: 'And you, sweet-heart, get your wrists together ready so we can snap them on you, don't be silly and argue about it.'

The two uniformed men jerked him towards them and cuffed him and Scalo screamed: 'We've got our own means of jus-tice, too.'

I whipped round on him and snarled: 'Then use it on yourself, cunt, because I am going after Suarez's killer no holds barred, and hell itself won't stop me, let alone ten long ones.'

'We usually deal with reasonable people,' Scalo said.

'And you are,' I said, 'you squalid little man, and our reasoning is that we are going to send the lot of you down for twenty years if we can.'

'We'll be down to see you when we're through,' Stevenson said.

'We'll bring a report over with us from the Westminster Hos-pital,' I said, 'and settle down in what we call the clever room over at the Factory and have a long serious talk about AIDS.'

Stevenson said to the officers: 'Take this load of disgusting shit away, will you—I want shut of it.'

'Suarez?' Scalo gasped as the men started hurrying him out. 'What? The little singer that flogged her arsehole? Why, Christ, we get hundreds of them a week!'

'To infect people with what you gave her?' I said. 'Is that the brand-new scam? That girl died in agony, you broke her, I've just read what she wrote where she was going to kill herself, only she was axed to death first; we've just come from the morgue. Herpes simplex, CMV, Karposi's sarcoma, dental abscesses, a group of mucocutaneous warts in her anus bigger than barrage balloons.'

'And the punters,' said Stevenson, 'got to spend up with you, haven't they? Because once they've got it, they can only screw at your places—nobody else will have them.'

'We'll see,' I said, turning away. 'Could be. Friendly little club, the Parallel.' I said to Stevenson: 'Come on. Let's break all this wide open.'

They dragged Scalo off across the black carpet of the club with its cigarette burns. He still didn't believe we could do it to him, and left with the assured insolence of a credit card presenting itself at the thin mouth of hell.

As I made for the stairs with Stevenson:
   Suarez.

I am a Spanish Jewess by birth; of course that explains a lot of things. Being a lonely woman, both shy and proud, I found myself thrown into surroundings where I was bound to be raped because my aloofness was a challenge to others—first at school, then later in the street, at the supermarket checkout point where I worked for a time, or at the pub Saturdays when the boys pinched, slapped and felt me to see what I was made of. 'Not like the rest of the mob, are we then, Queenie, what did you say your name was again, Queenie?' How could they know the sorrows and darkness behind my face, or know that in my own realm, inside myself, in my private relation with the world, I believed myself, in spirit, silently to be a queen, although disinherited, disrobed and discrowned? I wanted to keep my sense of my own dignity, but it is the most difficult thing of all to keep when you are poor. I was constructed to have a nature that could neither bend nor speak, nor be of a kind to ask for help—but, like all beaten people, had to retreat through the thorns until my hopes were rags and I had no sceptre or crown but what I could carry across London in my shopping bag. Once I went to Spain for ten days—it is called *Castilla*—by bus and, getting away from the others for a while, inched my way down the rocks of a considerable ravine to a

water bed which, because of its being summer, was entirely
dry. On enquiring in the broken remains of what was formerly
my own tongue I was told that they called such a place a
*cañada*. There I picked dry flowers burned as swiftly dry to
their colours in that heat as the rocks where I had found them,
and I held them against me for an hour before leaving them
tied as a bouquet with a twist of weed and climbing back up
to the bus. But I was happier than I had been before, being
certain in my inner way that I had found myself there in that
stricken yet proud country for a moment and left myself there.
For I have read that my father's name, Suarez, is a very ancient
and respected Spanish name, and indeed, until I became so ill
as to be able to think of nothing but my physical suffering,
which contracts all horizons, including that of dignity, I, too,
believed that I was worthy at least of my own respect. I used
to murmur to myself in bed: 'You are Dora, Dora Suarez'—
and who knows if I may not have the blood of princes hidden
in me? On my mother's side, of course, she being Jewish, I
had no country by inheritance, and so, what with my father's
origins on one side and my mother's lack of any, I was lost,
just as their marriage was lost, and so we were all lost, and I
had to go on alone as best I could. . . .

Is it because I never knew who I was after all that I walk
with my head bowed?


To work in A14 is to see everything that no one ever sees: the
violence, misery and despair, the immeasurable distance in the
mind of a human being that knows nothing but suffering between
its dreams and its death.

Every death I have ever seen in my work—in bars, at the edge
of motorways, in filthy rooms, suicides, people who have thrown
themselves from high buildings, under cars, buses or the underground, are all for me casualties on a single front. Each to me,
even some killers, have been men or women deprived of any
reason for going on—children even, sometimes—and one bright

desperate day they awake and say to themselves, 'I'll end it,' and they write themselves off in one single stroke of negative, savage joy, since there was nobody to meet them at the station.

Then, afterwards, the ravens, the vultures and the vampires that had been into them come to us to claim or complain over their now irrecoverable debt in the bloody, silent field, while the government, trailing the press after it like a shabby skirt stalks off to dine, wonders if it is still popular.

But for me the front is the street, and I am forced to see it every day.

I see it, eat it, sleep and dream the street, am the street. I groan in its violent dreams, see it under the rain and in the sun, the hurrying people on it, killers as well as victims, flying past absorbed as if they were praying. The way I am, I sense tears as well as hear them.

Dead people are very clean, too clean. They have been purged, white and even as the light on snow, but why? Where's the justice in it? That's what I want to know.

Why is it that the simplest questions are the questions that have no answer?

Why?

The narrow stair wound up to the next floor and ended at a small landing and a white-painted door, which was locked. Stevenson found his flashlight and looked at the lock. 'Banham,' he said. Then he got the keys out that we had taken. I looked at them in the palm of his hand.

'Not one to fit,' he said.

I said: 'That's easy. Give us a hand. One, two, three, both of us, OK?'

'When you're ready.'

We took all the space across the landing and gave the wood our right shoulders. It shuddered: it wasn't the kind of door constructed to answer back.

'Again,' I said, and this time the lock did our work for us, tearing the mouth it was bolted into out of the jamb so that the door fell back open.

'That's better,' I said, 'let's have some light on in the place.' Everything was in pitch darkness.

But before he moved, Stevenson stood still on the threshold and said: 'Wait. Do you smell something?'

I paused to breathe in and then said: 'Do you mean something live? Is that what you're saying?' I added: 'Yes.' Something small moved in the darkness.

'Don't you smell straw?' said Stevenson. 'And vermin?'

'Light,' I said.

We found a switch with our flashlights and lit the place.

It was full of cages.

'Let's see what's in the cages,' I said.

Roughly there had been silence in the place until we lit it; now there was an increasingly flourishing rattle in the straw, a rustle of little bodies. Aroused by the light, things darted about trying to bury themselves in the deftness of their panic, fleeing the light, trying to hide as prisoners in a cell do in their bedding when the people come for them.

'Why,' I said, 'they're little rats.'

'Nearly,' said Stevenson, 'but not quite.'

'What are they, then?'

He said: 'They're African by origin, I think they're gerbils, let's see.' The cages opened from the top; Stevenson opened one and grabbed an occupant. He held it up by its tail; it seemed to die; it drooped, almost motionless.

'What does it mean?' I said to Stevenson.

'It replaces a hard-on. It's a tunneller, it goes in where I think it does, it nibbles, it excites, it panics, it dies, and then you pull it out again by the string that you've attached to its tail. Of course you have to shave its skin off first so it gives the same nice smooth feel as a prick.'

'Why breed them here?' I said, 'on top of a nightclub?'

'Don't be innocent,' said Stevenson, 'this is the upstairs.'

'How do you read it?' I said.

'I read money and desire.'

'Explain,' I said. 'Tell me everything you know and think.'

'When it comes to AIDS,' said Stevenson, 'you're rich, but you've got it—you're loaded with money, but you're infected, you want to fuck still, but with whom?' He put the gerbil down and said: 'There's money in that. You know what organised crime is— it's supply and demand.'

'And Suarez?'

'Well, she was bound to get it,' said Stevenson, 'wasn't she?'

I said: 'Well, that's murder and you don't even die.'

Stevenson said: 'That's a lot of people.'

'I know,' I said.

Stevenson said: 'My dad was a miner in the north; he died in an explosion a thousand yards down, Geordie Main Colliery.'

'Do you understand that poor girl Suarez,' I said, 'watching herself die in her mirror day by day?'

'Oh yes,' said Stevenson, 'absolutely. You go out to work for next to nothing, and you run a mortal risk.'

'Poor darling,' I said, 'that's just what I can't stand, you see?'

'Ah, stop it,' Stevenson said, 'stop it, will you?'

'How can we stop it, the way we see our work, though?' I said. 'What? Just let it all slide?' I said: 'My father had a little corner shop, drapery, South London; yet he was in the Engineers during the war and defused mines on the beaches, and I'm very proud of him, glad to be his son. He told me once: "They made me an officer so that I could ask the sergeant for the right tools to go up to it." I said: "Weren't you frightened, Dad?" He said: "All the time, but you reckoned you were protected—it was important what we were doing. I wouldn't have had our boys treading on one of them." '

'All right,' said Stevenson, 'so what do we do now?'

I said: 'We get Scalo and Robacci out again and grill them.'

It is so difficult for a police officer to be part of the people that he is paid by the state to control: and yet it is sometimes not because he does not want to be part of the people, but because he does not know how to recover his origins until, as in my case, he is faced with a great personal catastrophe, which then becomes every catastrophe, and which changes everything both in himself and around him. Like Socrates, I think that all men must be just towards their own code if they are going to be at all, because in the end one code is all the codes, given that one is a just man. It is possible in my view that a just man should be indifferent to the fate of Carstairs and Suarez—one might as well be indifferent to one's own fate whereas, as we all know, we are not.

We went straight over to the Factory and walked into Scalo's cell; Scalo was sleeping on the army blanket, or as near as he could get to sleeping.

I shook him and said: 'On your feet. Get up. Move.'

He started wiping the sleep out of his eyes and said: 'What now?'

I said: 'A few questions upstairs.' I said to the officer who was with us: 'Get him dressed and bring him up to 205.'

When Scalo arrived, I said: 'Look, the choice is easy, Scalo. You either reply to us—otherwise it's the old game, bright lights and three teams of three officers relieving each other, nine men. They drink the beer, eat the sandwiches and fire the questions—you get fuck all. Well, that's it. Depends the way you want it, but make up your mind and let's get started anyway.'

'You prove I was responsible for these three so-called murders,' said Scalo, 'and OK, I pick up the tab.'

I said: 'That's right. That's how it works.'

'Right,' said Scalo, 'so go on and try and prove I'm involved.'

'Stop looking so happy, will you?' said Stevenson. 'As a police officer I hate that. As a police officer I'm not happy in my mind anyway, and so I doubly don't like it when I see cunts like you looking happy, Scalo, and that's where your face don't fit in this room, sweet. I just don't like your face, Scalo. I don't like it when I look at happy, guilty people; our code, Scalo, our code.' He caressed Scalo's fingers and said: 'Did anyone ever tell you you had very pretty hands? Well, fancy that, berk, now it's me, just a humble detective sergeant, that's telling you.' He stroked Scalo's fingers again and said: 'With sweet fingers like you've got there on the end of your hands, you want to go balls out so as not to get them broken then, don't you?'

Scalo said: 'What are you trying to say?'

I said: 'What we're saying is, you've gone too far, Scalo. Over the Parallel and the three deaths you're wrapped up; you're yesterday's wet newspaper, you're way over the edge.'

Scalo said: 'There's no price on it?'

I said: 'Not on yesterday's news, no.'

I got up, yawning. 'We're going on a short trip now, the three of us,' I said.

'Oh yes?' said Scalo. 'Where are we off then?'

'Back to The Parallel,' I said. 'Where else? We're going on a quick trot down there, and you're going to be the guided tour.'

'Why so?' said Scalo.

'That's the question people ask themselves as they die,' I said.

'I'm not dying,' said Scalo.

'No, not yet,' I said.

We ran him away downstairs to the car and took him round again to the Parallel at that dead hour between day and night when even in London there's no true light. Driving there, I said to Scalo: 'How well did you know Dora Suarez?'

He shrugged and said: 'The name means something, but do I know every little scrubber that comes into one of my places to sing?'

'Reflect on the question,' Stevenson said. 'It was she took the axe in the face, not you.'

When we arrived and I unlocked the place, Scalo said: 'Can I just go for a shit?'

'Why not?' said Stevenson. 'If it'll make you smell less bad.'

Stevenson and I waited against the long bar decorated in black and gold, and I switched on its single brilliant spot. Somewhere an automatic fan started up as we stood in the shadow which that one light underlined; it also showed up a thin drifting haze of dust that the fan sent over to the stacked bottles on the shelves, the buckets with their melted ice—all the ceased activity of a closed-down bar.

'Scalo?' I called out. Distantly, the long hollow crash then the cistern rang out, its noise important in the silence, and then at last the loo door slammed.

'Ah, there you are,' Stevenson said to Scalo when he finally arrived round the far end of the bar, doing himself up at his crocodile belt. 'Good, because we wouldn't have wanted you to leave us the way the turds go.' He said: 'OK, now this is a further introduction to the easy method. Not that you need it—our methods are the same as yours. Now, are you going to take us on the tour here, or do you want your doorman, Robacci and yourself doing the uphill run, the three of you separately, in front of twenty-seven trained men—because don't worry, we've got them.'

'That's it,' I said, 'do we start you off with Bowman, Drucker and Rupt, or would you rather tell us what this zoo you've got upstairs is about?'

'Zoo?' said Scalo. 'What zoo?'

'Ah, now you're starting off terribly feeble,' said Stevenson. 'We're talking about the gerbils you've got pulsating away upstairs.'

'Inform us, Scalo,' I said. 'You're looking twenty years in the face.'

Scalo said: 'Look, I know nothing about it, OK?'

Stevenson said: 'Look, we're not monsters like you. We just

want to meet the farmhand, that's all. Like friendly, make an acquaintance.'

'Scalo,' I said, 'who was the short man in the grey sports gear running out of the back door of the club? Now look, we really mean it.'

Scalo said: 'I really couldn't be helping you there.'

I said: 'British jails are filthy dirty, Scalo. We don't have the public funds to get you colour telly, and your Bolivian passport will just be a memory for a very sick old man by the time you get out.'

Scalo said: 'You like to break a man. There ought to be a law.'

'We're all the street,' I said.

Scalo said: 'So I don't make my plane for Milan two o'clock.'

'No,' said Stevenson, 'but there's a police bus to Brixton at half past ten, and believe me you'll be on it.'

'Talk some more, Scalo, guilty man,' I said, 'talk some more.'

Stevenson said: 'These rats were hard fucks for sick condemned men, weren't they? Weren't they? Weren't they?

'And even more fun if girlie took the rabbit up hers first while your punter jacked off and then maybe followed it,' he said.

'And another thing, the girls were easy, weren't they?' I said, 'because once they were infected, they were caught, just like the punters.'

'I'm not telling you a thing,' said Scalo.

'Not going to show us your rats, then?' I said.

'I'm saying nothing. Nothing at all.'

'Still, you're beginning to understand what serious police work really means, now, aren't you, Scalo?' said Stevenson. 'Because you might have been in danger of forgetting. It's dead simple. We find the punter and grill him.'

I said to Scalo: 'By the time our people round at the Factory have finished with you nine-handed, anything you know about these three deaths, we'll know it; you know how we work.'

'Next time you put money into London clubs,' Stevenson said, 'invest a little more wisely, try and be appreciated, come on less heavy next time when you've done your bird.'

'Meantime, nothing you can tell us about the Suarez/Carstairs/Roatta killer at all?' I said. 'Your sportsman with an axe handy, reckons himself in a mirror, fast with a Quickhammer?'

'It's your last chance,' said Stevenson.

Scalo said: 'I couldn't help you.'

Stevenson reached a glass off the bar, got his cock out and pissed in it. He handed the glass to Scalo.

'Drink,' he said. 'They say rats get thirsty.'

Session two. We were still all three of us sitting at the bar. I said to Scalo: 'Now we're going over the whole lot of this again, and then we're going to go on and on and on going over it. Your time is our time, and our time over at the Factory is our own time, and that, darling, is your hideous fucking bad luck.'

'The law says you can hold me for forty-eight hours,' said Scalo, 'no more.'

'You're going back, way back to the days when you still were someone and had a passport,' I said. 'I pity you.'

'And besides, why take a steam hammer to crack a nut?' Stevenson said. 'Five or six hours is all we need, Scalo, and you'll already never be the same again.'

'I feel like a beer,' I said.

'That'll be on the club, I suppose,' Scalo sneered.

'Who wants to drink your fucking rubbish?' I said. I went out and got the cans I kept in the boot of the Ford.

When I brought in the Kronenbourgs, Stevenson snapped one open and said to Scalo: 'Cheers.'

Scalo said: 'Don't I score for one?'

I said: 'You do not, scum.'

Scalo said: 'What are you doing right now to Robacci, that doorman, Margoulis?'

Stevenson looked at his watch. 'What, right now?' he said. 'Right now the two of them are being broken up separately over at the Factory by Rupt, Drucker and Snaile.' He added: 'And it won't take long either. Margoulis will have grassed by now, he's a peeper. Peepers always grass.'

'You people are fucking inhuman,' Scalo said.

'All right,' I said, setting my empty can down. 'let's get at it again then, shall we?'

'I know what I think, Scalo,' said Stevenson. 'I think you must either have got your shares in this club here very cheap, or else you must want to protect them very badly—but in either case you look as if they were starting to weigh heavy round your neck, Scalo, my life and fucking mazel tov; I mean, just look at the trade the place suddenly isn't doing.'

Scalo said: 'Normally the police come in tactful.'

Stevenson said: 'Well, now you see how the police comes on when it's working on three murders, and like when it's not being tactful.'

'Suarez,' I said. 'You might as well spill, Scalo, we've got all our time. The sporty little man in the running gear.'

'Look if I knew anything,' said Scalo, 'I'd have made a deal with you hours back, but the fact is I'm mostly abroad, and I tell you, I know nothing about these deaths. Felix Roatta was a cunt who come on too hard and greedy and lost his chops down to it, but these women's deaths, I tell you, I know fuck all about.' He added: 'Anyway I don't understand. There's a tariff with you people upstairs; it was set up long ago.'

I said: 'Yes, well, this time your tariff's gone off the edge of the plate.'

'Come on now,' said Scalo, 'let's be reasonable, can't we, there must be a price on this. OK if it's steep.' He looked at his watch and said: 'Christ, I have to be in Milan tomorrow afternoon like I said, the plane won't wait, so how about it?' He said: 'OK, so, one, I drop the Parallel Club, there's been trouble, nasty, right,

OK, it got its knackers caught in its knickers, so we get out at a cash sum and I throw you the folk in with it, do I care, I do not—easy with the noughts at the end of the banker's draft is all. So. Cash,' said Scalo. 'Right, well, let's dream of a figure—I say just dream of one for openers, is all.'

I said: 'You pay in dollars?'

'Always, always in dollars,' said Scalo with a pacifying smile. 'Yes.'

I said: 'A case of advanced AIDS. An axe death. An old lady of eighty-six thrown into the front of her clock. What does that run out at in dollars?'

'Now don't fun me up,' said Scalo. 'Now please.'

I said to Stevenson: 'I think we'll just run him as far up the mast as he'll go and see what happens to him when he gets to the top.'

Stevenson said to Scalo: 'So that we're to understand that you're by way of offering a bribe to two police officers.'

Scalo said: 'When you've got your knees a little browner, you'll understand. You're both quite new on this, I would think.'

Stevenson said to me: 'Hasn't hell suddenly got so fucking crude these days—it makes you feel like putting on clean clothes.' He added: 'How long shall we try and get them with the DPP?'

'Twenty years each wouldn't be long compared to eternity,' I said, 'which is all Carstairs and Suarez have in front of them now.'

Session three, still in the Parallel bar. I was saying to Scalo: 'Perhaps you were more on the management side only, but for me you still knew all about the gerbils and what they were there for.'

'And we haven't all our time,' said Stevenson, 'so which version are you choosing? You either own shares in the Parallel Club and no vermin, or else you own both the vermin and the shares.'

'I still badly want a word with the sporty man in the photograph, Scalo,' I said. 'In fact, more I think about him, more he turns me on.'

Scalo said: 'Names? I know no names, folks. What are names?'

'The wrong ones carry a lot of porridge,' Stevenson said.

I said: 'So you know nothing about Roatta, you know nothing about the gerbils, nothing about our disappearing man in the club photograph—so what are you, some kind of immaculate fucking birth or what? It would be a right marvel to hear something you did know about, because if you go on not knowing about anything like this any more, you're going to turn into a fairy tale, my old darling, and I don't know a crown court in the land who believes in them.'

'Anyway,' Stevenson said to Scalo, 'there's no point spreading butter on a heart attack is there? We've got Margoulis, we've got Robacci, and now we've got you—so until we get answers here that really really interest us, we're just going to go on and on like this, eating you up one after the other until in the end some fucker suddenly farts and decides he does know something, OK? And until that moment comes, you, Margoulis, Robacci and every other saint in the calendar is going indoors to take shade at the Factory, and don't think Mr fucking McGuffin the lawyer is going to get you out of there because we'll fire three murders and the Parallel Club at him straight in the mush, and the press will have a lot of fun with it. We'll see to that end of it, don't worry your heart out.'

Scalo said: 'I didn't realise it was that bad.'

'Well, it is,' I said. 'It's very, very serious, even our folk upstairs at the Factory are sneezing hard. The press is starting to poke about in it now, too, and as for us, a policeman being an expensive thing, the public wants a run for its money, so there we are. It's pathetic, isn't it?'

'So you see, Scalo, don't you,' said Stevenson, 'that these

three murders here are a really rotten rotten case, and that we at the Factory so far have every reason to think that Dora Suarez was deliberately infected with AIDS for financial reasons—that the Parallel Club offered a service of infected call girls for rich, seropositive young cunts, who, knowing that they no longer had a chance of coupling with the pure young daughter of a duke, had no option other than sexual relations with women as infected as themselves for the rest of their lives, which is to say on average three years with AIDS, and when I see villains making money out of that, we don't like it. Strange folk, aren't we?'

'You'll never prove that,' Scalo said.

'You're quite wrong there, Scalo,' I said. 'I've proved much harder things.'

'Well, it's true it would have been more difficult if you hadn't been going to help us,' said Stevenson. 'Only the fact of the matter is, darling, that you are. You'll be falling over yourself to help us over this once you've understood what twenty years in Maidstone with not one hour's recommendation really means, let alone the reaction of your co-detainees once they know what you're in for—some of them have high moral, even priestly aspirations as they purge their crimes in there, didn't you know?'

'I'm tired of standing around in here,' I said suddenly. 'Let's go back to Room 205 and start this all over again. Let's see if we can't get the glimmerings of a statement into shape.' Turning to Scalo, I said: 'You don't look as if you knew the Factory very well yet, but you'll soon see that it's a place where time no longer exists for people in your position. You're in for a stupefying ride, but there you are. Sorry, I'm afraid that can't be helped.'

Scalo said: 'I'm a Bolivian citizen, and you two are going to suffer because of that.'

Stevenson said: 'For a little lad on the away ground you come on strong, don't you?' He yawned. He said to Scalo: 'You got your passport on you then? Let's see it, just to see.' He put his hand out.

Scalo showed the passport and Stevenson took it from him. He stowed it away in an inside pocket and said to Scalo: 'Now who are you? Suddenly you're no one, are you?'

Scalo shouted: 'Give that back.'

'Round about 2009 you might draw lucky,' Stevenson said. 'When you get out, you have to go and ask the court.' Turning to me, he said: 'Let's get the car.'

Waiting for the car with Scalo, I felt old and depressed; then all at once I looked across a space inside my head and saw Dora with perfect clarity; I suddenly had an absolutely clear view of her through pine trees massed on a towering slope. 'So you were there after all,' I said, as though she had kept a vital appointment. She was pretty far off. She was walking quietly among the trees, her head bent thoughtfully, half-turned away from me, bowed over a white dress that she was wearing now. She seemed self-absorbed and moved very slowly. If she were still wounded, that was too far off for me to see, but what is sure is that for an instant, in that forest clearing, as she moved away to its other side I saw her entire shape half-turned from me and it was most certainly the sweetest shape I have ever known; she made me feel clumsy and stupid. I was not disappointed that it did not happen but thought it might well have been that for all the distance between us, she was about to turn, look up, reach out and touch me; and in that instant all the love that I ever had in me rose up and overwhelmed me in a wave of unimaginable joy; everything was worthwhile after all. If only she had been enabled to turn them to me, I knew that her eyes would no longer have been the hard, blinded fruit, the tough glossy almonds pitted with dust that had stared upwards past me when I found her at Empire Gate, but would have been, if only I had been allowed to see them, peaceful, reflective and alive with a meaning that on earth

I could only guess at: and it was hard for me to reconcile her quiet arms as they were now, her white hands calmly joined, with that other dislocated arm, stiff, thrown upright as a challenge, a menace, a demand—a sword in the freezing room where I had found her, flung forward.

# 8

When we got up to the second floor, I said to Scalo: 'You wait out here, all right, just heat your arse in that chair there.'

'Look,' said Scalo, 'be polite. Where've all the manners gone?'

'This is the Factory,' I said. 'There never were any.'

'Yes, to you it'll seem like a different world for a little while,' Stevenson said to him. But he added comfortingly: 'Don't worry, you'll adjust—they all do.'

We left him there and went into 205. We had hardly done that when Charlie Bowman stuck his snout in the door. 'Hey,' he said, 'either of you know about a Greek around here some-where name of Margoulis?'

'I wouldn't trouble him just now if I were you,' said Stevenson. 'He's had a rough time with Rupt and Drucker; he's trying to sleep it off in Cell 3.'

'What do you mean "sleeping it off"?' said Bowman. 'He's thrown off his first-stage rockets in my office not half an hour ago.'

'After Rupt and Drucker and the two of us,' said Stevenson, 'he can't have many rockets left.'

'I'll tell you one thing,' said Bowman, 'trying to get the truth

153

out of him's like extracting a molar out of a middle-aged virgin without anesthetic, not easy.'

'They know you knock them about, Charlie,' I said, 'and that doesn't help really.'

Bowman said: 'Who's the little swarthy feller wasting public plastic chairs out with his arse outside your place here?'

'That's Scalo,' I said, 'ex-boss of the Parallel Club. He makes up a wheel in Carstairs/Suarez, and that's not the kind of thing you want to know about at all.'

'Normally, no, I wouldn't,' Bowman said, 'only tonight I feel like restless, and I've got that desire to make people talk to me.'

'He could have a go at Robacci, I suppose,' Stevenson said. 'He's had a chance to sleep, and Charlie couldn't do much harm there.'

'No,' I said, 'I don't want this person in the script at all; I explained it all upstairs.'

'It's your man Scalo out there that suddenly interests me,' Bowman was saying.

'Fuck off,' I said in a voice like half a ton of ice. 'Get back to suicidal Japanese millionaires—I'm not hiring, you've been told the deal, get lost. You or anyone from Serious Crimes lays a finger on Carstairs/Suarez, just one, and I'll electrocute you, now shamble the lower cheeks, Charlie. Out.'

'I'll tie your scrotum round your neck in a double Windsor!' he screamed.

'Put the dialogue on account and leave,' I said. 'I'm busy, so why don't you find something exciting to do, too?'

'You certainly have a way with detective chief inspectors,' said Stevenson when Bowman had left, slamming the door in two.

'It's because I don't care,' I said, and added: 'Mediocrity always knows when there's no tit going, pity the poor bastard.'

The phone rang; it was Cryer. 'I've got an interesting one here,' he said. 'It's a million to one it's anything to do with you, but I still thought it was worth a call.'

'Go on.'

'It's Clapham, not far,' said Cryer. 'That's what made me automatically think of Roatta.'

'Go on.'

'I've a young free-lance photographer on the strength, lives right there; he wants a job on the paper and he's going balls out for one with his camera.'

'Fine.'

'Well, he sits out evenings, wet or shine, on Clapham Common North Side, camera always ready for anything.' He said: 'You know an area called College Hill?'

'I'd have to look it up on the A to Z,' I said. 'That's somewhere off Balham/South Circular Road, isn't it? Lovelock Road?'

'You're on it,' Cryer said. 'Well, he's sitting out opposite the 37 bus stop opposite the Grove Mansions block and this man comes past jogging.'

'You've five hundred of them,' I said.

'Not with blood on their balls and an extraordinary step like a man bicycling fast, only without a bicycle.'

'A nut,' I said.

'Maybe,' said Cryer, 'but I thought I'd just give you a bell, that's all.'

I said: 'Your man get any pix?'

Cryer said: 'A bundle. This jogger intrigued him. Consequently my feller sits out on the same bench for five nights, and the jogger comes past five nights.'

'I'd like to see the pix, I think,' I said.

Cryer said: 'You can. But if it's the spot-on number, my feller did even better than that because tonight he followed the man home.'

'Home?' I said. 'Where's home? Where does the mat spread?'

'I told you,' Cryer said, 'College Hill.'

Suddenly I saw College Hill. I said: 'Isn't that where that big rubber factory burned down in '85?'

'You've got it,' said Cryer. 'And that's where the jogger went. But there's even more than that. When this free-lance sleuth of mine gets back there, your jogger don't go in by the front door, but by means of the fire escape—that's to say what's left of it, it's rusted out—races straight up the front of the building and through a high-floor window with no glass in it, and that's it. No light goes on in the place, so none goes off, does it?' He added: 'I wouldn't have bothered you with it if it hadn't been for Roatta being topped half a mile away.'

'How soon can I have those pictures, Tom?' I said. 'It's immediately worth a visit.'

'Now,' he said. 'I'll have them biked round to you.'

'You seen them?' I said. 'The face of blokey tell you anything? This jogger, little or large?'

'Not duck's arse, but small.'

'Fair or dark?'

'Dark.'

'Worn down with luggage at all?'

'A sports bag.'

'Ah,' I said. 'This sports bag, ask your man if it made a jangling noise at all.' I added: 'Another thing, any physical peculiarities? The way he carried himself at all?'

'I don't know what I'm looking for the way you do,' Cryer said. 'You'd best do more than look at these new pictures.'

I said: 'Why? Something struck you? Your photographer man?'

'Right hand between his legs as he ran,' said Cryer.

'He run a bit doubled over then?'

'That's right.'

'Any Bordeaux on his clothing—I mean blood?'

'You'd better see the pictures,' Cryer said.

'I'm waiting for them.'

'They're coming,' Cryer said. 'By the way, people are saying you've been through the Parallel Club like a dose of salts.'

'That's right.'

'And that you've nailed two or three—man by the name of Scalo, Robacci, and the doorman, a Greek called Margoulis.'

'You're bang up to date,' I said. 'We're putting them through the machinery right now.'

He said: 'You're working very closely with Stevenson on this, that's right, isn't it?'

'Neither of us can see any reason not to.'

'In other words,' said Cryer, 'you're both pretty sure that Carstairs/Suarez and Roatta are connected.'

'Nothing so far's told either of us that they aren't,' I said. I added: 'This jogger of yours, did your man shoot him full face?'

'No,' said Cryer, 'he tried everything but he just couldn't seem to get him full face.'

'But his pictures are better than the others?'

'Well, I've got the copies in front of me,' Cryer said. 'Of course these are shot with a much better lens than yours. I'm looking at your man now. He's dark, late thirties, Mediterranean origins maybe. He's wearing funny little thin sports shoes, he's very high-stepping—funny, that—big shock of black hair, thick grey sports trousers, wool, dark socks, looks like he reckons himself.'

'Say you met him on a dark night.'

'I'm not afraid of a battle,' Cryer said. 'But since you ask me, I'd rather not.'

'Why not?'

'That's your question,' Cryer said, 'not mine.'

I said: 'Supposing these pictures did interest us, what's the deal here?'

'Well, my news editor is getting very interested in this story,' Cryer said, 'like really keen.'

I said: 'Does he know I'm on it?'

He said: 'Yes.' He added: 'It's not my fault. Things get around, we knew it the minute you were back. The *Recorder* likes your cases. They always turn out differently, the ones you get stuck into.'

I said: 'We'll leave it this way, then, usual deal. I'll feed you the story as and when it becomes fit to sell newspapers.' I felt my voice crack as I added: 'I'm going through some sort of personal crisis with this case that I can't describe, Tom.'

'What?' said Cryer. 'You? A crisis?'

'All I can say is that I've got to be careful not to go over the edge this time,' I said.

'For Christ's sake don't fall.'

'In the end we all do.'

'You'll find whoever killed Suarez and Carstairs,' said Cryer.

'I know,' I said, 'but at long last the way lies through myself.'

'Come round and see Angela,' said Cryer. 'Why don't you ever come round to the house? You remember the Mardy case? Angela said you'd had enough with the Mardy case. I know you've got your sister Julie, but still, come and talk to her; she wants you to come and talk to her—why won't you ever let any of us help you?'

'You know me, Tom,' I said, 'I can't. Must I explain? How can I explain? I'm a very lonely man, deep buried, and so I love you from in the earth.'

I rang off.

Cryer's photographs of the jogger arrived in the hand of a police clerk. I held my hand out and said: 'Put me a magnifying glass into that.'

'What? At this time of night?'

I said: 'You heard me. You've got five minutes, four by the time you've left this room at the speed you're going.'

The officer left; he looked irritated and confused.

When I had the glass and had brought up all the detail with it, I thought for a while; then presently I went into Room 202. I said to Stevenson: 'Here, have a look at these.' Stevenson was sitting there with Scalo still facing him across the littered desk. Scalo looked tired.

'Something new?' said Stevenson. He jerked his head at Scalo. 'You want me to get rid of him?'

'No,' I said. I took a chair round and sat down on Stevenson's side of the desk. I took one of Cryer's photographs and spread it out under two ashtrays.

'What have you got there?' Scalo said.

Stevenson said: 'Fuck off.' He was frowning at the photograph through the magnifying glass. 'This Japanese film really works right down to the last crab, doesn't it?' he said.

I said: 'Is it the same man as we've got in the club snap with Suarez and Roatta there, that's what I want to know, what do you think?'

'It probably wouldn't stand up to a good lawyer just yet,' said Stevenson, 'but then on the other hand, we're not lawyers, and my instinct tells me that it very likely is. These are terrific, where did you get them?'

'What matters is that here they are,' I said. 'Particularly this shot here, I think with your man's back half to the camera again.'

'Exactly,' said Stevenson. 'Same funny step, same half-turned head, those weird little running shoes—what are they, spiked or something?—the same look of the man running through the door in the club?'

I shoved all the pictures under Scalo's nose. 'You're lost,' I said. 'You don't even know who you are any more. But if you want to buy yourself some open air, do you know this man's face?'

It was obvious that Scalo didn't.

I said to Stevenson: 'For my money it's the doorman that knows.'

Stevenson shouted: 'Officer!'

When the duty constable appeared, Stevenson said: 'Weigh this off back to its cell and bring the Greek back on—Margoulis.'

'Oh, by the way,' I said to Scalo, 'before you go, how far have we got on the subject of the little rats upstairs there? Have you been telling my colleague here everything you know about those rats?'

'Rats?' said Scalo obstinately.

I suddenly flew into one of the greatest rages I have ever got into in my life. 'You miserable fat cunt!' I yelled at him. 'There are hundreds of little rats in cages right on top of you at your stinking little club! They must have earned you otherwise they'd never have been there, and now all at once no one wants to know a dicky-bird about these rats and I have had your fucking ignorance up to here and I will bury you under five foot of cement, you little bastard, if you don't start bleating about it in under ten seconds, that's all the time you've got, now sing, shitbag.'

'Yes, now come on, Scalo,' Stevenson said, smiling, 'as we are beginning to get very tired of you. Who fed the rats and looked after them? Who picked them out and peeled them? Who tied the string to their tails when they vanished up inside Miss Suarez and others? Who paid that person? Who was he? What did he look like? What else did he do for a living?'

I pushed the photograph over to Scalo, picked up a ballpoint and ringed the face that turned away in shadow towards the door at the edge of the dance floor. I banged my fist down on the photograph and said: 'Talk, cunt.'

'I think he probably went with his face shawled into the rooms next to the cages where they had it off,' said Scalo. 'I think that went with the kick. But I never employed him, whoever he was.'

Stevenson said: 'Somebody must have.'

Scalo said: 'I think that must have been Roatta.'

'That's handy, isn't it?' said Stevenson. 'Roatta being dead.'

'And how much did the club take each time there was a spectacle?' I said. 'How much for a little rough-shaved rat up the sphincter? Two hundred? Five ton? A long one?'

Scalo panicked. He swallowed and said: 'Your last figure's your nearest.'

I said to Stevenson: 'This Scalo's repeating himself—let's get the doorman up and offer to break him because we're wasting time and besides I've got another idea.'

'Yes, only before you go,' said Stevenson, 'let's just both listen to the Greek for a moment, I don't see the harm in it.' He said to the officer who was bundling Scalo out: 'Put that one into the cheery room in case we need him back—no point his going back to his cell—and let's have the Greek on.' The officer removed Scalo and Stevenson yawned. He leaned back, stretched and said: 'Hard work, isn't it?'

'It's like trying to drill through concrete with a matchstick,' I said.

Presently the Greek appeared. I pointed to Scalo's old chair and said: 'Park.'

Stevenson said: 'You look in shit order, you do, really frightful, as if you hadn't had a tart for a week. What is it then? Corns playing up?'

Margoulis said: 'Now what do you want?'

'It's pictures,' I said. 'Lots of pictures. We're going to turn you into an art critic. Now you're going to look at these pictures closely, and give a considered opinion here.'

'I was never a great one for faces,' Margoulis said. 'Funny that, but still, it's like that sometimes, isn't it?'

'Not this time it isn't,' I said. 'This time you're going to find it isn't funny at all.' I picked up the phone and said into it: 'Are Sergeants Drucker and Rupt in the building? Good, ask them to come up.'

'You're in for a lot of wear and tear, Margoulis,' I said, putting the phone down, 'On the other hand, you're a big tough West End club doorman and we know you shit them all.' I said to the officer: 'Just fix him in that chair, will you, and let's have some proper light, I can't see my finger to pick my nose with right now.' So the officer placed Margoulis in the chair; then he brought out a big lamp stand with a one-thousand-watt bulb in it and set that up, too, till it faced Margoulis on Stevenson's desk.

'You had your chance,' I said to Margoulis. 'Well, now this is your last one before we switch on and put the juice through this. Also if you don't cooperate, you'll find yourself doing some basketball around the place. I don't like it much, but there's a rush on for the answer with this one.'

As I spoke, the door opened and Rupt and Drucker appeared, Drucker first. He was in boxing gear—spotless white T-shirt, sneakers and pink nylon shorts. 'Evening,' he said. He wasn't a big man; he was vast, and when he flexed his shoulders, Room 202 seemed to like get in the way.

'How's the sporting life?' Stevenson said to him.

'Getting better,' Drucker said. 'Three hours' punchball tonight; it's the heavyweight semifinals with Wembley police Saturday night. You coming? I can get you tickets.'

Rupt had been looking Margoulis over. He said to Stevenson: 'Was this all you could find for us today then?'

'The point is he knows things we want to know,' Stevenson said.

'Even so, I think they might send them up a bit tougher,' Rupt said. 'Seems a pity somehow, having to mark up old men.'

All the same he took hold of Margoulis' cheek between his thumb and first finger and pulled hard. 'What do you think?' he said to Margoulis. 'Fancy getting into training then, Grandpa?'

'They get worn out climbing all the way up from the street I reckon,' Stevenson said. 'They seem to get kind of weary on the stairs.'

'Well, three days in St Stephen's after we've finished with this one,' Drucker said, 'and it'll be like a bank holiday for the geezer.'

I said to Margoulis: 'Well, you see, this is the sergeants' mess.'

'And what a mess,' Rupt said. He said to Drucker: 'Let's see if I got that bit of karate right this evening.' He smacked Margoulis' chair with the cutting edge of his hand; the top rail of the chair shattered and bits of Ministry of Works woodwork flew about the place. 'Sorry,' said Rupt. 'Had a row with the old woman earlier, always makes me nervous.'

'How do you feel, Margoulis?' I said. 'Up to looking at some pictures now? You just speak up loud and clear and then I swear there'll be no bother.'

Margoulis made a noise of some kind, so I handed him Cryer's photographs. 'And try telling us something interesting about him for a change,' I said as I gave them to him, 'like his name or something.'

'That way we can eliminate him from our enquiries,' Stevenson said. He switched the appalling light on and off several times.

Presently Margoulis said: 'Roatta hired him.'

'Why?' said Stevenson. 'For the rats?'

'I know nothing about rats.'

'Can't you smell if there are rats in a place?'

'I know nothing about rats.'

'He don't even realise he is one,' Drucker said.

I said to Margoulis: 'We probably wouldn't even be so interested in the individual except that for some extraordinary reason, no one in this case so far appears to want to know about him with a barge-pole.'

Margoulis said: 'I've heard that Mr Roatta reckoned that the geezer owed him money down to something, and that he might help pay it off by working upstairs, something like that.'

'Was it the man in the photograph who brought the rats in?'

'I don't know anything about any rats, I keep telling you.'

Stevenson said to Rupt: 'Just slap him. Not hard, we don't want him bedridden.'

In the confined space the blow went off like the roar of a 303 rifle. Stevenson said: 'OK, now pick him up, dust him off, set him up in his chair and we'll start yet again.' He took the doorman by his back hair and turned his face up to the ceiling. He said: 'You all right? Makes your ears ring a bit at first, doesn't it?

Still, as you are a hard man . . .' He didn't finish the sentence; there was no need. He added: 'Cooperate. You can see we haven't much time and that we mean business.'

I said: 'Until you do answer these questions we're just going to go on and on putting them to you, Margoulis, it's our only way, so what you need to do now is be clever and cut this as short as you can.'

Stevenson said: 'This man again now. The man in the photograph taken by the girl with the burnt legs the night of Roatta's party at the Parallel, and the face in this new set, do you think the face is the same?'

Margoulis said: 'It might be.'

I said: 'Come on, love, is it or isn't it?'

Margoulis said: 'I think it is.'

I said: 'You'll be required to make a statement.'

Margoulis said: 'But I enjoy life.'

'Street accidents are the scourge of this city,' said Stevenson, drowning a yawn with the back of his hand, 'but what do you expect the police to do about it; we're seriously undermanned.'

I said: 'This boy in the photograph, he got a name?'

Margoulis said at last, in the same sighing tone with which a man dies or has an orgasm: 'Tony.'

'He's only learning!' Drucker said with admiration. He picked Stevenson's ashtray up off the desk and spun it to Rupt, who caught it and spun it back again. They were getting bored.

I said: 'Any second helping like a surname to go with it?'

'Just Tony, I knew him by.'

'There has to be a bit more to it than that,' said Drucker.

'Go on,' I said.

'In and out of the club every night, was he?'

'Three, four nights a week,' Margoulis said. 'Staff hardly noticed him, he was just around. Mr Roatta gave me the word on the door that it was OK for him to be around and I let it go at that.'

I said: 'Did he frat at all?'

'Frat?'

'Yes, like chat up the bird that worked in the place, you know.'

'Yes, well, he did a bit.'

'Fancied himself?'

'Well, yes,' said Margoulis, 'he certainly thought he was OK. Look,' he added, 'I don't know what I'm getting into here, telling you people all this—I might as well be dying, what I'm telling and getting myself into.'

'You just concentrate with all your might on what you're trying to get out of,' Stevenson said.

Drucker said to Rupt: 'They say there's a life after death, but by Christ this one don't look in good shape for it.'

Rupt said reasonably: 'That's because the people up there don't play enough football. They want to get some of them doubling out there Saturday mornings up north in the wet at Driffield Park; that way they'd soon get a bit of lead in their pencil.' He trod heavily on Margoulis' West End doorman's hunting boot; it squeaked.

I said to Margoulis: 'Take all the time you need to think, then tell me how many times you ever saw this Tony with Dora Suarez, say during the three months before she died.'

Rupt stirred in the shadows. Margoulis said in the end: 'Six times anyway.'

I said: 'Was it like trouble talk they had? Like was it animated?'

He said: 'Well, it was quite intense.'

I said: 'Describe this intensity.'

'No, well, it was just like sort of quite intense,' said Margoulis helplessly, 'that's all.'

'Did they ever disappear upstairs together?' I said.

He said: 'Well, I couldn't always be looking because of the customers on the door, but I made them having it away together three, four times, yes.'

'They stay up there long?'

Margoulis sighed. He said: 'The time it took me to drill a hole in a floorboard.'

'Shut your mouth,' said Rupt.

I said to Rupt: 'Don't touch the friend, he's starting to be helpful now.' I said to Margoulis: 'We're not in the business of knocking folk about.'

Margoulis felt his big face where it had been tenderised and said: 'Really?'

I said: 'It's only when we're in a hurry to catch a man, and then the frightened folk that could lead us to him won't talk.'

Margoulis said: 'You know what the West End is, and a man's health does sometimes come into it, yes.'

'You should have seen the state of Dora Suarez's health,' I said, 'and you'd have thought yourself well off with both your legs smashed with an iron bar.' I stood up. 'Well, that'll do for the present.' I said to Drucker: 'Get all that down in front of the stenographer and turn it into a statement for blokey here to sign, everything he's just told us.' I added to him and Rupt: 'Be kind to him, show him the family spirit a little because he's been helpful and besides we'll need him in court.'

I went towards the door. Stevenson said: 'Where are you going?'

'I've got this other idea,' I said. I picked up three or four of Cryer's photographs and a photocopy of the club one; I put them in my pocket.

'Do you know what time it is?' Drucker said.

'No,' I said, 'and until I've nailed this man I don't care.' I added: 'You don't either. Nobody does when there's this work on.'

I was starting to leave, but then the phone rang; Drucker picked it up. He covered the squawk end and said to me across it: 'Robacci wants to come up.'

'All right, then,' I said, 'let's have him up.' I said to him and

Rupt: 'You both stay here, help us get a shape put to all this.' I said to Stevenson: 'Something's giving.'

Stevenson said: 'Yes, let's do it now.'

Drucker said: 'Well, we don't want this prick around if Robacci's dropping by.'

'No, quite right,' said Stevenson, 'Mr Margoulis can now get to bed, wheel him away.'

We had Margoulis wheeled away; he looked glad about that.

Presently Robacci arrived. He looked a bit afraid when he saw the scene in 202; even so, he smiled like an old trouper, a weary and familiar smile, and said: 'Look, I've been thinking this lot over.'

I said: 'Good, that's what your brains are for.'

He said: 'I was just the floor manager.'

'And my name's Adolf Hilter,' I said. 'Did you know Tony?'

'Tony?'

'Don't start,' I said, 'the man who looked after the rats upstairs.'

'The rats?' Robacci said. 'The rats? What rats?'

I said to Rupt and Drucker: 'Find this gentleman a comfortable seat.'

They put him into what was left of Margoulis' chair. Drucker said: 'You'll be sitting on a few splinters, but by the time this is over, you won't give a fuck.'

Robacci said: 'Am I likely to get hurt?'

Rupt said: 'It could happen.'

'When?' said Robacci.

Drucker said: 'Any time. Depends on you.'

'My graft was to deal with the customers', Robacci said.

I said, 'Everyone who screwed up there had AIDS.'

Stevenson said: 'When we've got time, we'll go into your membership list for upstairs, but right now this is a triple-murder enquiry and we want to nail the man, which we think is the same man who did all three of them, and we are beginning to think his name is Tony. So tell us about Tony, and don't tell us you've never heard of rats at the Parallel Club, darling, the time for silly stories is really over.'

'The point about AIDS in a man is what it does to his member,' I said. 'I've found time to do a little reading.' I placed a book down on the table and opened it. 'Have a look at these,' I said. 'Are you in tip-top screwing form yourself, Robacci? Here are photographs of Kaposi's sarcoma lesions on the penis, and do you feel you could screw with your cock in that state? Well?' I said. 'Look at the pictures and answer my question, do you or don't you?'

Robacci shook his head.

'I entirely agree with you,' I said. 'However, what you do if you're infected and got the money for it, is watch a man or a woman have an orgasm by means of an animal put into her fundament and even get your rocks off over it. Singers at the Parallel Club?' I said. 'People with no money and a pretty face, you mean, trailing round with a mike to make it look good for half an hour, and then it's away up to the punters on the first floor. Your backers seem to have thought there was money in it.'

Stevenson said: 'So now you see why you're here, Robacci; it's to keep the dirtiest part of this city from turning jet black.'

'I deny everything!' Robacci shrieked. 'I tell you I didn't even know there was an upstairs.'

'That won't do at all,' I said. 'You're beginning to look as if you were in need of a bit more polishing.' I looked at Drucker.

Drucker came forward with eight fingers out. 'Good,' he said, 'I was getting bored.' He said to Rupt: 'Let's try it out on this old cunt here if this Japanese trick here really works.'

Rupt said: 'Well, I don't know, but I burst a bag of straw in two with it only this evening.'

Robacci said: 'Christ, stop them.'

'I don't know if I could,' said Stevenson. 'In any case, what's sure is that time's money in this room, and your time don't count a great deal. So don't tell us fairy tales, we're very busy, we've heard them all, and besides they get like very boring.' However, he looked at Rupt and said to Drucker: 'Still, just wave your crazy mate down for a moment, will you?'

I said to Robacci: 'You're in the most dreadful bother, black-head—as far as the Parallel's concerned, you'll be up in front of other officers, Serious Crimes, most likely, Chief Inspector Bowman and that mob as like as not, God help you; but that'll be the subject of another enquiry. What we're interested in here are these three deaths—the rest of it will go on from there.'

'Tony, now,' said Stevenson, 'the man in these photographs. Are you sticking to it that he never existed? Are you telling us that just like the others? Is that it, then? Is that what you're saying?'

'Be very careful now, Robacci,' I said, 'You are waltzing Matilda, you're just gambling away your long-term future here. The more lies you tell now, the bigger and filthier the splash this is going to make on page one when you go to trial. A prosecutor hung all over with L-plates could pull the trick—and I will tell you, the way you're going now, you are steering the straightest possible course for Canterbury; if I was blind myself, I couldn't miss it.'

'I'm trying to help you as best I can.'

'Well, it's not good enough,' said Stevenson. He said to Rupt and Drucker: 'Take him away and like carpenter him into a statement. I want it like yesterday was too late. When you're satisfied, have the berk sign it.'

Drucker said to Robacci: 'Come on then, sweetie. Folks are always so glad when they get away from signing with me.'

Robacci shouted at Stevenson: 'I want to live!'

Rupt took him by his left ear and whispered into it: 'What for?'

Drucker marched him out, saying: 'Tony now.'

Rupt said: 'Yes, let's hear about Tony.'

'Tony.'

'Tony.'

I said: 'It's going to be a long hard night for you, Robacci.'

I picked up my photographs and left before anything else stopped me.

I went up Meard Street and round the corner into Wardour; it was a basement club called the Spiaggia di Napoli; it lay under a bankrupt dress shop called the Nth Wave. I caught sight of my face as I passed the bouncer's mirror at an angle facing the stairs as I went down; it looked to me as though I had died a thousand years ago. I went in past the public telephone that was always busy and said to the barman: 'The boss in, Mario?'

'Over on the jackpot there, top end of the bar.'

'How's the family?' I said.

He said: 'Reproducing.'

He neither trusted me nor didn't; I was a copper with contacts both sides and that didn't make sense to him.

Mario's face always reminded me of a horrible case I had had years ago. It was a hard morning in winter, December, just past dawn, and two of us in a patrol car were sent by radio to this body fallen down outside Luton. It lay spread-eagled, covered in frost, at the foot of a high-tension pylon in a great field where the cables marched across carrying the electric current towards the city of Luton. The dead man's shoulders were so wrenched by the shock when he short-circuited the terminals and killed himself that it looked as if he had somehow buttoned himself up wrong inside his grey jacket. He hadn't. But it was a rotten jacket to die in anyway—the kind you get from national assistance that doesn't keep the cold out. His hands had been burned away where they had gripped the cables at the top of the tower till the energy had hurled him off them. His eyes had been fried directly into fishballs; there was nothing else left of his face but his eyes in sockets that were now huge, and his glaring teeth. He had been thrown by the shock from the two hundred feet that he had patiently climbed among the girders so that he could make an end, down into that flat, endless field that bordered the motorway under a colourless sky, and so had purged himself of existence. Young as I was then, I could easily have managed his fragile relic alone, but as it was, the two of us, and the two men from the ambulance, all lifted him together. We laid him on the stretcher, having covered his face, as carefully as you place a dead match in an ashtray, and then we carried him away to the hospital there at Luton.

In the Spiaggia everyone could speak English all right, but no one ever did except at work. They were all Italian, and so Italian was the language they all spoke—waiters, cab drivers, porters, small-time villains, dealers and gamblers seconds off the back and so on going all the way up to the hierarchy, which had not only marked out the foreign London territory but was also respected for ancestry and reputation. The young men looked after the older men not only because they were family—which was reason enough—but because they were legend; everyone knew what losses they had taken in the Soho wars. Racy old haw-haw British folk in overcoats and polka-dot ties who thought it would be fun to take their women down there after a Chinese lunch and show off with the old Positano Italian in the afternoon were told to fuck off, because everyone in the Spiaggia was oversexed and it was a club where women only started fights.

At a table in the corner by the jacks, eight men in demolition coats were playing *scopa*. They had a bottle out in front of them and the look of men who did not want to be disturbed. Coming in, I looked at the telly high up on the wall with the Kempton Park card coming up for the 3:30 and then at the gobbling row of fruit machines underneath, each with its dark young punter with a face like a stained knife blade gazing into the screen and feeling for the payoff. Mostly they were off-duty waiters from the restaurants up the street, but at the last machine to the right by the wall was the man I wanted to see, a man my own age wearing an old mac wringing the bandit's arm with his back to me. He wasn't alone, though. As he felt me come in a small man wearing a blue Burberry put his right hand in his pocket and turned towards me expressionlessly, only I was busy thinking, and so was unaware of him.

I went up to the older man playing the machine from behind and put my hand on his shoulder.

'Mauro,' I said, 'I want to talk to you.'

The next thing I knew was that I thought I was dead, bent backwards over the bar at an impossible angle for a human spine; and the cutting edge of the short man's right hand was an inch above my throat—meantime I just had time to see the barman filling the sink with water in case I did scream so he could dowse me in it and send me out with the rest of the garbage. The other drinkers had their backs turned; the young dealers went on knocking and calling the bets as though nothing were happening. The man I wanted said to the man in the Burberry just in time: 'Let this man stand up, Fabrizio, let him breathe.' He watched the machine jerk out silver intently till it had finished, picked it all up and pushed it across the bar. He said to me, meaning the man in the blue raincoat: 'He's new, he's young, just in from Sicily, he don't know a lot of folk yet, but you must be sick to come up to a man in here from behind.'

I said: 'I suppose I am, only I'm distracted by a matter in my mind.'

'Sure.' said Mauro, 'money. You're a fired policeman and not young. How much do you need? A hundred? Two hundred? A long one if you like.'

'No, this is murder,' I said, 'and I'm back on the police suddenly at the Factory on account of it.'

Mauro said to the barman: 'Give him a ring-a-ding, but a

double, and hurry.' He said to the watching man in the Burberry that had nearly dug my grave: 'Take your eyes off from my friend.'

When the drinks came up, I said: 'Mauro, I feel I've just got to talk to you for five minutes, it's a human matter, can you make us a corner free?'

Mauro leaned over the bar and said to the barman: 'You see this man?' He stabbed a finger at me. 'You never forget him, all right? He took me in out of the pissing rain one night years ago back over to his place when I hadn't a light nor a roof and treated me like I was his son, and that's not forgotten. So move the folk over and make us a table, move those boys there over, the folk in here think there's nothing serious in life but playing cards; mind, I know they spend money.' When the place was ready under the thick Nazionale cigarette smoke, Mauro said: 'Stop watching the soft porn on that video, come over with me now and sit down.' He said to the barman: 'Bring on the Bell's. Bottle. Two glasses. Ice. It's with me.' When we were served, he said: 'Well now, tell me.'

'It's bad,' I said, 'very bad. Only not for me—it's the others this time, which is much worse.'

He said: 'Is it true you're back at the Factory? I got a whisper, but is it true?'

I said: 'Mauro, yes I am back with the law. They called me. I'm not concealing anything, I'm back at A14.'

He said: 'Is it Suarez? Carstairs? Felix Roatta?'

'Yes,' I said.

He said: 'Roatta was dirty; he got his head in the way.'

He lit a Westminster. 'Is it true what I read, that the girl had AIDS?'

'Yes,' I said, 'Suarez was dying.'

'Why take the trouble to kill her then?' Mauro said.

'Mauro,' I said, 'I'm here in friendship, but this case is full of Italians, and that's why I'm here; I need your advice.'

He said: 'Go on.'

I said: 'I'm coming round to the idea that she was killed by whoever it was who gave her AIDS, and that suited people.'

'She worked at the Parallel Club, didn't she?'

'Yes,' I said, 'and we've buckled three of them. They're over at the Factory now.' I drank some whisky. I said: 'Mauro, this is very nasty, and I need no lectures.'

'Italians,' he said. 'You mean Scalo, Robacci—they're the Parallel.'

I said: 'Have you heard about the rats?'

'No,' he said. The barman brought us more ice. 'What rats?'

I told him about the rats; I told him about Suarez in the morgue, about the pathologist, about Wiecienski, about everything. I said: 'Suarez, ah poor child, she thought too much, she wrote too much, she ended up knowing too much. Remember, she wasn't just killed, Mauro, she was axed to death, and it took the killer several blows. He also wanked in her blood and drank some of it. He also killed Betty Carstairs, the old lady who was sheltering Suarez because she interrupted him while he was finishing Suarez off.' I added: 'And it's even worse than that. I think Suarez was in love with her killer, or at least had been.' I said: 'Mauro, try and help me get justice for this girl.'

He said: 'How?'

I said: 'How many Italians here do you know called Tony? Very sporty and can't get their rocks off, so they kill the woman.' I leaned over to him across my glass and said to him very quietly: 'Suppose Suarez were our wife or daughters, what would we do?'

He sat very still.

Taking his hand, I said to him: 'Help me, Mauro. We've known each other for a long while now. I've declared myself, told you who I am again, what I'm doing, what I'm on. You don't have to help me unless you want. But all I know is one thing, this man's got to be caught, you can see that, you can see he's a maniac.

I'm here talking to you because I'm desperate to catch him, for if you had been with me in the flat at Empire Gate and then at the morgue to see her body, then you would have known.'

'An axe,' said Mauro, staring at the table, 'a nine-millimetre Quickhammer. A name? The idea of a name?'

'Just Tony so far,' I said. 'Suarez never named names. I can go on squeezing the three men we've hammered till hell gets tired, but we haven't that kind of time. I have to find a shorter way.'

'You got any kind of face for this Tony?'

'I've took these,' I said. I got the photographs I had out of my pocket.

He looked at the pictures, then started pouring out a drink without looking where the bottle was. In the end he said: 'This is very very difficult.'

'Family?'

'Well, the clan,' said Mauro, 'but he was always wrong-sprung.'
The light turned darker over our table.

'A big girl died very abruptly in a hotel room in Kings Cross once,' said Mauro. 'I'm going back seventeen years now. She was found by the maid that came in to do the beds with her head half cut off and her nose in the bedside ashtray. Do you remember?'

'Yes,' I said. 'Big, fat girl. No story in it; Serious Crimes didn't want to know, the press neither. Three lines on page three. It was Frank Ballard dealt with it while he was still sergeant at A14 and I was on the beat in Chelsea. Vicar's daughter up from the sticks, liked a fuck, frankly. Razored and bottled—we never got anyone.'

'No you didn't,' said Mauro, 'you hardly could, because we covered it that time.'

'Only that time?'

'Yes, he made a mistake with one of our women, so we went up against him several of us, and you could say that that was when he started to take up running in a very serious way.'

'Mauro,' I said, 'who is it?'

He said: 'It's very hard for me; I'm just not a man to talk to the police.'

'Ballard, Stevenson and I, we exist because of these photographs,' I said, pointing at them. I said: 'Think of Suarez. Think of the blebber's daughter. They were fat, ugly or sick; but they were still lives.'

In the end he said: 'Now he calls himself Tony Spavento.'

'That his real name?'

'No,' said Mauro. 'Spavento is the Italian word for terror. I'm not allowed to tell you what his real name was.'

'Was?'

'He doesn't exist for us now.'

'Sounds bad.'

'His own family have a permanent contract on him here.'

I stood up; I was a bit pissed and trying to think, too. I said good-bye to Mauro. I walked up the moth-eaten carpet of the club stairs to the street; I went back to the Factory thinking of Suarez's body, lying axed and naked on our earth as if, poor child, she were all our loved ones, all of them.

Do you know I cry in my sleep? Do you think a man can't cry in his sleep?

# 9

I opened the door into Room 202. Stevenson was there with Robacci. Robacci was smiling; I decided to cure that, put an end to the smile. Stevenson said to me: 'Robacci's talking. He's happy.'

I said: 'I'm not at all happy.' I said to Robacci: 'Tell me about Tony Spavento now, let's have it straight up, darling.'

'I just went on and on appealing to the facts and to his conscience until he spat the whole lot out,' Stevenson was saying. 'I was just about to send down for a nice cup of tea each.'

'Spat what out?' I said. I took Robacci softly by the jacket and said: 'I am fed up with your lies, now start telling me about Tony Spavento.'

Robacci went dead white and said: 'What? I can't—we all have to live.'

I said: 'You went the wrong way about it.' I didn't touch Robacci; I didn't hurt Robacci. I just massaged the lapel on his jacket and went on doing it. 'Spavento,' I said. 'Talk.'

'We don't talk about him,' Robacci whispered.

I said to Robacci: 'You're now in a dreadful jam, Robacci. If you don't talk to us, we throw you to Canterbury, that's twenty years. That's the wolves. You'll be seen to when you get there. While if you do talk to us, your own folk'll see to you before you're even charged.' I said: 'Anyway we're both sides watching you now, so you've really no way out, you're fucked.'

Robacci said: 'OK, OK, so I do some bird, but I'm for nothing with this man Spavento.'

'Wrong,' I said, 'anyway for us, it was you folk took the contract out on Roatta.'

'Not me, not me!' Robacci screamed. 'If it was anybody, it was Scalo.'

'When robbers start thinking safety first,' I said to Stevenson, 'it really is pathetic, isn't it? It really says good-bye to everything pretty well, doesn't it, and isn't that a funeral for you, it's really very very sad, I find.'

Robacci said: 'Roatta was into Spavento.'

'Never mind all that now,' I said. 'Basically it was down to the rats, wasn't it?'

'OK, yes; well, Tony minded them.'

'He minded them and then guided them into people at the end of a string,' Stevenson said. 'Didn't he, though?' He smashed his fist down on the desk. 'And there are three bodies to show for his behavior. Didn't he? Didn't he?'

'Spavento is physically sick, isn't he?' I said. 'With AIDS, isn't he, you elegant little cunt?'

'Nobody talks about him,' Robacci whispered, looking at the floor. 'I keep telling you.'

'I don't know who these virtually witless people think we are,' I said to Stevenson. 'I keep telling them and telling them that we're serious folk, that this is really real police work, and they still don't want to know; my life, will they swallow it, my life, they fucking well will not.'

I said to Robacci: 'Now this is going to come as a brand-new horrid surprise to you,' I said, 'but you, Scalo and Margoulis are being bred up here in the Factory to talk about Spavento in front of a court. I'll let you into a secret; you're both going to get very mediocre counsel, we'll fix that from our side with the DPP, and you're both going to go down with a monster bang; because Margoulis will be our witness and he'll have the very best counsel; we fix all that, too. These lawyers have to make a living, the money on the brief's the same whether they perform well or badly, see?' I said to Stevenson: 'But that'll just be tidying up.'

Stevenson said: 'I think we'd better just go off and see Spavento now and tackle him with a few questions, thus eliminating him from our enquiries, if you see what I mean.'

'It's being worked on by folk who are in the job of selling newsprint,' I said, 'so it might take two hours or not even.'

'Well, I don't think we need this individual cluttering this room up any more,' said Stevenson, indicating Robacci with the edge of his thumb. 'He makes a small room smell even smaller.'

'Can I go back down to my cell now and get some sleep then?' Robacci said.

'No you can't,' said Stevenson. 'What you can do is sign a statement with Rupt, Drucker and a WPC, go up in front of the beak in the morning at nine and then straight to Brixton on remand, your feet won't touch.' He said to me: 'Fucked if I can see why these people should snore their heads off and us wearing our boots out.'

He rang for the duty constable. When the officer appeared, Stevenson waved at Robacci and said: 'Take this lot away.'

'I want my lawyer,' Robacci said, 'I want him now.'

'I'm in hell and I want a fucking snowball,' Stevenson said.

He burst out laughing. He added: 'Fuck off, cunt.'

Dora had written: 'Oh, it's sure that the more beautiful you are on this earth, the fewer they are to protect you.'

When Robacci had gone and 202 was empty, I repeated those words of hers to Stevenson and I said: 'Don't you see, we're too late to save Suarez, we're too late as usual to save her, but it doesn't work like that at all, and so don't you see that we must have rules, even if they're apparently obscure rules—for if not, we'd all be murdered, and then there'd be no one left at the bar at six, which is the civilised hour.'

'I suppose we're still men, then,' said Stevenson. 'Is that what you're trying to say?'

'If you're my friend, yes,' I said, 'that's exactly it.'

'Apart from finding who killed her, what else can we do, though?' he said.

'We must try and bring her back,' I said, 'just as if her death had never happened.'

'That's mad,' Stevenson said.

'It's no madder than what surrounds us,' I said, 'and it must be done, even if I can't think out exactly why, it's as if we were back saving people back in the war.' I thought for a moment and said: 'We save Suarez and somehow we save everybody.'

Thank God I am neither particularly human nor beautiful, Stevenson neither—for it must be as terrible to be a beautiful human being as it must be to be rabbit or a partridge, threatened on every side by cunts: nobody and everybody wants you, and you become everybody's prey.

I stood up and went over for a moment to stand by the window, still bleeding for Suarez inside; like all the wrongly dead, she was a heroine in her own right for me, poor child, and it was for her that I existed in the police or elsewhere: my poor darling sweet Suarez, my darling Suarez.

I dreamed of times when my mind was not so old—of brilliant sun and then of grey rain, of going out into days in the morning as though these things were not old but brand-new and that I still belonged in them, as did everybody I had ever known, quite equally, which is to be a true citizen in any place.

I said out into the night: 'We'll get our dignity back; whether alive or dead, we shall all be as we used to be.' I found I absolutely had to state those words out loud because, through the deaths of Suarez and Carstairs I found myself suddenly in a state of great doubt, despair, and in a testing time, not only because of the way the two women had left us but because of the fury I felt on account of it. I found my own life set on the scales as though it were theirs; and the worse I found I was in my mind, the more I thought and clung to my memories of gardens, springtime and vanished times in my attempt to rid myself of the evil that saturated me through being obliged as a peasant is to go into a cellar and kill a snake—although, in the world I worked and lived in, good was a feeble dream compared to the reality of evil unless she were conjured up again by the grasp of a vanished but loving hand, a night out, the deep passion of a kiss made particular for you alone and printed to your cheek by the one being created to you for the purpose. I don't and can't know how the new times will come—I only know that Suarez and Carstairs must, by our forces, be put to rest; because until that is done, the new future will never come, and so none of us can ever be at rest.

It has always seemed certain to me that there is only one way to go about anything or go anywhere—it is as straight as possible. I must end with my hands right in my work and solve it; and although I have made terrible mistakes through ignorance, I see justice under that light—everything usefully done is done for others. Now Carstairs and Suarez, too, in their new state, will surely find and join hands with us in a mysterious and valuable way that the rest of us can't yet know.

It's a silly, frightening world but our own, I suppose.

I suppose.


(They say that faith can move mountains; so I have heard and do in part believe it, that's Shakespeare, that is. I hope he was right; that's me.

For Betty Carstairs was murdered because she loved Suarez as the daughter she never had, and at eighty-six she tried to save her; and Suarez was killed because she was beautiful, poor, sick and at our mercy, and we showed her none, and may our country hang its head.

I see now, clearer than I have ever done, that my work is a matter not just of my personal honour, but of our national honour, as if, in spite of everything, there were still a spark in us as there once was when we loved the dead as ardently as we did the living and believed in their continued being as I still most certainly do, and then I am really not capable just by myself of explaining just what went wrong after that.)

Did you know I sometimes cry in my sleep? Did you ever hear of a man who never cried in his sleep?

By examining other people's lives and deaths I am half consciously showing myself how to approach my own.

Strip horror; face it naked. Don't hide or run, and then the good will come, even if it has to go through hell to find you.

I remember, a long way back, talking to Frank Ballard about a flasher he had arrested on the banks of the Serpentine. 'Nine flashers out of ten are harmless,' I said. 'The tenth is a killer.'

The tenth could be a Tony Spavento.

The Voice rang. 'I don't like the way you're going about this Carstairs/Suarez case,' it said in a tone somewhere between authority and nervousness. 'I don't like it at all. You're acting as if you were the law, not just a sergeant working for it.'

'There ought to be a law that made murder impossible,' I said, 'but there isn't, so I'm filling the gap until there is.' I added: 'As for being just a sergeant, don't assume I'm not ambitious merely because I turn down promotion; we've had this conversation before. In my own way I'm very ambitious. Most hardworking people are—also my twin ambitions are positive and useful. One, I want to be a pioneer, not a pawn—two, I want to find out everything I possibly can about myself and others, because the more I know, the better equipped I am for catching killers. What would I find out as a detective chief superintendent? Nothing.'

'We don't want any pioneers at A14.'

'Well, it's that or take me off the case,' I said, 'in which case I'll continue it as a private citizen. I told you what the contract was at the word go, and you agreed to it.'

After a long pause the Voice said wearily: 'All right.'

It rang off.

I went into Stevenson's office. 'Well?' I said. 'What happened to our three lovely detainees?'

'They went over to Great Marlborough Street, where they were remanded in custody pending further enquiries, application for bail refused.'

'Well, that's one part of the vomit cleared up,' I said. 'Now let's see about the big lot.'

As I spoke I found I was remembering my grandmother from my childhood, for no reason perhaps but that, like my sister Julie, she represented innocence. It was summer, and my gran sat reading in a deckchair in our small garden under the only tree, an apple tree, wearing a straw hat tilted over her nose; she was still a very handsome woman, even at forty-eight. A hot wind raved vaguely among the leaves, turning up their pale undersides, and just the memory of her helped disentangle my spirit from all the squalid filth that was my working life. For an instant, Stevenson and Room 202 vanished and I was running towards her through the long grass that hot afternoon—oh Didi! Didi!—taking her by the hand and pulling her up out of her chair to bring her up for tea, which my mother had set out on the verandah—tea, bread and butter, jam and cake on a cloth spread over a green-painted iron table.

What I do know is that if my grandmother were in my place now, and if it were she who had to deal with the deaths of Carstairs and Suarez, she would have acted just as I am doing—

she was stubborn, independent and compassionate, and that was why I had always loved her so. She never uttered a word when her two sons died in that car accident, but a cancer which, according to the doctors she had had for a long time but had said nothing about, now suddenly declared itself, perhaps because of the shock, so that she had to go into hospital very shortly after the funerals. Sensing, as she told my mother, that the operation had failed, she called for all her makeup and put it on, asking sister for the loan of her pocket mirror, and she hummed a little music from *The Coronation of Poppaea*, her favourite opera, the morning she died.

Voices from so far back now that they are still young fly calling, searching in the darkened wood of my mind and I see at long last that the pain of her loss helped me make me what I am.

Sometimes I feel so oppressed by evil that I feel I could go out of my mind like my wife Edie did. It's not just the terror that the facts of a murder inflicts on me, but the needless agony that threatens and visits people—that's my sadness. Life, people, the places they made for themselves, the traces they leave behind them like the wake fading behind a ship, the earth itself—life is so precious that I fear one day it might blind me, just as it blinded Suarez.

But I will equalise everything for you, Dora, just as I swore over your body in the morgue that I would.

(I saw the photograph of her again, taken in the Parallel Club while she was still alive. The shot was taken from slightly behind her and close to her right side with a flash, and the light brought her cheek out dazzling white in contrast to her black hair. Her almond eyes were three-quarters open under thick lids, only they were responsive and living, not fixed absently upwards as they had been when I saw them in death. She was heavily made up— I understood why now, of course—and on the monochrome film her lips showed as black as her eyes and hair. She held a microphone in her right hand and her lips were close to it, parted and singing. Beyond her, looking with the camera, were tables jammed with the solid, impassive faces of villains—Parker and Sharpe, the iron-bar specialists, were there with their women, also Mike Slattery and Phil the Gap, and of course the dark-haired man, in the act of turning his face instinctively from the camera, that I had shown the Italians.)

I was worn out suddenly; we were trying to do work in hours that needed weeks. I said to Stevenson: 'We've known each other awhile—can I just tell you something that makes this case different for me? Different from all the others?'

'Of course. What is it? You sound really serious.'

'I don't care what you think when I say this,' I said, 'but I think I would have been in—'

The phone rang. Stevenson picked it up, saying: 'It'll have to wait a minute.' When he had finished listening, he put it down and said: 'That was Barry from Records.'

'Well?'

'Suarez had form, did you know?'

'Don't tell me,' I said, 'I can guess—theft and prostitution?'

'Well done,' he said. 'Three months theft, thirty days for the other.'

'As if she were the only one,' I said, 'and as if it mattered.' I added ironically: 'Desperate people will do almost anything these days, won't they?'

'He was only trying to help,' said Stevenson.

'Oh I know that,' I said. 'Nothing on Spavento, I suppose.'

'Nothing.' He added: 'What were you just going to tell me when the phone went?'

It rang again. Stevenson picked it up, listened, and handed it to me.

'Cryer.'

I took the phone and said: 'Yes, Tom?'

'We've found him—my photographer's got his picture again, but this one's different. In this one he's at home.'

I said: 'College Hill? The old rubber factory?'

'That's right.'

'How long ago was this?' I nudged Stevenson and put the call on the loudspeaker so that he could listen.

'Less than an hour ago. He's taken lots of them; he's taking them all the time.'

'Where the hell is he taking them from?' I shouted.

'He's up on the rooftop opposite. Spavento's place has three big windows, and from where my boy is he can cover them all.'

I said: 'Are you in contact with him?'

'Yes,' said Cryer. 'By walkie-talkie. I'm down in the street. So what do we do?'

'Keep on doing exactly what you are doing till we get over there, which'll be as quick as it takes four wheels,' I said. I added: 'What's Spavento doing right now?'

'Wait,' said Cryer. There was a pause while he contacted the photographer on the roof. When he came back on, he said: 'Nothing. He's lying on a bundle of old rags in a corner, staring up at the ceiling; he's using a black Adidas sports bag for a pillow.'

'Christ, where is this photographer of yours?' I said. 'In the room with Spavento or something?'

'You know it makes no difference,' said Cryer. 'With the lenses we use it's as if he were.'

I said: 'Where do we find you when we arrive?'

'Public call box halfway up College Hill.'

I said: 'Right.' I said to Stevenson: 'This is it. Come on, let's motor.' As we started downstairs I said to him: 'No chance of any of our people being over there, is there?'

'How could there be?' said Stevenson. 'Nobody knows where Spavento is except you, me and the press.'

'It's the press that bothers me. Anyway, thank God for that— I don't want a single leak here.'

'Any particular reason?'

'Yes,' I said, 'I'll explain later.' We reached the Ford in the police park and got in.

'I've got reasons of my own,' I repeated, 'I'll explain later.'

We had reached the south side of the river when Stevenson turned to me suddenly and said: 'By the way, you've got a serious-looking bulge in your right-hand pocket. You're armed, aren't you?'

'Yes,' I said, 'I am for once.'

'When did you draw the pistol?'

'I didn't,' I said. 'It's my own pistol, a .38.'

'Look,' he said, 'it's none of my business, but you know it's against the law for you to be carrying anything other than a police weapon when you're on duty.'

'I know what the law is,' I said calmly. I added: 'What about you?'

He said, 'No, I'm clean the way you usually go. I hate fire-arms.'

I said: 'So do I, but this is different.'

'Why?' he said. 'Why is it different? Spavento's neither more nor less dangerous than any other maniac.'

'That's not it,' I said. 'This is just different. I repeat, I'll explain to you later, when we get down there.'

He said: 'You've not treated this case the way you treat other cases—not since the first moment you were put on it. Can I ask you, just between ourselves, as two men, why that is? Is it the victim that's different?'

'Yes,' I said, 'yes. For me Suarez is totally, utterly different.'

'But why?'

'I can't tell you why,' I said. 'To me she's not just reference A14 stroke 87471, she's just different.'

'Just Suarez?' Stevenson said. 'What about 87472? What about Mrs Carstairs?'

'She too, of course.'

'But it's Suarez, really.'

'Yes,' I said, 'it's Dora, yes.'

'Dora?'

'I don't want to go into it any more. Please don't try and make me.'

'Be careful,' Stevenson said.

'Why?' I said. 'There are plenty of careful people around—too many.'

We didn't speak any more for a while but drove on down the South Circular, making for the Lovelock Road turnoff which led to College Hill. Dora was in my mind—Dora's box, Dora's book, the photographs of Dora. It suddenly started to pour with rain.

'I wish you'd tell me what you were going to do,' said Stevenson.

'I will in a minute.'

'Do you know yourself?'

I said: 'Yes.' A light turned amber and we sat in a silence broken only by the dirty rain pelting on the dirty windscreen.

'I wish I understood.'

'You understand all right,' I said. 'Anyway part of it—the part about realising how it was for Suarez, being axed to death; I'm convinced her arm was cut at the shoulder like that as she reached out to try and plead with her killer. The rest of it, thank God, she knew nothing about—being drunk from, masturbated into; and all that the very night you had decided to kill yourself anyway.'

'Yes, I suppose I do,' he said.

'We can never suppose in our job,' I said.

The whole dreadful mosaic was in my head, my saying to the crew of the morgue ambulance, yes, I've finished now, you can take them away, taking a last look at Suarez in what was left of her new dress as they covered her and put her on the stretcher; at the two overturned bottles of wine which were to have been her send-off to the other world, at her new shoes lying in a corner, at the magazine lying open at the advertised holiday in Hawaii. There, too, in my head as I drove through the heavy, early-night traffic was her uninjured arm, stark white, which appeared to be waving us all freely onward into a different world; and there were her thighs again under the thin material of her dress, too heavy and out of proportion to her now, swollen on account of the blood which, because of the position she had died in, had drained down into them. There was the tightly-clenched little fist that belonged to her bad arm, the one half hacked off; there were her black eyes eternally devouring the secret of an empty corner.

Off the South Circular Road I started reading off the names— Neanderthal Avenue, Sobers Street, Gunters Passage. I said to Stevenson: 'Lovelock Road ought to be third on the left after the next set of lights.'

Cryer came on; I always gave him the frequency. He said: 'Where the hell are you?'

'Nearly there,' I said. 'Why, what's happening?'

He said: 'How can I start explaining to you what you've never seen before?'

'Your feller still up on that roof?'

'Yes.'

'His nerve holding out?'

'Just about.'

'What's Spavento doing?' I said.

'You might call it some kind of training,' said Cryer.

I could hear his voice shaking even over the radio. 'We're coming,' I said, 'we're two minutes away.'

'You're going to have a nightmare job.'

'I was constructed to have nightmares,' I said.

'Don't drive up all the way to the factory,' Cryer said, 'Mike says he seems like nervous, uneasy. There's an Indian take-away fifty yards before on the left as you come up off the South Circular, you can't miss it, I can see it from the roof here, it's all lit up.'

'We'll meet you there,' I said. 'What does it look like in Spavento's room?'

'Horrible,' said Cryer. 'It's unbelievable what he's doing—anyway, Mike says it's too disgusting to print, and it's a story I couldn't write for the paper, it belongs in Krafft-Ebing country.'

I saw the take-away and said: 'Don't bother, we're here. Come down to the caff, Tom.'

# 10

The killer was looking carefully round the very edge of the middle of the three glassless windows of what had been the old machine workshop down into the street. He didn't know why, but he was nervous. He told himself he was really well hidden out and so had nothing to worry about, but it didn't help; instinctively he was sure something was gliding over him.

He was taking the fifteen-minute break from training as he did every three hours, timing himself with his plastic multiprogramme wristwatch, and had just now balanced the trainer neatly in its corner, noting that the rusted spokes were satisfyingly covered with his blood—he was only sad that there was no one on the dishes placed around the workshop to watch him perform. He put his thick lips to his blood as he placed the trainer against the wall burned grey by fire; then, having looked out of the window, he moved slowly backwards and stood where he could see the street from a point in the workshop that lay in deep shadow, where neither daylight nor streetlight ever reached.

He was in very great pain after the last session, but he nodded slightly to himself about that, knowing that the pain was necessary—as with creation, destruction overrode every other desire. He opened his fly, that he had only just zipped up, and looked down at himself in there for the sheer pleasure of it; in the middle of the mat of blood that lay in the crotch of his sporting joggers now there was practically nothing left of that at all, just red shreds. Pain was a liking which you grew to love.

'I'm really honed now,' he whispered. 'Honed.'

Some hours before he had felt it imperative that he should go down to a boozer called the Double Barrel not far off in Oakley Grove, and so he had put his running shoes on, the new spiked ones that he had found for himself over in Brent Cross, paced himself over there and trotted in. Neither people nor alcohol had ever interested him, but he was often, though outwardly impassive, excited to see the effect that both had on others, and himself on them. He could never share their lives—the very idea of being involved with others made him shudder, though he had a series of carefully observed copies which superficially worked to attract a victim. He could be entrancing, serious with his good looks; only it was death to peel off the image, even to interrupt or in any way trespass on him, as thirteen dead people could tell if they could tell. He had been constructed to remain outside in the dark, alone; so he avenged himself by seizing one of these creatures from time to time as the ferocity of his desire seized him, and when his training permitted. Because of this self-punishment, when he did attract and ensnare a victim, any form of death was allowed.

He also killed for a living; look at Roatta. Like everyone else, he had to live.

Just now he had looked down at his new car parked in the street—he had wrecked the Fiat and dumped it. The replacement was a nice Volkswagen Golf, 1988, suburban-villa clean, silver grey with Kent plates. It had been standing opposite the Double Barrel and he had watched the owner, minor businessman by the look of him, go in there and order what looked like a glass of Chianti at the bar in a haw-haw chummy voice.

He had looked the Volks over carefully and decided yes, it

would do for him—he liked the car. The interior upholstery was
pale, but that didn't matter; he had a special little absorbent mat
in his sports bag which would prevent any blood getting on the
driver's seat. He thought of everything.

When the owner of the car drained his glass, stood up and left
the pub, the killer let him leave, then followed—he suddenly felt
like a bit of motoring, out in the quiet of country places somewhere, get his lungs clean. He went and stood over on the pavement not far from the Golf. A half-cut punter, staggering past
him, said to the killer: ''Scuse me but your balls are bleeding.'

'Thanks for the good news,' the killer said.

'Don't work the old mechanism too hard.' The punter laughed,
tottering away into the dark of South London, 'that's the motto,
old boy.'

'I won't forget,' the killer said, but luckily for the old drunk
his attention was on the car; he suddenly had to have it.

The man, the owner of the car that the killer was waiting to
drive, came over to the Golf. He was about to unlock it—had
the keys shining in his hand, in fact—when the killer strolled over
on his spiky shoes and appeared beside him suddenly as a shadow,
very close—so near that the car owner could breathe him.

'What do you want?' the man said.

'Your car,' the killer said, 'luckily for you.' From behind he
locked an arm which felt as if it were made of steel cable round
the owner's neck, taking care that his face couldn't be seen. The
car owner's face brightened redly under the pressure till it looked
like a darkroom bulb. The killer grabbed the keys; then he
smashed the owner across the face with the back of his hand,
felling him. The killer's wedding finger carried a ring with a big
false ruby stone in it, cut sharp, which he always wore in memory
of the bride he had never had.

And now there was the car, parked out in the street, glittering
and clean, with only fifty extra miles on the counter that hadn't

been there before, and not a scratch to show for it. He had just been driving around; he had rationed himself a rest from training.

It had been a day of cold bright sunlight, but now College Hill had swiftly darkened into night, and that made the killer feel curiously sad, empty and depressed; he had a horrible feeling suddenly, which he had never had before, that all at once there was no further point to him. He turned quickly to his reflection in a remaining piece of corner window glass for reassurance, but because of the position of the sinking sun, he somehow could not get himself into focus. He travelled through all his usual magic, his formulae, his women, his killing, his physical beauty—but this time the magic turned him down flat, bypassing him; it seemed to be telling him good-bye, it had gone somewhere new.

Now, feeling out of luck, and against his will, he remembered some words that he wished immediately that he had never heard of but that he must have at some time heard: 'Sweet Thames run softly, till I end my song.' By an association that he did not try to place because he was unable to, the rhythm of the words recalled not only the river but also a boat on the water that had a still, painted look about it. There were two people in the boat—a couple—and then by a relentless progression, a tall old clock came to his mind; the clock was broken and there was someone like an old woman who smelled bad lying partly inside it. The memory was fresh, startling and new, and it worried him empty, sick; it made him feel old and ugly, though he had no means of knowing why. It also tore him up inside because he was not equipped to have memories. He could not imagine what memories he would have if he was able to have them.

Again he felt instinctively that he was being watched—the thing he most feared and hated. He slipped sideways on back to the window corner a second time, but he could see nothing unusual either down in the street or across it in the few other windows.

Stripped naked as he was, if you took care not to look at his privates, he still superficially looked good—short, but hard and muscular, a curly-haired beachboy except for the gear he wore across his stomach for his training, which struck a wrong note. He was pouring with sweat after his last session and he was strapped into yet another brand-new pair of racing-cycling shoes, black with bright pink bands this time. The big black mat of his pubic hair satisfyingly stated his maleness, replacing what had once been the shy pinkness of his penis, which, while it still existed, used to hide its tiny head in it, looped permanently sideways; yet otherwise there was no reason why he shouldn't be feeling great, thanks to his slow but sure mastery over the rest of himself through training and punishment. Indeed, in an effort to re-create this old sensation in himself he snapped the great leather band strapped around his dark waist with his contorted thumbs, but the sound came back at him from the burnt, blackened walls of the place as a bark of laughter so realistic that he whipped round to see if some joker was actually there.

Anxious, restless for a reason he couldn't name, he sped—he always moved very quickly—around the room and checked that the door that led onto the black staircase, still choked with the rubbish left after the fire, was well blocked. He couldn't lock the door as he would have liked to because there was no lock and no key. He had already checked all the outdoors while the light lasted to find the source of the warning message that his instinct brought him, but the area was a mass of high buildings festooned with chimneys; any enemy could find a vantage point and watch him. He had to be so careful—the simplest precautions were always the best; he had learned that in his childhood. It was the only memory he had of it—when he used to piss the bed, after the first few beatings from the captain, wet or shine, he slept on the floor with the end of his penis in the neck of a lemonade bottle. As long as he was first up in the dormitory of forty he could empty the night's result down the jacks.

His nameless anxiety increasing, the killer now put on a pair of racing-cycling gloves and began hurrying, flitting about in the room, its darkness relieved only by the faint, general glow of the city, cleaning away every place in the room where he might have left fingerprints. He pissed once into the rusty old bucket the other end of the workshop from where he slept. The movement made him groan with agony; he had to noodle and massage his penis with a fierce gentleness until somehow the water could finally pass.

He could be quickly packed if he had to be. He would have to leave his training gear behind him; it was too unwieldy to take and besides would hamper him if he was in a rush. It was a pity, because he had got it just the way he wanted it and it was really well run in. Still, it could be replaced at any breaker's yard, or even a council rubbish dump.

# 11

Stevenson and I parked well downhill from the take-away on the side of the street where, according to the large-scale map we had, we couldn't possibly be seen from Spavento's building at all, getting out of the car which was automatically a good thing because the street was calmish now that it was well dark, and so the less movement there was around, the better. Cryer saw us arriving from the entrance of the little bar-restaurant and made a sign, but seeing that the place inside behind him was packed with folk, I made a negative sign at him with my forefinger and then waved at him to cross the street our side.

When Cryer joined us, I said: 'We can't possibly talk in there.'

'Where, then?'

'Under this lamppost why not?' I said. 'It'll do fine.'

When we were there, Stevenson said to Cryer: 'What the hell is going on up there?'

Cryer held out a big envelope to us and said: 'This, Mike threw the film down into the street and here are the prints.'

'Before I start,' said Stevenson, drawing the blowups out of the envelope, 'am I supposed to go into a state of shock over these?'

'How do I know?' Cryer said. 'All I can tell you is that I'm a married man and that I did; in fact, I'm still in it.'

'That's because you're not a copper,' said Stevenson. He divided the stack of photographs in two and passed on half to me.

'Go easy with them,' Cryer said.

We started to look at the pictures and presently Stevenson said: 'What does he think he's doing? Is he an acrobat cycling on one wheel or something?'

Cryer looked over his shoulder and said: 'He isn't properly mounted yet.'

I said: 'He's mounted with the ones I've got here.'

Stevenson looked over my shoulder at the pictures I had and said: 'Holy Christ.'

I said: 'The scroll of wire that it had to go through was lovingly made, wasn't it?'

Cryer said: 'But what's the shape of that wire?'

'Can't you see it's the shape of a vagina,' I said. 'The penis is locked into the far end of the wire and so stretched into the semblance of an erection, and the man on the tyreless wheel rolls backwards and forwards, keeping himself balanced with his hands on the floor, as you can see here, as if in the act of intercourse, and the process has to continue until he comes, and that could take hours.'

'Good for the muscles,' said Stevenson.

'All except one,' I said.

'Why that big band across his stomach?' said Stevenson.

'To stop the wheel rim from biting into him,' I said.

'It's insane,' said Cryer.

'Of course it is,' I said. 'Pain is inflicted by those who have no idea what it means,' I said, 'because they inflict pain on themselves. A man, a butterfly—it's all the same to a torturer. Violence replaces love with the psychopath. Or, better still, violence is love with them. The psychopath has no means of knowing what he's doing. Otherwise,' I added, 'he's perfectly normal—drives a car, goes to work, even marries sometimes. It works fine for a while, kiddies and all, until something explodes, and then we're called, don't I know.'

Stevenson said: 'I don't believe these pictures.'

'There are others,' I said.

'You can see we can't print these,' said Cryer. 'Half our readers would have a heart attack, and the other half would switch papers—we'd be broke in a week.'

'Yes, I know,' I said, 'the press can't afford to roll the carpet back too far.' I added: 'I told you it wouldn't be a big story.'

'Oh, it's big all right,' said Cryer. 'Only it's too big.'

'Well, I'm not standing here all night,' I said. 'Let's stop wasting time.' I said to Cryer: 'Show us the way up to that roof of yours; I want to have a look at him. Your boy up there, has he got a night-sight camera?'

'Of course.'

I said: 'Then let's get there. No chance of his seeing us?'

'None,' said Cryer, 'even in daytime. We go up the fire escape at the back of the block opposite; the roof's the same height as Spavento's floor.'

'OK,' I said, 'away we go.' We started walking over there through the rain.

Cryer said: 'Getting him out of there's going to be dangerous.'

'If he doesn't feel like coming with us,' said Stevenson, 'yes, very.'

I said: 'Well, then, it's a good thing we had a good look at Tom's photographs here, particularly the one which shows him loading the Quickhammer, isn't it?' Cryer said: 'All right now, through this gate and up that path, then round the back of the building and to the right.'

I said: 'And no torches, no lights at all.'

Indirectly, from an angle beside the window, standing in an intense draught which grew from the night wind, the killer had come back to stand again and stare down at the Golf which was his wings of a dove; but it was growing steadily less visible in the sparse streetlights of College Hill and the massing dark. He was all packed, and had a growing desire to go down with his Adidas bag, take the car and drive; its keys tinkled in his hand—they were the escape from his feeling that he was shut in and being watched. He felt driven to move; the impulse to move was beginning to drive him like steam behind a piston, the gauge steadily rising. He had bandaged himself up roughly between his legs. True, he had had to leave legacies of himself behind in the place, the assorted dishes on the floor with their ancient stains, the wheel—he couldn't take the risk of going out into the street laden down with all that, and anyway he was a man who travelled light. And yet his instinct urged him above all not to move—not to open his door and go out into the street, whatever he did.

A peculiar lassitude, a sadness, began to take charge of him now as he stood with his face leaning against the corner of masonry by the window, and a growing certainty that he had stolen the car for nothing; some voice told him that he would never get the chance to use it. Lost between counterstorms of rage and fear, he bellowed aloud at this invading anguish which was quite new to him; he had never before been forced into conscious knowledge of his own hopelessness. It was a condition of complete interior absence, the emptiness of collapse which, although he had known it fleetingly after he had been in action, he had never known settle in him like a dark, flapping, sharp-beaked bird before as it was doing now, or torture him as his scattered periods of sleep had done, or as his filthy dreams did. This motionless, seemingly permanent pain that had suddenly kicked its way into him— new in that for the first time he was aware of it—opened him up as if he were nothing but a long-deserted, rotten front door, and moved in on him, a squatting black void that had moved in on him to stay. He was completely unprepared for it, coming for him as it did from a quarter and in a way to which he was fully vulnerable.

The worst part of what he was just starting to go through was that it seemed to him that the bird was exactly his own shape and was trying to burst it. He could feel it crawling in him, trying to exercise its great wings inside him. It precisely filled him; it filled him exactly as an egg fills its shell. Yet it was also his converse. Although it was as invisible as he was invisible to himself, it was as much at its ease inside him as he was in pain. It pecked deftly about in his interior when it felt its feeding time had come, just as it pleased, and he was sure it was beginning to pass its first stools inside him. They were stools of himself; the bird was banqueting on his husky, attractive body and then shitting in him, hopping slowly around inside him, coughing up rotting morsels of himself that it couldn't yet digest, or else storing them away in another place inside him with its beak for evaluation later. He felt that the presence inside him of this great black bird of absence meant that he by contrast was on the way out, screwed, fucked, finished, and that he was condemned to be pecked at slowly and eaten forever by this succubus, feeding greatly, as and when it felt inclined, delicately or voraciously, on those most delicate parts of himself, which, up to this moment, only he himself had felt entitled to destroy. For the first time in his thirty-eight years of life it occurred to him whether his own death might not be preferable to the death of others if his only future was going to consist of being rotten prey until he did die.

He wanted to act; but for the first time the gale of action roared through him as though he were a rotted sail which it blew to tatters, leaving him listing and beached above a sullen reddish brown tide; he had already, in the first few minutes of his new state, lost too much of his strength and violence to what was now inside him. Hopelessly, he pulled the shreds of his cock out and tried to knead it, thrash it, stretch, force, excite it into some semblance of an erection, staring with a rapt, glassy expression of exaltation up at the blackened cement of the ceiling. After what he had been doing to it all day, it was streaming with blood; there was nothing left of it for him to get hold of, so that in the end, groaning, he smacked himself there on it in his frustration, crying, whimpering and drivelling with rage, with one of his youthful little racing shoes whose spiked heel went straight into the thick black mat of his hair there.

Then, with his two bands still round his waist, naked, he pushed his training machine back out into the room again and got onto it with a weariness that was being rigidly observed.

We watched him through the lens of the photographer's camera.

'How are we going to get him out?' Stevenson said.

I said: 'I'll get him out.'

Cryer was saying: 'He's getting back on his wheel again.'

The photographer said: 'Christ, look at him ride, look, there's blood going down all over the floor.' He took a lot of film. 'Nobody's ever going to believe this,' he muttered, 'if it weren't for the film.'

'Christ, his cock,' said Cryer, 'there can't be anything left of it.'

'See for yourself through the lens,' said the photographer, 'there isn't.'

We all watched Spavento by turns. He moved slowly on the wheel, backwards and forwards, propelling the wheel with his hands along the floor and balancing himself with his muscular legs. Every time his prick declined, part of it bulged through the wire scroll and was forced to brush harder and harder against the revolving spokes.

Cryer said: 'It will take me three weeks before I can face Angela and the kid again after this.'

'You should have gone in for literary criticism,' Stevenson said, 'not crime reporting.'

The photographer said: 'I'm sorry for the poor cunt.'

I said: 'Don't be. We reckon he's responsible for the deaths of Suarez and Carstairs, also for the deaths of twelve or thirteen other people. He has to be nailed and he's going to be. You're looking at someone in hell; you're looking at the truth that the British public never want to see in print. The public want just the grimy outline, not the intimate revolting details.'

'All right then,' said Stevenson, 'so what do we do?'

I said: 'We're going to start by sending the press home.'

Cryer said: 'You can't do that to me. Not now.'

I said: 'Now look, Tom, don't start. What I say goes. Now I'm sorry, but there it is. You won't be out over it; I never let my mates down. You're the only paper on the scene, you've got the pictures, you've lived the story, you print what your editor will let you print.'

'What do I have to say so I can stay on?'

'There are no words for the music,' I said. 'It's not on.'

Stevenson said to him: 'You heard the man.'

I said: 'Let's get back to street level.'

Cryer and his photographer got into their car, Cryer saying to me: 'You've been a real bastard over this.'

I leaned in at his window and whispered: 'I'm not. You'll see later. I've got my reasons.' I added: 'I don't know how to thank you for tracking Spavento down.' I added: 'I have special feelings over Suarez.'

'What?' The photographer laughed. 'Over a dead girl?'

'Shut your mouth,' I whispered to him, 'just shut it and make sure it stays that way.' I said to Cryer: 'I'll ring you when this is over, Tom; then you and I and Angela can have that meal together.'

'You'll never come for it,' he said. 'You never do.' He did a swift U-turn and I watched his car vanish left into the South Circular Road. I turned back to Stevenson, who was leaning with his back to the wall by the entrance to the block where Spavento was.

'Well?' he said, 'now what?'

'The plan's easy,' I said, 'it's the execution that's moody, I'm going in there.' We stood in deep shadow and spoke very quietly.

'Right, let's go, then.'

'No,' I said. 'You're going back to the Factory, and you're going now.'

He shook his head. 'No chance,' he said. 'Sorry.'

I said: 'Spavento is down to me. Suarez and Carstairs is my case.'

'No,' he said, 'It can't be done.'

'You don't understand,' I said. 'Look, you've got family responsibilities. I haven't. You've got some kind of career in front of you; I haven't. A14 only fetched me back up off the beach because they'd got no other moron to put on this. I've always been expendable as far as the brass is concerned, and I tell you, that's the only reason they're using me—they'll junk me again once I've done their work for them.'

'You're making no sense at all,' he said. 'The two of us can cut this madman out upstairs there, all right, but just you on your own, that could go either way.'

'You still haven't understood,' I said. 'This'll only go one way. There'll only be one to come out. There's going to be no paperwork on this.'

He said: 'I believe you love Suarez.'

I said: 'That was what I was trying to tell you in your office earlier; only when I found her at long last, she was dead.'

Stevenson said: 'For God's sake.'

I said: 'You are a friend of mine, but even so you can't know what I know or feel, you are not me, and I am going to avenge her now, as I swore I would when I kissed her head, and you have heard nothing, seen nothing—so now go—this is between me and the responsible man. I tell you again, there'll only be one to come out, so now go.'

'You're armed at least,' he said.

I said: 'I'm out of practise but I am, and for the reason I've given you, if it is a reason. Now take the car and leave, the keys are in it.'

'You've got no defence in court at all,' he said, 'if you kill him.'

I said: 'If I'm dead, I shan't need one. If I live, then the only man who can put me away for twenty years is you.' I said: 'That depends on you, and I depend on you—knowing what you know, you must do as you think best, but you won't stop me now. My mind is made up and that's the end of it, so now will you just leave me be?'

'I can't let you risk your life like this.'

'It's my risk.'

'I repeat, you're taking the law into your own hands.'

'It's better in my hands than in no hands.'

'It isn't for us to make the law,' Stevenson said, 'we're here to uphold it.'

'Suarez was your sister,' I said, 'your daughter, your wife.'

'You're not meant to think like that,' he said. 'You're a copper.'

'If I didn't think like that, I wouldn't be a copper,' I said. 'If I didn't think like that, there'd be no point in being a copper or anything else.'

'Drop it.'

'No.'

'All we've got to do is get into the car and call the mob up—wait till the mob comes round to get him out, that's what they're paid for.'

'No,' I said. I pushed him over to the Ford.

'Will you stop being such a cunt,' said Stevenson. 'Everyone in the Factory knows they want to take you back and promote you; don't fuck it up over this maniac now.'

'I don't want to be promoted,' I said, 'I've never wanted to be promoted.'

'What do you want then, for Christ's sweet sake?'

'I don't know if what I want exists,' I said, 'but that doesn't alter the fact I want it, and I'm sure I'm not the only one. And don't raise your voice,' I added, 'I want him quiet till I get up to him.'

He saw that the game was set out; he understood now and got into the Ford. As he started it he said: 'I'm not going home, I'll be in 202. Ring me the second you're finished.'

As I watched Stevenson leave and prepared to go up against Spavento I wondered if even those really close to each other and comfortable in their lives now understood any more what that means, the ruin and end of a life in a disgusting way, or if perhaps they have forgotten what that mortal sickness which we call despair really means.

For so many people, and good people, too, are now, thank God, at last well based in their lives after the miserable horrors of the war that they are perhaps no longer capable of imagining themselves as a face against a wall with no further to go. But I had joined the police in order to protect the weak in the same spirit as any volunteer for the same cause in any domain—only with me it was not the hospital, but the street.

If you want to deal with evil, you must live with it and know it. In my work you have no chance at all of beating what you don't know, whose language you can't speak; the margin is very tight, and the risk of being corrupted accordingly very near.

I loved Dora, not only because I found her beautiful for me, but also because I felt so ashamed that we should have allowed her to fall so far; and so I was sure that in human law, by going up to Spavento now, I was at least acting as the shield that she should have had; I even felt that I was perhaps taking a step towards that time when others like her would be protected from the death that she and Betty Carstairs had suffered. For the span of my own lifetime I would always arrive too late, but I felt I must try to look forward to a day when that would all be altered, so that we would no longer only be able to obtain justice for people after they were dead. I know that if it were for me ever to command anything, I would have a centre where people frightened for their lives could come and be seriously listened to, their fears sifted, analysed and acted upon, and not just be told to fuck off and stop wasting police time.

There was a door, a heavy steel one, that had once, before the fire, given access to the factory building on the high platform at the delivery bay end which had been barred across and yet still presented no problem since the door had been half torn out of the cement wall and lay half sprawling on its lower hinges. I checked my pistol before I went in and then jammed it between my belly and waistband just in front of my right hip, pushing the right-hand end of my jacket into the back of my belt so that there would be nothing between the weapon and my hand. I felt very afraid. By a blink of my flashlight I saw that although the staircase ahead of me, rising beyond the lorry weigh-bridge by the side of the glassed-in dispatch manager's office was blackened by fire, it was built of cement and intact. A cat shrieked on a minor note and flew towards the shattered jacks, and I started up the stairs, not slowly, but listening. Through the twisted window frames between the floors the city glowed blue and orange and made a sound like a gagged man trying to speak; but inside me Dora was saying to me all over again from out of her exercise book from Empire Gate:

When I was little, about eight or nine, my father took us back to Spain, and I left my parents and wandered until I found myself in a deep abandoned garden down between rocks where olive trees still managed to grow; there was a thin stream which bubbled up from underground into a pool hardly bigger than a hand mirror, and there I leaned on my arms against its edge and stared into it, wondering what was going to become of me. I never forgot that moment, I think because my experience happened in that country, whose race I am partly from.

I climbed another floor, and at an angle of the blackened stairs her lost voice rang inside me for the first time, high and clear, but imprecise, yet as if she were trying to thank me, reach out for me to help me and be helped.

I felt sure she was glad I had heard her and I whispered: 'Dora, look after me,' whereupon I felt her smile pass straight through me and knew that she was released forever from this earth and that I would come through all right, too, because of her.

I suddenly thought as I crawled on up the stairs, 'I wish Dora could have known my sister Julie.' I have always loved Julie; she lives just outside Oxford and she is the only family I have left now. For I knew that if Dora had come to her in trouble, Julie would have sat her down in the comfortable chair in the sitting room by the electric fire and made her a cup of tea or poured her a shot of whisky just as Betty Carstairs had. She would never have asked Dora any questions—Julie never did that—and in the end Dora would have confided in Julie as another woman and told her whatever she felt like saying, and Julie would have helped her in a way that Betty couldn't because she was too old, whereas Julie was only five years older than Dora would have been. At any rate I felt sure that if the two of them could only have met in time, Dora would be alive now and then I would have taken her to me; but in the meantime Julie would have lodged her in the attic bedroom where I always slept on my rare time off from the Factory, and as for her physical condition, Julie knew a lot of specialists in Oxford because she did hospital work, clerical, in the hospitals during her time off from her job in the town hall. Julie is a big fresh girl like an apple, a kind, intelligent girl, there aren't many like her left in Britain now, and she is my lovely sister, too, we have always been very close—and we would have saved Dora, only it was too late now.

What else had Dora said?

> We are all made to give what we have. (Be patient with me, love, just till I can face my end; that will be a great release for me, but I don't think you're equipped to understand.) I have always feared the great questions and now here they are, entering me just as I'm ready to leave my gross, sick body, and now I pray only, as I prepare myself, that nothing, nothing what-ever may be left over of me after my flesh. Oh please not: all I desire is to vanish completely, is it possible?

We are all much too far off from each other. 'For,' she wrote,

> one night Jesus came to me in a dream, carved, and in white, and told me that it was now time for me to fly, to take my wings back that I had put aside for a while and fly back to my own country. He told me it would be all right, and he held out his hand to me, which I took; I had never felt a hand like his before, and never shall again.

She added:

> I loved the man who has done me nothing but wrong and evil because he was in even deeper misery than I was. I said to him only, over and over, try not to hurt me. But he is going to hurt me.

She concluded:

> Once I had lost what I thought was my honour, I went on the streets for money at first as a means of trying to fight to get my honour back, but only lost still more of it there. But

then I thought, perhaps there is a different kind of honour in our case. And I suppose I must at least have been partly right because I found the sense of it at least did return after some years. True, it staggered back into me like a wounded sparrow, but I saw my honour differently when it came home to me like that, sick, than I could ever have done if I had never lost it.

The killer had stopped all training; he stood motionless, naked in his big bands, in the three-quarters dark because of the streetlights, his mouth slightly open, wondering if he had not heard a noise on the staircase, a soft noise which he had never heard at that hour before, if he had in fact heard it, he wasn't yet sure. The blacks and the rest of the district smashed the factory up for fun, but they always made plenty of noise about it; that never bothered him. But this was a soft, slipping noise that he believed he heard; it might be nothing, or else it could just relate to a pair of soft, deliberate feet.

Women! His old ones! Sometimes they came back to haunt him. At times he was aware of their faint dead voices in the silence that surrounded him; he frowned at the echoes of their babbling squawks as they perished; he caught again, like bile coming back up in his throat after a bad meal, a nose dipping into a Schweppes ashtray in a cheap hotel somewhere as its owner died, was at times, in his head, pursued by the tap of girls' shoes on a pavement, by the smell of their scent and sweat, by all the madness of his life's work.

He belched suddenly. He had just eaten a small scrape of his shit which he had saved in a cotton bag; it was all he ever permitted himself when he was on punishment training. He was incapable of wondering what he was doing it all for, what he meant or what he was proving, apart, of course, from the straight excellence of his bones, his limbs, his curly hair, his superb physique, trained to an ounce: he would never understand that to others he looked curved, tired, his eyes blank and dead, his hair dirty, his sodden trousers an embarrassment, his endless stories about himself in the pub frankly a fucking bore, his monotone insistence on death, punishment, how he would rather fuck a dog than a woman, not really what most folk wanted to listen to when they came down to the boozer for a pair of jars.

But the killer, listening to the stairs, did suddenly feel tired as well as, after his final stretch with the wheel, in pain. For now, casually, uninvited, this terrible bird had now come to nest and exist in him. It was now even darker, more insolently at home in himself than it had been at first, and behaved in him, in every realm of him, in a provocative and deliberate manner, turning and hopping round more and more nosily and aggressively inside him, arranging its greasy, poisonous wings with their green and scarlet sheen as it pleased with its predatory beak, suiting itself boldly to his interior; its presence created this new exhaustion in him, draining his strength, agility and beauty. Shocked, he waited in terror, facing the door, while the bird did its own thing inside him, independent. Even with the Quickhammer in his hand he had a chill, muddy certainty in himself that if anything was going to happen, this time he wasn't going to make it. He had felt himself being invisibly watched all day, and although he insisted to himself that he was as fast, fit, trim and well as ever he had been, inside he felt that with half his natural purpose, the one between his legs, destroyed, he might be going to fail, fall and die.

Earlier I had thought: 'How could Suarez and Spavento between them ever have known what love was?'

But she explained it for me in what she had written to him on a paper serviette that I found in her box at Empire Gate: 'You always drew me to you in spite of everything—I know we can help each other.'

But all the killer remembered from time to time was the crisp smack of his axe severing her arm at the shoulder when she sought to reason with him.

As I went up through the dark to Spavento's place, Dora spoke and said: 'It's all right, I held Betty right to the end and we saw each other through, all right, even through the fire, and she's just resting now.' She added: 'It's wonderful for us to know that you love us.'

I said: 'I do love you.'

'Our door's always open.'

'It's finding it's the problem.'

'It's there.'

'I wish we could have met while we had time,' I said.

'It's always the same,' she said, 'we never do.'

'Why, Dora?'

But she only said: 'Good-bye now, and good luck,' just as Stevenson had.

When I got up to Spavento's floor, I saw, well before I had reached it, that his door some seven feet above me was open, a pale square in the blackness lit by the city beyond. I made sure that the gun was loose, easy in my waistband, just how I wanted it, then I walked up the rest of the stairs. When Spavento spoke from somewhere in the dark room, saying he was armed, I said: 'I am a police officer and I have a warrant for your arrest, so whatever you're holding in the way of fire irons, sonny, drop it.'

'It doesn't work like that with me at all,' said Spavento, and fired at wherever he thought I was.

It certainly wasn't one of those pistols you drill defaulting gamblers with across a coffee table. The bullet was a huge one: it flattened itself into an iron stair rail just behind me; bits that were left of it whined off into the darkness of the silent floor above and did a lot of damage to glass and plaster that had already been ruined—stuff fell, rang, showered and tinkled downwards till they hit the ground floor.

I didn't draw my own gun but just went straight into the place.

I was in a state where I found I didn't care. I said to Spavento: 'Do you make me?'

'I make you.'

'Well, in that case,' I said, 'you can see I'm armed.' I cocked the pistol and said, as if introducing two people at a party: 'This is a Smith and Wesson .38.'

He said: 'Are you a police officer?'

I said: 'The way you're placed now it makes no difference to you who I am; I'm here.'

'Why?'

'Suarez,' I said. 'Carstairs.'

'What are you going to do about them?' he said, aiming at me in the blackness.

'I'm going to kill you,' I said. 'Now either drop that gun you've got or else fire it. Go on, go on!' I shouted. 'Let's see who's fastest, fuck you.' He aimed at me, hesitated, then turned half aside. 'All right,' I said, 'if you're not going to fire it, throw the fucking thing on the floor; come on, I haven't got all night.'

He dropped the Quickhammer on the floor. 'I loved Dora,' he said, 'I couldn't let her alone.' He added, with a hint of shy pride: 'She loved me, too, of course.'

'I know,' I said. 'I saw the proof of that in the morgue; don't let's go into it.'

I went up closer to him; for the first time I noticed how both he and the place stank. 'What are these dishes doing on the floor here?' I said.

He said: 'There's no secret—I stood their heads on them so they could watch me while I punished myself.'

'How many?' I said.

'Ten. Twelve maybe. I'm not sure.'

'What happened to the heads when they finally got tired watching you?' I asked him.

'Well, you know what it is,' he said. 'Confidentially speaking, they started to smell so bad that I had to junk them in the death. Pity, but there you are.'

'Let's have judge, jury and accused all on a friendlier basis here,' I remarked. 'After all, we're all in the same room, so let's chat for a minute before any action's taken.'

He didn't seem to mind, just said: 'Excuse me if I hold my balls in for a moment, I'm bleeding there rather hard.'

I took no notice of him; I was poking about in a heap of dirty rags with my gun barrel. Finally I said: 'What are all these filthy old knickers doing here?'

He said: 'They're my souvenirs. You know, like a photograph album kind of thing. I like sniff them and so on sometimes when I'm in the mood, I sort through them at times, they kind of remind me of things that are over.'

'You should have gone for treatment,' I said, 'but it's too late now.' I added sharply: 'Get up.' Spavento had gone to sit down on the rags he had for a bed; there he had splayed his thighs apart and stroked away the blood from the crotch of his grey jogging trousers with his finger ends, sniffing it, considering it, even licking it from them. But the dull light still caught the Quickhammer which lay too near him for me. I said to him again, louder: 'I said, get up.'

He moved with the speed of a snake for the Quickhammer. I aimed at his heart and said: 'Forget it, Tony, you can't win.'

'Aren't you afraid I'm going to let you have dumdum number two?'

'No,' I said, 'I'm not. Now get up.'

When he was on his feet, I said: 'Now pick up that gun of yours. Go on, pick it up.'

'Why?' he said.

I said: 'Don't ask questions, just do as you're told.'

He picked the gun up and I said: 'Now I want you to hold that gun very tight, Tony.' Once he was doing that, I said: 'Now you could fire that at me if you liked, couldn't you?' I said: 'You'd be dead before you'd taken first pressure, but you could still have a sporting go.'

He didn't say anything, so I said: 'Now here's your second chance—are you going to try and kill me with that or not?'

He said: 'No.'

'Because you're frightened to?'

He said: 'No.'

'All right, then,' I said, 'well, in that case you can put the gun down now if you want to. Throw it away into any old corner, that's right, away you go.'

So he threw it away; it made an appalling clatter on the concrete floor by contrast to our quiet voices and the black, silent room.

'All right then,' he said, 'now what?'

I said: 'Right, now move over to by that window there where I can get a shot.'

He moved over. 'One thing,' he said.

'Are you asking for favours?'

'Two,' he said. 'First, don't look at my privates.'

'All right,' I said. 'If that's your will, strip with your back to me, then I'll throw these smart new cycling shoes of yours over to you and you can come over here and cover yourself with them. Just simply string them on that band you're wearing on your lower belly there.'

When he was ready, I said: 'Well, then? And what's the other favour? Don't be greedy.'

He said: 'No, just do it quickly, before I have time to think.'

'Right,' I said. I had already aimed, so I fired immediately and cut him down. My bullet hit him in the top left of his chest with the added roar that all loud noise makes in places built of cement. The killer's face assumed a severe, numbed expression as though he had come in to find his wife in bed with his brother. His right hand, already dead for a quarter second, slapped itself to the wound while the force of the bullet spun him backwards as if he were dancing a tango at twice the speed of the music. Then he slammed into a wall and fell on the floor face downwards on all fours in a crouching position like a runner suddenly turned lazy; his fingers scrabbled busily in the dirt for a second as though they were trying to write, stopping as I shone my flashlight on him to see if he needed finishing off.

I took the magazine out of the pistol and dropped it and the .38 into my pockets. I felt nothing.

A fresh-looking young sergeant in uniform from the local law appeared in the doorway with two other police officers behind him and hurried over to look at the body in the corner with a torch. When he had had enough, he stood up and, turning to face me, said: 'You?'

'That's right,' I said.

'Are you a police officer?'

'Yes,' I said. I showed him my card.

'Self-defence, was it?'

'The facts will speak for themselves.'

'Did you fire that shot with a police weapon?'

'No,' I said. 'I fired it with my own weapon.'

He said: 'I see.' He held his hand out. 'I shall have to have that gun of yours, I'm afraid.'

I gave it to him. 'But don't forget the nine-millimetre in the corner,' I said.

'The others are on their way over.' He coughed and said: 'You'll have to come down with us, I'm afraid.'

So then I put my hands in my pockets and followed the sergeant down and out into the pouring rain. It was dawn on March 1, a season of storms, and there was a near hurricane blowing in from the east up the Thames. I had tears in my eyes for the first time since I had broken my arm at sixteen playing football, but my tears were not for me—they were for the rightful fury of the people.

Le Puech,
July 7, 1989

TITLES OF THE AVAILABLE PRESS
in order of publication

THE CENTAUR IN THE GARDEN, a novel by Moacyr Scliar*
EL ANGEL'S LAST CONQUEST, a novel by Elvira Orphée
A STRANGE VIRUS OF UNKNOWN ORIGIN, a study by Dr. Jacques
  Leibowitch
THE TALES OF PATRICK MERLA, short stories by Patrick Merla
ELSEWHERE, a novel by Jonathan Strong*
THE AVAILABLE PRESS/PEN SHORT STORY COLLECTION
CAUGHT, a novel by Jane Schwartz*
THE ONE MAN ARMY, a novel by Moacyr Scliar
THE CARNIVAL OF THE ANIMALS, short stories by Moacyr Scliar
LAST WORDS AND OTHER POEMS, poetry by Antler
O'CLOCK, short stories by Quinn Monzó
MURDER BY REMOTE CONTROL, a novel in pictures by Janwillem
  van de Wetering and Paul Kirchner
VIC HOLYFIELD AND THE CLASS OF 1957, a novel by William
  Heyen*
AIR, a novel by Michael Upchurch
THE GODS OF RAQUEL, a novel by Moacyr Scliar*
SUTERISMS, pictures by David Suter
DOCTOR WOOREDDY'S PRESCRIPTIONS FOR ENDURING THE END
  OF THE WORLD, a novel by Colin Johnson*
THE CHESTNUT RAIN, a poem by William Heyen
THE MAN IN THE MONKEY SUIT, a novel by Oswaldo França, Júnior
KIDDO, a novel by David Handler*
COD STREUTH, a novel by Bamber Gascoigne
LUNACY & CAPRICE, a novel by Henry Van Dyke
HE DIED WITH HIS EYES OPEN, a mystery by Derek Raymond*
DUSTSHIP GLORY, a novel by Andreas Schroeder
FOR LOVE, ONLY FOR LOVE, a novel by Pasquale Festa Campanile
'BUCKINGHAM PALACE,' DISTRICT SIX, a novel by Richard Rive
THE SONG OF THE FOREST, a novel by Colin Mackay*
BE-BOP, RE-BOP, a novel by Xam Wilson Cartier
THE DEVIL'S HOME ON LEAVE, a mystery by Derek Raymond*
THE BALLAD OF THE FALSE MESSIAH, a novel by Moacyr Scliar
little pictures, short stories by andrew ramer
THE IMMIGRANT: A Hamilton County Album, a play by Mark
  Harelik
HOW THE DEAD LIVE, a mystery by Derek Raymond*
BOSS, a novel by David Handler*
THE TUNNEL, a novel by Ernesto Sábato

*Available in a Ballatine Mass Market Edition.

THE FOREIGN STUDENT, a novel by Phillippe Labro, translated by
    William R. Byron
ARLISS, a novel by Llyla Allen
THE CHINESE WESTERN: Short Fiction from Today's China, translated
    by Zhu Hong
THE VOLUNTEERS, a novel by Moacyr Scliar
LOST SOULS, a novel by Anthony Schmitz
SEESAW MILLIONS, a novel by Janwillem van de Wetering
SWEET DIAMOND DUST, a novel by Rosario Ferré
SMOKEHOUSE JAM, a novel by Lloyd Little
THE ENGIMATIC EYE, short stories by Moacyr Scliar
THE WAY IT HAPPENS IN NOVELS, a novel by Kathleen O'Connor
THE FLAME FOREST, a novel by Michael Upchurch
FAMOUS QUESTIONS, a novel by Fanny Howe
SON OF TWO WORLDS, a novel by Haydn Middleton
WITHOUT A FARMHOUSE NEAR, nonfiction by Deborah Rawson
THE RATTLESNAKE MASTER, a novel by Beaufort Cranford
BENEATH THE WATERS, a novel by Oswaldo França, Júnior
AN AVAILABLE MAN, a novel by Patric Kuh
THE HOLLOW DOLL (A Little Box of Japanese Shocks), by William
    Bohnaker
MAX AND THE CATS, a novel by Moacyr Scliar
FLIEGELMAN'S DESIRE, a novel by Lewis Buzbee
SLOW BURN, a novel by Sabina Murray
THE CARNAL PRAYER MAT, by Li Yu, translated by Patrick Hanon
THE MAN WHO WASN'T THERE, by Pat Barker
I WAS DORA SUAREZ, a mystery by Derek Raymond